TITUS RETURNS

"Fans of inspirational romance will appreciate Lillard's vivid characters and positive message."
—*Publishers Weekly*

JUST PLAIN SADIE

"A beautifully written romance with an adoring character who sees herself as merely ordinary looking. When an outsider comes into the mix, the outcome will shock readers. The story is fast paced and believable. Lillard writes stories readers can relate to."
—*RT Book Reviews*

LORIE'S HEART

"This is a charming, contemporary novel with no-nonsense characters who are struggling with who they thought they were and who they are now, while trying to figure out in which world they belong."
—*RT Book Reviews*

CAROLINE'S SECRET

"Sweetly inspirational . . . Rich with the trappings of Amish culture and tradition, the novel informs as well as entertains."
—*Publishers Weekly*

"Lillard's evocative prose, well-drawn protagonists and detailed settings result in an inspirational story of romance, faith, and trust. Caroline's search for forgiveness and happiness will appeal to fans of Wanda Brunstetter and Beverly Lewis."
—*Library Journal*

Also by Amy Lillard

The Wells Landing Series
CAROLINE'S SECRET
COURTING EMILY
LORIE'S HEART
JUST PLAIN SADIE
TITUS RETURNS
MARRYING JONAH

Published by Kensington Publishing Corporation

The QUILTING CIRCLE

AMY LILLARD

ZEBRA BOOKS
KENSINGTON PUBLISHING CORP.
http://www.kensingtonbooks.com

ZEBRA BOOKS are published by

Kensington Publishing Corp.
119 West 40th Street
New York, NY 10018

All Kensington titles, imprints, and distributed lines are available at
special quantity discounts for bulk purchases for sales promotion, pre-
miums, fund-raising, educational, or institutional use.

Special book excerpts or customized printings can also be created
to fit specific needs. For details, write or phone the office of the
Kensington Sales Manager: Attn.: Sales Department. Kensington
Publishing Corp., 119 West 40th Street, New York, NY 10018. Phone:
1-800-221-2647.

Zebra and the Z logo Reg. U.S. Pat. & TM Off.

First Printing: November 2017
ISBN-13: 978-1-4201-3982-2
ISBN-10: 1-4201-3982-7

eISBN-13: 978-1-4201-3983-9
eISBN-10: 1-4201-3983-5

10 9 8 7 6 5 4 3 2 1

Printed in the United States of America

Contents

ഗ ഗ ഗ ഗ

MORE THAN
FRIENDSHIP

Again, ye have heard that it hath been said by them of old time, Thou shalt not forswear thyself, but shalt perform unto the Lord thine oaths

—Matthew 5:33

Chapter One

Clara Rose Yutzy pulled the buggy to a stop and set the brake. "She's a good horse indeed, Mammi."

Her grandmother smiled. "I got her at the Clarita auction."

"I know, Mammi. I was with you, remember?" Clara Rose slid from the buggy. Her *grossmammi* was as sharp as a tack. Of course she remembered. Mammi just wanted the reinforcement that she had gotten an excellent animal when she bought the retired thoroughbred.

"She's a beauty, huh?" Her *mammi* got out as well, smiling to herself as she patted the shiny roan on the rear.

"That she is." Clara Rose slipped her arms out of her black sweater and folded it across her arm. It was warm for early October, but that was the way of Oklahoma. It seemed, come fall or spring, she always carried a sweater whether she thought she would need it or not. The weather was so unpredictable it was certain if she didn't have one she would most certainly need it.

"It'll be fun to get started on a new project, *jah*?" Mammi pulled their basket of materials from behind the buggy seat and hooked it over one arm.

Though she was nearing sixty, Verna Yutzy had a spring in her step and a sparkle in her eye that Clara Rose had forever admired.

Verna attributed her glow of happiness to her longtime marriage to Clara Rose's grandfather. Abraham Yutzy had gone to his reward the year before, and yet Verna plodded on. Secretly, Clara Rose felt that her grandmother was enjoying life on her own. It was really no matter to her. All she cared about was that her grandmother was happy.

"Do you think Helen and Emily will be here?"

"Maybe," Mammi replied.

Clara Rose unhitched the horse, even as her gaze searched the yard for Emily Riehl's familiar buggy. She always enjoyed spending time with her friend. Though they weren't in the same buddy bunch when they were running around, Wells Landing wasn't that large, and everyone knew everyone else.

She turned the horse free into the pasture, watching as her *grossmammi's* favorite new beast snickered and approached the other horses already there.

"Verna, Clara Rose, come in, come in," Eileen called from the front porch. "You're late."

Verna shook her head. "Five after is not late, Eileen Brenneman. Keep your apron on. We're coming."

"You've been racing that new horse on the back roads."

Verna shook her head, but her eyes twinkled mischievously. "Just because she's a former racehorse doesn't mean Daisy Lane wants to run any faster than necessary these days."

Clara Rose hid her smile. Her grandmother's new buggy horse was a retired racehorse from Tulsa. The owner had donated her to the Clarita School Auction, and her grandmother had snapped the beautiful beast up as quickly as she could. Frankly, Clara Rose thought her grandmother had paid a bit much for the horse, but she knew that Mammi got a secret thrill out of owning a retired racehorse for a buggy horse like some of the folks in Holmes County did.

"I brought sugar cookies," Clara Rose said as she climbed the porch steps.

"Set them on the table with the rest. We'll quilt for a while, then we'll eat."

Verna led the way into the large room off to one side. The house had been converted from an *Englisch* house to an Amish house, and the rumor around town was that the room had previously been the owner's car garage. Now it held several large chairs. After their quilt squares were all complete, they would sew them together, then bring out the quilting frame to finish the job, but that wouldn't be for a month or so.

Clara Rose slipped into the seat next to her good friend Tess Smiley. Tess gave her a shy smile, then ducked her head. The girl really was the prettiest person Clara Rose had ever seen. Maybe even prettier than Lorie Kauffman. Though these days Clara Rose hardly recognized Lorie when she came to town, not since she'd turned *Englisch*.

"This should be fun, *jah*?" Tess said.

Clara Rose gave a small nod. "I was here last year. It was a lot of fun."

Their circle was the kind that met year-round, unlike some that only quilted in the wintertime due to the extra summer work of planting, farming, canning, and the like.

Tess gave a small nod. Everyone pulled out their needle and thread and started to work. The twenty-five-block square of beautiful pinks and corals would surely fetch a good price at the school auction next year.

The sewing group had been donating quilts to the Clarita School Auction for as long as Clara Rose could remember. And to be part of such a long-standing group gave her a secret thrill. After every meeting, she had to say a little prayer of forgiveness for her prideful nature in the beautiful quilts that they made.

"How much longer till the wedding?" Fannie Stoll asked. Was that a bit of jealousy she heard in Fannie's voice? The poor girl was nearing thirty with no prospects. It had to be hard on Fannie to see all her friends get married, while she was the only one who remained single. There was nothing wrong with Fannie. She was pleasing to the eye and a good cook. So why no man had scooped her up and married her by now was anybody's guess. Only the Lord knew.

"Six weeks," Clara Rose said. Her heart gave a little pound at the thought. In six weeks, she would marry Thomas Lapp. She would be Clara Rose Lapp. Marriage was something she had thought about for a long time. Not just the past year while she and Thomas dated nor the past nine months or so since they had announced their engagement to the community. Long before that. Back before she had even met Thomas. She had prayed and prayed for God to send a special man just for her, and He had. Now soon, so very soon, her dream would be a reality. She could hardly wait.

As she stitched, her mind wandered into daydreams. What would it be like when they moved into their own house? Would the garden be on the left or the right-hand side of the house? Would the barn be painted red? She hoped so. She also wanted chickens so she would have fresh eggs every day and a garden plot just for tomatoes because she loved them so much. She would can whatever was left over in the fall, come to quilting circle and make quilts, and she would change her church cape from black to the color of her dress, signifying to everyone that she was now a married woman. That thought thrilled her more than thinking about the upcoming November day when she would pledge her life to Thomas.

The other women began to talk around her, as her mind continued to wander. She could hardly wait to be married. She knew it might seem a little silly to some, a little overly joyous, but all she'd ever wanted to be was somebody's wife. She looked over to her grandmother, who sat across from her, chatting with Eileen. Her own parents were a sure testament to how to make a marriage work. Most people felt that Amish marriages were destined to succeed. She'd heard the talk in the grocery store, down the aisles of the market, but she knew how hard it was for people to make a good marriage. Her parents had made a good marriage, her grandparents had made a good marriage, and that was all she wanted for herself.

"Do you have your material picked out and your dress made already?" Eileen asked.

"*Jah*, of course." That had been done long ago. So why was Eileen asking?

"If you need any help, we could always work on some of it here," Mariana added.

Clara Rose shook her head. "Oh no, that is such a generous offer. But I wouldn't dream of taking the time away from making the quilts for the auction to do something like sew my wedding dress." As important as it was to her, helping others topped her own wedding by miles.

"I heard that you were thinking of taking in foster kids, Mariana," Verna said.

Mariana shook her head. "No. Not now."

Clara Rose wondered if the information was incorrect or merely outdated. She had been coming to the quilting group long enough to know that Mariana wanted a baby so very badly, but now she was in her forties and her husband was very sick. Ill enough that she had heard rumors that he had already had someone make his funeral clothes. But Clara Rose would never dare to ask. It was just too personal. Since his illness, Mariana had completely given up the idea of having children. At least she didn't talk about it these days like she had before.

"It was me." Eileen's words sent the group into utter silence. The only sound was the whir of the ceiling fan that was powered by the solar panel on the roof.

"You did?" Mariana asked.

"Well, sort of." Eileen stopped stitching and twisted her fingers together before dropping them into her lap. "I'm thinking about adopting." Like Mariana, Eileen was over forty and childless. The two women seemed to huddle together whenever they met, and Clara Rose wondered if it was this childless phenomenon that brought them together as friends. She knew there was a buddy bunch of childless couples, though she knew no more than that. They were a lot older than she was, of course. What they did at their meetings was their business. Not hers.

"That's wonderful," Tess said. Her words seemed to break the spell that had descended on the room, and everyone started stitching again except for Mariana. She just stared at her hands.

"You are?" Mariana said. Clara Rose chided herself for examining the two words for any hint of jealousy. Every night, she prayed for Mariana. Not for her to have a baby, but for her to have peace over her husband's illness. Clara Rose couldn't imagine what would happen if Thomas were to fall ill like Leroy had.

Her lips trembled, and Clara Rose said a small prayer of forgiveness. She had been so wrapped up in her own issues— the wedding, getting ready for the wedding, sewing dresses, and planning menus—that she hadn't thought much about Mariana and Eileen and how different their lives were from how she pictured hers. She wanted as many kids as she could have. Didn't every Amish woman? Little girls and little boys. Little Clara Roses and little Thomases all running around barefoot in their outfits made from matching fabric. She could almost see them chasing a herd of puppies through her coveted chickens. It was an idyllic fantasy and she knew it. But that was how she wanted to picture her life.

They continued to quilt and chat though the conversation seemed to turn to the lighter side. Maybe no one wanted to bring up weddings and children anymore. It seemed that both topics were a little bit weighted for some of their members.

"I was sure hoping to see Emily this afternoon" Clara Rose said.

"Their buddy bunch planned a day trip to Tulsa. Seems there's some big market at the fairgrounds and they all wanted to go and shop," Fannie said. She made a face that said she wouldn't want to go do anything like that, and Clara Rose wondered if the expression was sincere.

"And Helen stayed home to take care of the baby."

Emily's little girl could hardly be called the baby. Maybe a toddler, and Clara Rose wondered when she and Elam might have another. They were very good parents. And she loved to see them when they came to church.

Helen and Emily had both been steady members of the quilting circle, but in recent months it had become harder and harder for the two of them to attend. As the bishop's wife, Helen always had a full plate and since Emily had married Elam, her time had grown precious as well. Elam's father, James, had been kicked in the head by an ornery milk cow a few years back and needed special care. He was much better these days, but he had limitations to deal with. Limitations that affected his entire family. Clara Rose knew it had to be hard on them all.

Eileen tied her thread in a knot, cut it down low, then stood. "I don't know about the rest of you," she started, "but I'm hungry. Is everyone ready to eat?"

A round of *"jahs"* went up around the room. Everyone tied off their threads and prepared to snack.

Clara Rose grabbed a paper plate and piled it high with the cinnamon buns Eileen had made, one of her own sugar cookies, and the seasoned pretzels Tess had brought, along with two slices of cheese, a scoop of the pizza casserole, and a couple of bread and butter pickles that she knew for a fact had come from Fannie's mom's cellar.

"If you eat all that, you're not going to be able to get into your wedding dress come November."

Clara Rose whirled around, her hand pressed to her heart. "Obadiah Brenneman! You scared the life out of me."

Obie smiled, his green eyes twinkling. "That was not my intention."

"It is a sin to lie, you know. Don't make me go to the bishop."

His grin widened at her feigned anger. Though he had surprised her.

"What are you doing here?" she asked.

"This is my aunt's house."

Clara Rose took a big bite of the cinnamon bun and set it back on her plate before licking her fingers. "Yes, I do know. But what are you doing here during our quilting circle?"

Obie glanced around as if looking to see if anyone was paying them any attention. Only Fannie seemed to notice that Obie had come into the house. Everyone else was still milling around filling their plates.

"I was hoping I might talk to you."

Clara Rose nodded. "*Jah*, okay." She waited for him to start.

But Obie shook his head. "Not here. Maybe I could take you home this afternoon."

Clara Rose shrugged. "I guess so. I came with Mammi."

Obie relaxed a bit. Until that moment, Clara Rose hadn't realized how tense he was. He straightened up again. "Okay. That'd be good. Okay."

What was wrong with him?

Before Clara Rose could ask, he grabbed the plate and started filling it with the treats. Once he neared the table, the rest of the women noticed he was there. Everyone had to stop and talk to him, ask how things had been going, if he had any new golden retriever puppies, and if his twin brother, Zebadiah, was ever going to come back from Pinecraft and join the church.

Clara Rose watched as he talked to each woman in turn, then glanced back at her as if something was on his mind.

He had been her best friend for as long as she could re- member. Her own mother and Eileen, Obie's aunt, had been the best of friends growing up. She'd never experi- enced a time when she didn't know Obie. And she had come to depend on his crooked smile and perpetually messy black hair. He was as handsome as God made them, but he showed no interest in dating. Or at least none that he told her about. They were such good friends Clara Rose was sure that she would be the first one he would tell—aside from the girl, of course—when he finally fell in love.

"Something's up."

She whirled around, caught off guard for the second time in less than fifteen minutes. "Tess."

"What are you daydreaming about?"

Obie's name sprang to her lips, but she managed to keep from saying it out loud. It didn't sound proper to be daydreaming of Obadiah Brenneman when she was so close to marrying Thomas Lapp. But most people in these parts knew what good friends she and Obie truly were. Even Thomas was understanding of her unusual relationship with Obie. Lifelong friendship was a true gift from God, and no one should take it for granted.

"Nothing," Clara Rose mumbled.

Tess shot her a knowing look.

"You don't believe me?"

Shaking her head, Tess went back to the table for another cookie without responding.

"Mammi." Clara Rose approached her grandmother from the side, as she talked to Mariana. The woman still wore that same dazed look she had when Fannie had asked her about foster children.

"Yes, dear?" Mammi asked.

"I'm getting a ride home with Obie. Is that okay?"

"Of course, dear."

"I'll see you at home. And don't drive too fast, *jah*?"

Her grandmother only chuckled.

"For someone who wanted to talk, you sure aren't saying much," Clara Rose said. They had been riding in the buggy for almost twenty minutes, and Obie had yet to tell her what was on his mind. And there was something on his mind. Clara Rose could see it. His shoulders were tense, and the muscle in his jaw was jumping like a bullfrog on hot tin.

"It's not Zeb, is it?"

"No. Zeb is fine. Do you mind if we go out to Millers' pond?"

She frowned. "What's at the pond? No one's there this time of year." It had been warm lately, but not warm enough to get in the water.

Obie shook his head, but she noticed he had turned his tractor toward the Miller place.

But still he didn't talk as they chugged along. He'd said nothing was wrong with his brother, but something was definitely amiss. Obie was normally bright and bubbly, full of laughs and jokes and mischief. But today it seemed as if a dark cloud had descended on his personality and was raining on his normally jovial spirits.

Whatever it was, she would have to wait to find out, though. He seemed intent on reaching Millers' pond before he let her know exactly what was on his mind.

In no time at all, they had pulled to a stop in front of the crop of trees that sat in the middle of the Millers' cornfield. A well-beaten path led from the road at the edge of the field and into the trees, where the pond hid like an undisclosed oasis.

Obie came around to her side of the tractor and helped her down. But he was still acting strangely, jerking away from her as if her touch had burned him. Had he always been like that? Was she just hypersensitive to the fact that he was acting strange now? "Do you want your sweater?" Obie asked.

She nodded. It was warm enough out here, but once they got into the trees it would be much cooler by far. Fall was definitely upon them. Obie handed her her plain black sweater. She folded it over her arm, but was careful not to let it snag on the fence as they ducked through it into the cornfield.

But she was oh so aware of Obie walking behind her. It was strange, for she had never felt this way before. Was it because he was acting so weird? Or was something else happening today?

He didn't say a word, just followed behind her as they walked to the crop of trees.

The pond wasn't huge by any stretch of the imagination. Just big enough to allow the kids a place to cool off in the summertime. It boasted a thick rope swing, though everyone knew to be careful jumping in. The pond wasn't deep enough to support too many antics.

Clara Rose walked into the clearing and over to a fallen log. How long the tree had lain there was anybody's guess. But it had become a customary seat for the pond's visitors.

She folded her arms under her sweater and waited for Obie to tell her what was on his mind. Her heart started to pound in her chest, as if what he was about to say was going to change both of their lives.

Obie took off his hat and twirled it in his hands as if he needed something to do to disperse the nervous energy coursing through him. "Uh . . ." he started, but those green eyes darted to everything around but her.

"Obie," she started, "you're scaring me. Is everything okay?"

He stopped running his hat and trained his suddenly hard gaze on her. "No, everything is not okay." He practically yelled the words.

She'd never seen him like this, angry and agitated. She jumped to her feet. "What's happened? Please," she beseeched him.

"I can't let you marry Thomas Lapp."

Clara Rose's mouth went instantly dry. "What?" She licked her lips to no avail. "What are you saying, Obie?"

He started that hat-twirling thing again. "I'm saying that I've kept silent for too long. And I can't see letting you marry Thomas."

Clara's heart kicked up another notch. It beat like the bass drum in the marching band they had each year in the Christmas parade.

"Can you tell me what's wrong?"

He shook his head. "You just can't marry him is all."

Clara stared at him, unsure of what to say. "Did he do something? Does he . . . love someone else?" The words were painful to say. How could he love someone else? She had known they were going to get married ever since the first time she had seen him. They had naturally fallen into friends the minute they met, but she knew they weren't friends like her and Obie. Theirs was a different kind of friendship.

She and Obie had been friends for so long, his friendship was like a warm winter coat to wrap herself in and keep her snugly always. But Thomas was different entirely. It was a more mature feeling. She knew he was going to take care of her, and she would take care of him. They would have a farm and raise chickens and babies, and life was going to be perfect from there on out. She just knew it. So why was Obie bringing all this up now?

"Obadiah Brenneman," she started, her voice stern with her growing annoyance. "If you don't tell me what's going on right now, I'm leaving." The situation had lost its humor, if it had ever had any to begin with.

"You can't marry Thomas Lapp," he said again, as if those simple words explained it all.

"Why not?" Clara Rose shot back. Her words echoed in the alcove of trees where they stood.

He shook his head and took her hands into his. "I have a bad feeling about this. Just don't marry him, Clara Rose. Promise me."

Chapter Two

Obie dropped her off at the end of her driveway and chugged his tractor toward home. He hadn't said a word to her as they drove back to her family's farm. Not one word. She had expected something. Maybe him explaining himself as to why he thought she needed to call off her wedding to Thomas. It just didn't make sense. They had announced their engagement in January; everything was set and ready to go. In just a few short weeks, she and Thomas would say their vows and eat wedding cake, and she would start her life anew as a married woman.

She let herself in the house, wondering if Obie had gotten too hot that day. Maybe that was it. Heat stroke. So it wasn't extremely hot, but it was warm for October. That should count for something.

"Clara Rose, is that you?"

Her *mamm* came out of the kitchen, wiping her hands on a dishtowel as she walked.

"Yes, Mamm?"

"It's good to see you home—my goodness, child! Whatever is wrong?"

Clara Rose supposed the shock and surprise of her conversation with Obie was evident in her expression. But it wasn't something she wanted to talk about. Not with her mother. Her mother was levelheaded, staid, and true, and Clara Rose was certain the only answer she would get from Nancy Yutzy was that Obie would get over his doubts soon enough and that Clara Rose had already made her promises to Thomas. No, what Clara Rose needed was a different perspective.

"Is Mammi back yet?"

"She's in the *dawdihaus*."

Clara Rose gave a small nod and headed toward the back door.

"Only stay a minute. You have to come back and help Anamaria with supper."

Her sister was eighteen and fully capable of cooking for the four of them by herself, but Clara Rose stopped that thought in an instant. She was being selfish and ungrateful.

Lord, forgive me, she prayed. This whole ordeal with Obie had her thinking all messed up. "I just need a minute to talk to her about something." Clara Rose rushed past her mother without a second look.

"Okay then," Mamm called after her. But Clara Rose could still hear the questions in her voice.

It was a short walk from the back door to the front of the *dawdihaus*. In fact, before her father had died, he had built an aluminum cover that stretched from the porch of one house to the other so his mother wouldn't get wet when she came in to eat. Clara Rose remembered looking out the back window at her *dawdi* holding an umbrella over Verna's head as they walked together to come eat in the main house.

Things had seemed so simple then. She hadn't thought about it at the time, only now, when it seemed that everything was more complicated than ever before.

She knocked lightly on the door, then realized that Mammi, with her hearing, might not respond right away. She knocked louder.

"Keep your apron on! I'm coming."

Her grandmother threw open the door, those sassy blue eyes scraping over her from head to toe. "My goodness, girl. What's wrong?"

Clara Rose opened her mouth to speak, but no words came out. She shook her head and stepped into the house. She closed her mouth and opened it once more to try again.

"Spit it out," Mammi said.

"I don't even know where to start."

"The beginning is always the best place." Mammi took Clara Rose by the elbow and led her to the blue upholstered couch in the living room. Once upon a time, it had sat in the living room of the main house. Clara Rose could clearly remember so many days spent sitting on that couch and playing with her dolls, Anamaria next to her. Again, she was confronted with the simplicity of life then and the complexities of life now.

"Obie told me I can't marry Thomas Lapp."

"It's about time that boy said something."

"What?" Surely she hadn't heard her correctly.

"It's about time that boy said something." Mammi pronounced each word clearly and slowly as if speaking to someone who might not have ever heard English spoken aloud.

"I heard what you said," Clara Rose said as respectfully as possible given her current situation. "I just don't understand what those words have to do with anything I just said."

Mammi shook her head and came around to sit in her rocking chair. She reached into the basket next to the chair and pulled out her mending. One of her mother's church capes in a beautiful green. The same shade as Obie's eyes. Once again, he was right there in her thoughts. "You young people," Mammi started, but then broke off as a shake of her head was more expressive than mere words could be.

"What?" Clara Rose asked, more confused than ever.

"Did you ask Obie why he didn't think you should marry Thomas?"

"*Jah*, of course."

"And what did he say?"

"He said he didn't have a reason. Just a bad feeling."

Mammi nodded knowingly. "That is telling in itself."

"What does that mean?"

Mammi shook her head once again, then peered at Clara Rose over her silver-framed glasses. "And that, child, is what you must figure out for yourself."

Her grandmother's words stayed with her as she cooked dinner, said the silent prayer before the meal, ate, and said the silent prayer afterwards. She and Anamaria cleaned the kitchen, put up the dishes, finished the outside chores, took quick showers, then retired to their bedroom. There were two extra rooms upstairs so each girl could have her own if they so chose, but they never had. She and Anamaria were like opposite ends of bookends. Mirrors of each other, only a few years apart.

Tonight, Clara Rose was even more thankful that she shared a room with her sister. She sat on the bed and brushed her hair, hoping the familiar activity, as mindless as it was, would shed some insight into the turmoil this afternoon had brought.

"Are you going to tell me what's going on?" Other than Obie, Anamaria was her best friend.

"What would you say if I told you that Obie said I shouldn't marry Thomas Lapp?"

Anamaria's gray eyes clouded over like the sky during a summer storm. "Thomas is such a good man. Why should you not marry him?"

"That's what I keep asking myself. This is what I have wanted forever." Well, at least for the last three years.

"I know," Anamaria said, a strange tone coloring her words, but Clara Rose's thoughts were in such a jumble she couldn't pluck out another detail even if her life depended on it.

"Thomas is handsome. He has a good job with his father. He's kind and gentle. He'd make a good father to our children. . . ." What more could a girl ask for in a husband?

"But do you love him?"

Clara Rose scoffed. "Of course I do." But her heart pounded in her chest and the words dried on her tongue. Nerves. That was all. She had been planning this wedding for so long. This was exactly what she wanted from her life. Exactly.

"Then that's all that matters."

Clara Rose tossed and turned long into the night. She kept telling herself that she didn't have to decide this today. And what was there to decide? Everything had already been decided, from the color of their dresses to which female family members would serve as bridesmaids.

There was nothing left. She was getting married in six weeks to the man God had sent just for her. At least that's what she told herself. Yet that nagging feeling held on. She prayed about it, but still found no answers. She tossed and turned some more, said another prayer, then went through the whole process again.

She must've fallen asleep sometime around two o'clock in the morning only to be awakened by the rooster shortly afterward. The bad thing about Buster was that he didn't wait till sunrise to start crowing. He tried to get an early start to the day, usually beginning somewhere between four and four-thirty every morning. Anamaria thought he was out to get them for the times they chased him out of the henhouse when they wanted the hens to lay, but Clara Rose suspected that he secretly wanted to belong to a dairy farmer. Either way, his summons had her up at four when she'd barely gotten any sleep at all.

Quietly, she got out of bed and padded down the stairs and into the kitchen, careful not to wake anyone else. Maybe having an early start to her day was a good thing. The more time she was awake, the more time she would be able to figure through this mess of her thoughts. But after a cup of coffee she realized this wasn't a mess. Obie was nervous that their friendship would change once she and Thomas got married. It was completely understandable, but she couldn't let Obie's fears tarnish her own hopes and dreams. And those hopes and dreams were just about to become a reality. In just a few more weeks, she would be Mrs. Thomas Lapp. And once Obie saw them together, happily married and standing side by side, he would know without a doubt that she and Thomas definitely belonged together.

* * *

"You're awfully quiet tonight, Clara Rose. You got something on your mind?"

"Well, actually . . ." She shook her head. "Never mind."

She and Thomas were on their way home from the Sunday night singing. The clop of the horse's hooves on the roadway was soothing after puttering around on the tractor all week. Most of Wells Landing drove their tractors during the week, if they had them, and their buggies on the weekend. Sunday was a good day to go at a slower pace. Though her thoughts were anything but slow.

"Nah," Thomas started. "You can't say something like that, then say never mind. What's captured your thoughts tonight?"

Clara Rose pleated her fingers in her apron and tried to find the right words to tell Thomas what was on her mind. But she knew better than to blurt it all out. Thomas might not be as understanding as she was about the situation with Obie. Sure, they had known each other about as long as he had known her, but it was something different altogether when love was declared.

"It's Obie," she said. "He . . . I think he's just worried that our friendship is going to suffer once you and I get married."

Thomas gave a stiff nod, then clicked the reins on the back of the horse's rump. It seemed his horse liked an even slower pace on Sunday. "Well then, he would be right about that, *jah*?"

"What do you mean?"

"It's not feasible to think that after the wedding things will remain the same. You won't be able to spend as much time with Obie as you do now. You'll be spending time with me."

For as much thought as Clara Rose had given to being

married and having children, she hadn't thought about the true impact of what it would mean for her socially. No more singings, no more youth group meetings, more time with Thomas. Less time with Obie.

"He is my best friend."

She looked over to Thomas. But his eyes were trained straight ahead. Only the thin line of his mouth gave away his annoyance. Most folks in Wells Landing didn't understand the relationship she had with Obie. That was something she'd accepted long ago. Everyone believed that a boy and a girl couldn't be just friends. Still, her relationship with Obie was so much deeper than her relationship with anyone else, with the exception of her sister. She and Anamaria were siblings and that put their relationship on an entirely different level. But Obie . . . he was the one thing she'd been certain of in her entire life. Always there, always there to listen, and always ready to play a game, read aloud from a book, go swimming in Millers' pond. He was a true friend, and she didn't want that relationship to suffer. Why couldn't she have both?

"I don't think I like that," she muttered.

Thomas turned, and even in the darkness that surrounded them, she could see the blaze of his normally docile brown eyes. "Are you saying you don't want to get married?"

"Oh no, no, no, no." Clara Rose shook her head. "That's not what I meant at all. It's just that . . . well, I don't understand why I can't be married and have a best friend too."

Her mother was good friends with Maddie Kauffman. Well, good friends might be a little exaggerated, but Maddie came out to the house from time to time and shared a cup of coffee and a plate of cookies with Mamm. And there was Tess. She came over often to see Clara Rose and visit for a bit. She had only been married for a little over a year. She seemed to be able to make time for her friends. Why did Thomas think Clara Rose wouldn't be able to?

She looked back to that jumping muscle in the side of his jaw. "Are you jealous of Obie?"

Thomas clicked the reins again, a little harder this time. His impatience with the horse's slow pace was clear. "Of course not. It's not him you're marrying in six weeks, but me." His own words seemed to reassure Thomas, and a little of the tension left his shoulders.

Clara Rose breathed a small sigh of relief. The last thing she wanted was her future husband and her best friend at odds with each other so close to her special day.

"I'm sure it's nothing," Clara Rose said. Surely, after the wedding, everything would smooth out and become normal again. Obie was just worried that she was going to forget all about him after she and Thomas married. But she vowed right then and there to do everything in her power to make sure that all their lives went on exactly the same, no matter what.

Chapter Three

Yet Monday came and Clara Rose had no more peace of mind than she had the day before. In fact, she felt more confused than ever. She didn't like her life feeling so uncertain. She'd heard about girls her age having wedding nerves and second thoughts and such. She prayed all night for the Lord to give her quietness of mind and peace of heart, but when the breakfast dishes were done, she knew there was only one solution to her problem.

"Mamm," she called, "I'm hitching up the buggy and going visiting."

Her mother came out of the living room carrying a dust rag. "You don't have to work today?"

Clara Rose had recently started working at Abe Fitch's furniture store, helping him keep things neat and orderly. Abe was something of a scatterbrain, too interested in wood and his wife, Esther, to care a whole lot about much else. It wasn't that he was self-absorbed; that wouldn't have been becoming for an Amish man. He was simply . . . distracted.

"Not until noon. I thought I would stop by and see Obie and then go on into town."

Her mother gave her a questioning look. "Okay," she said, the word not matching her expression at all. "If you think that's a good idea."

"Why would I not think it was a good idea?" Clara Rose asked. "I came up with it."

Her mother shook her head and started back into the living room. Clara Rose followed, wanting to hear what her mother had to say and yet not wanting to hear it just as much at the same time.

Nerves. They were making her a little batty. But until she found out exactly what Obie was thinking and reassured him that nothing was going to change between them after the wedding, she didn't think she could find a way to settle her mind and her thoughts. And until she did that, she wasn't sure she would ever sleep again. No, this had to be taken care of. And it had to be taken care of now.

"Do you have something on your mind, Mamm?" Clara Rose asked as she followed behind her mother.

Mamm shook her head. "I told myself I was staying out of this."

"I asked your opinion. Surely you can give me that much."

Nancy Yutzy dropped her hands to her sides and turned to face her daughter. "Marriage is a wonderful thing, Clara Rose. Perhaps even the most wonderful thing in the entire world, but when it starts off, it can be fragile. I just don't want any of this problem with Obie to hurt your relationship with Thomas. That's all."

"Problem? You think that this is a problem?" She would not have called it that. Then again, she wasn't sure what she would call it. A situation, perhaps? An issue? But not a problem. Obie was never a problem. He was her best friend.

"Don't go splitting hairs, daughter. You know what I

mean. Sometimes a girl just has to face it. And when she gets married, her husband has to become her best friend. You're going to be partners in life." Mamm tossed her dust rag across one shoulder, then clasped Clara Rose's hands in her own. She squeezed her fingers reassuringly. "Change can be scary. Really scary. But it'll be worth it in the end." Her mother smiled, but Clara Rose noted her lips trembled as she spoke. "Of course Obie is going to have a tough time of it right now. Your relationship is going to change, and he's not sure where he's going to fit into your life anymore. But if you allow it, his insecurities can ruin the bond you and Thomas are building. I just don't want to see you let that happen."

Clara Rose squeezed her mother's fingers in return, then pulled her hands away. "I would never do that. I love Thomas. And I would do anything to keep him happy and by my side."

Mamm gave a quick nod. "Good. That's just the way it should be."

Clara Rose tried to smile. "I'll see you after work." She turned on her heel and left the room, thoughts of Obie and what she would do to keep him happy ringing through her mind.

The Brenneman farm looked as it always did. A little on the shabby side. But that's what happened when four bachelor men lived in one place without a woman. They had no need for flowers out front or even the simple, welcoming wreath on the door. There were no pots of ferns or children's toys, just a small vegetable garden and a pair of muck boots sitting crookedly on the porch.

They really needed a woman's touch around here, Clara Rose thought as she skipped up the steps. She rapped lightly on the door, ignoring the tripping beat of her heart. She was just a little nervous, that was all. Anyone would be when faced with the prospect of losing her best friend just because she was getting married to her other best friend. But somehow, someway, she would make Obie understand that, after she and Thomas were married, nothing would change.

The door opened and Paul Brenneman stood on the other side. "Why, Clara Rose! How good to see you today. Come in. Come in." He stood back to allow her entrance. "I'll get Obie. Obie," he called, the one word ringing loudly in her ears.

"Yeah, Dat?" Obie called from the landing.

"You have a visitor."

Obie loped down the stairs, stopping halfway when he caught sight of her. Clara Rose ignored the start of her heart as he slowed, then came down at a normal pace. "Clara Rose," he said.

"Can we talk?" She cast a quick look at his father, then back to him. "Alone?"

Obie gave a jerky nod, then grabbed his hat off the peg on the wall and crammed it on his head. "Take a walk with me?"

Clara Rose gave a small smile in return, then followed him out the door. Without a word, they strolled around the side of the house and toward the backyard and the field on the other side. It was nothing but a hay pasture, now mowed down, and she could see Eileen's house over in the distance.

"What do you want to talk about?"

Clara Rose opened her mouth to speak, but the words seemed to get stuck somewhere along the way. "It . . . I mean—" Where did she begin? She had no idea. She took a deep breath and tried again. "I just wanted you to know that you will always be my best friend." Her mother's words from earlier floated around in her head, seeking some kind of purchase with the statement she'd just made. But there was none. How could she have two best friends? And how could she choose between Thomas and Obie?

Obie frowned. "I know that."

She nodded awkwardly and cleared her throat. Why was this so weird? She had never been this uncomfortable with Obie before.

"I just wanted you to hear that from me."

He flashed her that charming smile that she loved so much. "That's sweet of you, Clara Rose, but I know that we're friends."

She was messing this up, not being clear. "I mean for always. Even after I'm married."

His eyes dimmed just a bit and his lips pressed together, but he gave her a nod.

The tension left her body in a big whoosh. He understood. "So now you don't have to worry about me and Thomas, *jah*?"

He shook his head. "I don't think you understand." He let go of her hand. The minute he pulled away, Clara Rose began to fret.

"But I do understand. I do. You're afraid that you're going to lose me as your best friend after Thomas and I get married. But I know that's not going to happen." Sure, Thomas was a little jealous right now. But once they were married that jealousy would disappear. And everything would settle back into the pattern it had been in last week before all of this happened. Thomas would be her fiancé—or rather, her husband—and Obie would be her best friend. And she would still have that passel of children, the herd of puppies, and all the rest of her dreams that went along with marrying Thomas Lapp.

"He's not the man for you," Obie said.

"He is too," she countered. Obie knew. He had been there when she and Thomas had seen each other for the first time. Thomas and his family had just moved to Oklahoma from Missouri to expand their horse-breeding business, and someone had invited him to their youth group meeting at Millers' pond. Clara Rose had been laughing at something Obie had said when she'd tripped over a fallen branch. She would have sprawled headlong onto the bank if Thomas hadn't caught her. That's when she'd known her prayers had been answered. God had sent Thomas Lapp to her, just as she'd asked.

"He's not. I don't know how I know. I just do."

"He's a good man," Clara Rose said, daring Obie to contradict her.

"I know that."

"He's a hard worker and will provide for me and our children."

"I know that too." Obie ground his teeth together so hard she could hear them cracking.

"So what is the problem?"

He turned and looked out over the field. "I don't know."

"You can't just say he's not the man for me and not have something to go with it, Obie. You've been my best friend for as long as I can remember, and I trust your judgment. But I can't defend my decision if you don't give me something to go on here."

Obie shook his head. "I don't know." He gave a jerky shrug. "I just got this bad feeling, you know?"

"A bad feeling about Thomas Lapp." He was the best man Clara Rose had ever met, and she considered herself the luckiest girl in the world that he had picked her to be his bride. His family did well for themselves, had a beautiful farm, raised magnificent horses. And they were all-around loving and God-fearing people. There was no bad feeling to have about Thomas Lapp. "You know what? I think you're scared."

Obie scoffed. "Me? Scared? Of what?"

"I don't know." But she did, and God forgive her the lie. But it sounded so vain and arrogant to say that she believed that he was afraid of losing her friendship when she married Thomas. And she couldn't say that out loud. Not even to Obie.

"See, that just goes to show that you're wrong." His mouth was twisted into a weird angle, and Clara Rose knew that he was struggling not to say more.

"I've prayed for so many years that God would bring somebody into my life who would love me, and cherish me, and want to marry me, and be with me forever. And He did. He gave me Thomas. I don't understand why you can't be happy about that." She turned on her heel and marched back toward the house. As she walked, she listened intently for sounds that he was following behind her, maybe running up to her to tell her that he was sorry, that he was wrong, and that he knew that she and Thomas were going to be the greatest couple Wells Landing had ever seen.

But he didn't. When she got to the top of the hill, she turned back to where he stood in the middle of the field that separated his house from his aunt's. He was just standing there, watching her as she walked away. Even from this distance, she could tell that his eyes were clouded over. His shoulders slumped and his head sagged. But he didn't come after her. Clara Rose blinked back tears and climbed into her buggy and headed for work.

* * *

"There are none so blind as those who will not see," Mammi quoted Thursday night as they stitched the new quilt. Of all the different parts of quilt making, this was Clara Rose's least favorite. Everyone sat in chairs, close to each other but not connected. Everyone had their own quilt square in their lap as they stitched the individual pieces together to form the pattern. Clara Rose much preferred when the quilt top, the batting, and the bottom were all tacked together and stretched across the quilt frame. That's when the true quilting began. When that happened, they were all connected, all touching the same fabric as they worked in their tight circle.

Clara Rose missed the rest of what her grandmother was talking about as her mind went straight to Obie. He couldn't see. Did that make him blind? She supposed she couldn't fault him. He was her best friend, and he was worried that she was making a bad decision. But there was no call for him to worry. Thomas had never done anything improper toward her. He'd never stepped out of line. Except for holding her hand from time to time on the way home from the singings, he had been nothing but a perfect Amish gentleman to her, a fact that made her love him even more.

"Clara Rose? Is something bothering you?"

She started, then whipped around to look at her friend. Tess smiled encouragingly.

"No," she scoffed. Another lie to add to her growing list to ask forgiveness for. "Why would something be wrong?"

"Well, I called your name three times before you answered." Tess shrugged.

Clara Rose wilted a bit under her friend's concern. "No, it's just a lot, you know." It was about the vaguest statement she had ever made. But, with the wedding coming up, she figured her friend could fill in all the blanks herself. And that's exactly what happened.

Tess nodded. "Marriage is a big step."

Something in her tone took Clara Rose's thoughts away from her own issues and problems. "Is everything okay with you?"

She had never known Tess to complain about anything. Tess Smiley was sweet and kind, and never had a bad word to say about anything or anyone. She always looked on the bright side and was in general a complete joy to be around. Clara Rose always tried to keep a positive outlook, but that was one thing Tess did with seemingly no extra effort. To see her brown eyes dim and the corners of her mouth turn down had Clara Rose reaching out to her friend.

She patted Tess on the knee. "You can talk to me whenever you need to. You know that, right?"

Tess had recently moved to Wells Landing from the Amish community in Clarita, Oklahoma. It wasn't so far away, but it was far enough that in order for Tess to visit with her family, she had to get a driver to take her there. Seeing as how she'd lived on a farm right next door to her parents before she'd moved, having that far to travel was a big step.

"It's fine," Tess said.

Clara Rose wouldn't be the only one asking forgiveness for lies at night. She took her friend's fib to mean that she didn't want to talk about it.

"Just know that marriage is a big step," Tess said. "And you have to be sure. Are you one hundred percent sure, Clara Rose?"

"Of course I am," Clara Rose said. She looked up to find that all eyes were on the two of them. When had the conversation across the room stopped, and exactly when had it centered on her and Tess?

Her grandmother nodded. "Marriage is a big step. I don't have to tell you it's forever. Or until death."

"Do men sit around talking like this?" Clara Rose gave an uncomfortable laugh. It was a very poor attempt at changing the subject, but the tension in the room was starting to eat away at the air, leaving her breathless and wheezing.

Eileen picked up her quilt square and began to stitch once again. "It's different for men," she said, not bothering to look up as she worked.

"How so?" Fannie asked.

"I don't know," Eileen said. "It just is."

Clara Rose glanced around the room, realizing for the first time the differences in the women seated there. And for once she was glad that Helen Ebersol and Emily Riehl weren't in attendance. Emily was such a good friend, and Helen was the bishop's wife. It just didn't seem like a conversation she wanted to have in front of them. But these ladies . . .

Fannie had never been married and most likely would never marry, and Tess had recently gotten married and moved away from her family. Eileen was married with no children, and Mariana's husband was terminally ill. Then there was Clara Rose herself and her widowed grandmother. Each one of them had a different take on marriage; each one of them had something different to bring to the conversation. How was she supposed to sort through all that?

Prayer.

It was the only answer she had. And pray she would. For understanding, for peace, for knowing that she was making the right decision. She had prayed her entire life for a husband to love her, care for her, and help her raise children and tomatoes. God had sent her Thomas Lapp. For that, she would be forever grateful to Him. She knew Thomas was the one for her, so why was she having so many second thoughts?

Thankfully the subject dropped between them, and Clara Rose breathed a sigh of relief. They stitched for another twenty minutes or so and put away their quilt squares in order to fill their plates.

It took them nearly two months, meeting once a week, to make a quilt. But Clara Rose supposed that they could do it in half that time if they spent more time quilting and less time eating. But she had to admit that the eating was almost her favorite part. Everyone brought such delicious food—old favorites, new recipes, and something that Eileen liked to call copycats. It seemed that was when you took a recipe from a restaurant and tried to make it at home.

Clara Rose piled her plate high with seasoned pretzels, a new recipe for divinity that Mariana had been trying out for Christmas, and little chicken nugget sandwiches no bigger than half dollars.

Before she could make it back to her seat, the front door slammed. Clara Rose whirled around to find Obie coming in.

"Nephew!" Eileen said. "Funny how you always show up when it's time to eat."

Obie turned a shade of pink that made his eyes seem even greener. He shot his aunt a sheepish grin that bore traces of apology. "It's merely a coincidence, Auntie," he said. "I came to see if I can give Clara Rose a ride home."

It was as if a spell of silence had fallen over the room. The women all stopped talking and eating, and everyone turned to look at her. Such a statement usually meant a couple would be going out together, and most always once a couple started dating they ended up married. But Clara Rose was already engaged. To someone else.

"I mean . . ." Obie's color deepened to a truly embarrassed red. "I just thought . . ." He shook his head. "Never mind." He turned on his heel and found his exit as quickly as he had entered.

"I'll just go . . ." Clara Rose started. She didn't allow herself time to finish as she hurried out the door after Obie.

She found him easily enough. He hadn't gone far. His aunt had an old porch swing hung on the branch of a large oak just to the side of the house. Obie had found his way there and was now using the heels of his walking shoes to push himself into motion.

Clara Rose slowed her steps and made her way over to him. He didn't bother to look up as she sat down next to him. She offered him a bite off her plate, and he shook his head, then reached out and snatched the piece of fluffy white divinity.

"You think I'm crazy, don't you?"

Clara Rose laughed. "No, I don't. Yeah, well, maybe a little. But I know you care about me and that's where all this is coming from. That means more to me than anything else."

He nodded and swallowed hard, then finally raised his eyes to hers. "I wish I knew what it was. I wish I knew where this bad feeling was coming from. Maybe then you would take my advice. You could see why I don't think that he is right for you."

Clara Rose laid her hand on top of Obie's knee and gave a little squeeze. "Thomas Lapp is a good man."

Obie nodded. "I know that. And I know how well-established his family is. And I know that they have the best horses and buggies in the county. Heck, they have a tractor they drive to church."

Clara Rose nodded. It was the closest thing to a car the Amish were allowed to own, and the Lapp family had the nicest one. "But you can't tell me." It was a soft and simple statement.

Obie shook his head. "No."

"It's all going to be okay, Obie."

Obie nodded. "If you say so."

"I do," she said. "God sent Thomas for me to marry. This is all part of His plan. Whatever's going on in your head, just let it go. Everything is going to be just perfect. Just wait and see."

Chapter Four

But Obie just wouldn't let it go. Three days later, Clara Rose had had about all she could take of it.

"Every time I think about you marrying him, it makes my heart squeeze in my chest," he said.

She shook her head. "Quit confusing me, Obie. My thoughts are a jumble, and I can't keep them straight." She'd spent the evening before with Thomas and a couple more friends hanging out and playing Rook. It was a new game for them, and they had laughed and laughed as they tried to get the rules down and still come out on top. It'd been a great night: fellowship, fun, and food. And in that moment all of her doubts had disappeared. Obie was mistaken about Thomas. Last night she had known it for certain. Now, today, as she stood out in the yard and fed the chickens, the doubts resurfaced. And all because Obie "had a feeling."

"I don't mean to," Obie said, his voice pleading with her for acceptance.

She wanted to understand—she wanted to so badly. But none of it made sense. "I know that, Obie, but please. Stop."

He was shaking his head before she even finished the sentence. "How can I stop when you are making the biggest mistake of your life?"

Clara Rose dropped the bucket of feed at her feet and slammed her hands on her hips as she turned around to face him. "Mistake? How can it be a mistake, Obie, when you have not told me one thing? You have a feeling, but you have nothing to tell me. Have you seen him in Tulsa at a dance club? Is he going around with another girl? Is he violent?"

As she asked each question, Obie shook his head, his mouth a grim line.

"Then I don't see anything that makes this a mistake. And I wish you would stop saying that." He had been her friend for as long as she could remember, but her patience was wearing thin. She trusted Obie. She wanted to believe him when he told her that he was worried, but how could she continue on if he couldn't tell her his concerns?

"Just call off the wedding." He held his hands out to her, reaching for her as his eyes beseeched her to listen.

But she had had enough. "I'm not going to call off this wedding, Obadiah Brenneman. No matter what you say." Because everything that he said was nothing more than words. He kept denying that he was worried they would lose their friendship once she and Thomas got married, but she knew that to be what it was. Now their friendship was tearing apart and all because he was being stubborn and unclear.

"Not even for me?" His green eyes saddened as he continued to study her.

"I can't call off the wedding without a reason. We have been dating for almost two years. I'm twenty-one years old. I'm ready to get married. And my wedding is scheduled in less than five weeks. Then you come in here and tell me that I need to call off the wedding, but you can't give me any specific reason as to why. Why should I listen to you?"

"Because I care about you more than anyone else in the world. You know that."

"If you care about me so much, then allow me this happiness." Obie's doubts had started to bleed into Clara Rose's own thoughts. Last night, as they sat around the table, everything Thomas had said had made Clara Rose begin to wonder. Was he telling the truth? Was he being sincere? Never before in the two years they had known each other had she ever questioned anything that Thomas had said.

"I can't allow you a happiness that will eventually ruin your life."

"It's not ruining everything. You are." The minute the words were out of her mouth, she regretted them.

Obie straightened, his back stiff. He ground his teeth together and gave her a sharp nod. "If that's the way you feel." He stalked past her, toward his tractor.

"Obie," she called after him, but his steps never slowed.

She watched, her heart breaking as he swung himself into the cab of his tractor and started down the drive.

He'll get over it, she thought to herself. But never once did he look back. Never once did he wave. Clara Rose blinked back her tears and picked up the bucket of chicken feed. She sprinkled a few more handfuls around, then headed for the barn, her steps heavy.

Half an hour later, she could stand it no more. She checked the messages on the phone hanging just inside the barn door. But Obie hadn't called. She had known that from the start. She hadn't heard the phone ring. But she'd had to check just to be sure.

"There you are," Anamaria said. "Mamm wants you to take these eggs over to the Chupp farm."

Why can't you? jumped to the tip of her tongue, but she bit back the hateful words. Nerves, she told herself. She was jumpy and nervous and anxious and irritable. Part of it was Obie's fault, and part of it was the wedding looming in the future. The most joyous time of her life was being ruined, and she was so sick of it. This should be a happy time. As much as she loved Obie, she wasn't going to let him ruin this for her. She smoothed her hands down her apron and took a deep breath. "*Jah*, of course." She took the eggs from her sister and hitched up her horse.

"Are you coming in, or are you going to stand out there all day?" Mammi asked as Clara Rose stood on the porch at the *dawdihaus*.

"Do you have a minute to talk?" Clara Rose nodded to the purse handle her grandmother had slung over one arm.

Mammi nodded. "I was just going to go out for a drive." It seemed the novelty of having a racehorse as a buggy horse had not worn off yet.

Her grandmother set her purse in the chair by the door and started back into the living room, motioning for Clara Rose to follow behind. "What's on your mind, dear?"

"A lot of things," she said.

"You want to pick one to talk about it?" Mammi asked. Her no-nonsense attitude always brought a smile to Clara Rose's lips.

But this time, she couldn't muster even the smallest quirk of her mouth. "I had a fight with Obie."

"And?"

Clara Rose shook her head. "He keeps telling me that Thomas and I shouldn't get married, but he can't give me a reason why. He just keeps saying he has a bad feeling, and that he wants me to call off the wedding. But I can't call off the wedding. It's five weeks away, everything is set, everybody's coming. Four hundred people are going to be here in less than five weeks. And he expects me to just call it off?"

"Do you want to call it off?" Mammi's steady blue eyes studied her.

Clara Rose didn't hesitate. "Of course not. I've been waiting my whole life to get married. Why would I want to call off my own wedding?"

Her grandmother seemed to think about it a minute, then reached over and patted Clara Rose on one knee. "Are you sure that Thomas is the right man for you?"

Clara Rose jumped to her feet and threw her hands in the air. "Not you too!"

Her grandmother raised a calming hand. "Now don't get in a tizzy. I was just asking a question. If you think that Thomas is the right man for you, then what does it matter what Obie says?"

Clara Rose wilted like a petunia in the noonday sun. "Obie is my best friend. I want to make them both happy. I want to marry Thomas, but I want Obie to be happy for me. But he's not."

"Of course not," Mammi said.

"What's that supposed to mean?"

But her grandmother shook her head. "That is something for you to figure out on your own, child."

"Are you ready to go?"

"Thomas," Clara Rose breathed. She snapped to attention. "What are you doing here?"

"Maybe I should ask you the same thing. You don't normally work on Thursday."

"Abe asked me if I could work an extra shift. He's got a big load going out to the Baptist church in Bixby, and he needed someone to polish it up before they load it into the truck." She had readily agreed, needing something to settle her mind.

"We have a date tonight." Thomas frowned, his dark brows meeting somewhere in the middle of his forehead.

A date? They had a date tonight? It was Thursday—what would they be doing on a Thursday night?

"You forgot."

She started to shake her head and make up some excuse as to why she hadn't remembered and explain that she surely hadn't *forgotten*.

He cut her off before she could speak. "I can't believe you forgot."

"I'm sorry, Thomas. I've just got so much on my mind lately." That was the truth and an understatement.

Thomas nodded. "Uh-huh."

She wasn't sure she appreciated his sardonic tone. But she wasn't about to argue with him. Their relationship seemed so fragile these days. And not because of him. He seemed like the same old Thomas as always, steady and dependable and true. She was the one walking around on eggshells and monitoring everything that she said and he said and everyone around them said. And how he looked at her and what he wore and everything that he did, all the while trying to discern why Obie was so determined to keep them from marrying.

Her mother's warning from a couple of weeks back still echoed in her mind. As much as she was beginning to believe her mother had been right, she didn't want to have to choose between Obie and Thomas. They were the two most important men in her life, and she couldn't imagine it without either one of them.

"The children's hospital," she breathed. She had forgotten all about it. Thomas had asked her a few weeks back if she and some of the other members of their youth group could go over to Pryor and visit with the sick children at the hospital. Thomas had arranged it all. Rented a car and a driver and gotten everybody together. He'd even come up with some ideas for entertainment for the children. All she had to do was show up. And she couldn't even do that.

"I know you've got a lot on your mind and everything," Thomas said, "but I'm really disappointed that you didn't remember this."

Clara Rose felt doubly repentant. Thomas's own baby sister had died from a terminal illness when she was no more than four years old. That had been five years ago and still he loved to go to the hospital and visit with the children and brighten their day. He was a wonderful person for arranging this visit, and she was a horrible person for forgetting.

"Just give me a minute here and I'll be ready to go." She didn't need to change. She had only been at work for an hour or so, and her job was done. It wasn't like Abe was going to need her any longer. But that wasn't the point. She had had so much on her mind lately that she had forgotten this wonderful idea that Thomas had included her in.

He gave a curt nod, and that little muscle jumped in his jaw like it did when he was overly thoughtful.

Clara Rose turned on her heel and headed for the back room. "Abe," she called, "I'm leaving now."

Abe Fitch looked up from the tabletop he was sanding and squinted at her through the smudged lenses of his glasses. She could almost see him clicking everything into place as if he had forgotten for a moment where he was and maybe even who he was because he was so engrossed in the job at hand. But he gave a small smile and nodded. "*Jah*, okay then. Be careful and thanks for coming in, Clara Rose."

Clara Rose took off her wood shop apron and smoothed her hands down the black one she wore underneath. She wasn't dressed fancy, but it would do. The children at the hospital didn't know the difference. Though she wished she had a minute to go home and maybe put on her favorite purple dress instead of the blue one that she wore, the main thing was the children.

She grabbed her sweater and her purse and started toward Thomas. He was waiting just where she'd left him, and she was immediately overcome with her emotions and feelings for him. Obie was worried that there was something wrong with Thomas. Something about him that didn't sit right. But how could that be? Thomas gave so much to other people, just like today's visit to the hospital. And she would do better to remember and live by his example. Once they were married, they would be a couple, and things like this would be part of what they did. He was a fantastic person, loving and caring, and would do almost anything for anybody around him.

Suddenly she was surer about marrying him than she had been in a long time. Her heart fluttered in her chest, then settled down into its normal rhythm. Everything was going to be just fine.

The good feeling lasted all of fifteen minutes. Somehow, in driving around and picking everyone up for the trip to the hospital, Clara Rose ended up in the front seat, with Thomas in the back sitting next to Sarah Yoder.

Everyone knew that Sarah was crazy about Jonah

Miller, but Jonah wasn't over Lorie Kauffman yet. If he ever would be. At the rate that Sarah was flirting with Thomas, it didn't seem that it mattered much to her after all.

Clara Rose pulled down the visor and looked in the mirror to see behind her.

Thomas was smiling and laughing at something Sarah said. And, for an instant, Clara Rose wondered if perhaps Sarah had taken advantage of the situation and positioned herself next to him.

Clara Rose shook her head at her own wayward thoughts and snapped the visor back into place. Sarah— and everyone else in the van, for that matter—knew Thomas and she were going to get married in just a few short weeks. Sarah couldn't capture his heart this late. Not that his heart was even up for capture. It belonged to Clara Rose. She was just being paranoid. And she needed to stop, before it ruined everything.

Yet she turned in her seat and looked back to where Thomas sat behind her. "Did I tell you Mamm finished the last of the shirts for the wedding?"

Thomas glanced from Sarah to her as if he had just re-membered that she was sitting up front and he was sitting by another woman. But then he smiled, those brown eyes melting like hot chocolate. "Good, good. Is that every-thing now?"

Most men didn't care one iota about how the wedding preparations went. Thomas did his best every step of the way, making sure everything was in place for their big day. And that was just one more reason why she loved him.

"It is. Everything's ready for the wedding. Just a little over four weeks now." She smiled when she said the words, but her eyes cut toward Sarah.

The girl shifted in her seat and looked out the window, which was strange since she was sitting in the middle and had to look out over someone else to do so.

"I was surprised to see you here, Sarah," Clara Rose said. "You're not in our buddy bunch or even in our youth group."

"Oh . . . well, I was with Jason Chupp when Thomas came to invite him, and naturally it was such a wonderful idea I asked if I could tag along."

Clara Rose tried to smile. "How sweet." She looked to Thomas, but he seemed to be staring out the window, allowing them a conversation of their own. Not knowing what else to say, Clara Rose turned back to the front. She was being ridiculous. And had almost completely embarrassed herself. She needed to get a handle on her wild emotions, and she needed to do it quickly before she made everything fall apart.

"Are you awake?" Clara Rose asked into the darkness that night.

"*Jah.*" But Anamaria's voice sounded so sleepy Clara Rose wasn't sure if her sister had meant to reply at all.

"Do you think Thomas likes Sarah Yoder?"

"What?" Anamaria's drowsiness disappeared in an instant. "Sarah Yoder? Why would he like Sarah? Doesn't she like Jonah?"

"I don't know." Clara Rose was glad for the darkness that hid her expression and the pink heat she knew tinged her cheeks. "It's just Obie keeps telling me that he has a bad feeling about me marrying Thomas and Thomas is just so perfect. Makes me wonder."

"That Obie is off in the head?"

"That Thomas isn't what he seems."

From across the room, the bedsprings squeaked as her sister shifted in place. Then Clara Rose was blinded by a flashlight beam to the face. She held up one hand to shade her eyes. "What is that for?"

"I just want to see your face," Anamaria said. "How could you believe that Thomas is anything but what he is?"

"Obie's been my friend for so long."

Anamaria let out a frustrated noise. "Thomas Lapp is the nicest man I know. He's kind and gentle and caring. He does things for other people without being asked and without wanting anything in return. He's always helping out even when he's not asked. He's the first one in line when someone needs help and the last one to leave when they get there. No, Thomas Lapp is a wonderful person. I don't know what's the matter with Obie right now. Maybe he has some kind of vitamin deficiency, but there's nothing wrong with Thomas."

Clara Rose lay back in her bed. From across the room, she heard her sister do the same. At least a flashlight wasn't shining in her face anymore. Now the beam was trained on the ceiling with its little peaks and dips in the texturized finish. It looked like the picture of the surface of the moon that she had seen once in an encyclopedia at the library. The moon was so far away, and the Amish really didn't study science. She shouldn't be fascinated with the little dark spots and craters all over the surface of that big orb. But as mysterious as it was, it wasn't half as mysterious as why Obie felt the need to make her doubt Thomas. Or why she allowed herself to doubt Thomas.

"You're right," she said. Thomas was about as perfect as they came. And that was something she needed to remember.

* * *

The next day, Clara Rose woke with a peace in her heart that she hadn't had for days, not since Obie had come into the quilting circle and told her that she shouldn't marry Thomas Lapp. Last night, talking with her sister, hearing her sister's words about what a wonderful man Thomas was, had changed everything. Today she would have tranquility of the heart. And she wouldn't have to worry about those plaguing doubts. The nervousness over her upcoming nuptials was gone, and in its place were happiness and a joy that she hadn't felt in a long, long time.

She went about her morning chores with a spring in her step. And to make matters even more complete, tonight was Friday, the night of the annual Wells Landing hayride. She could hardly wait. It was just a good excuse for a bunch of them to have some farmer drive them out in the woods. Still, she was looking forward to spending time with Thomas, just the two of them. Well, there would be a few other couples around, but it wouldn't be like the night before when they sang at the hospital in front of children and doctors and nurses and hospital staff, not to mention each other. This was a little more intimate. And she was looking forward to rattling around in an old wagon through the woods while everyone told stories and enjoyed the changing weather.

"You look chipper today," Mamm said.

"I am." It felt good to say that, to have that burden of doubt lifted from her shoulders.

"You and Obie make up?"

Clara Rose felt a great cloud rain over her day. "No, he still won't talk to me." Not that she had gone to his house or anything. She had only tried to call from the phone in the barn, but when he hadn't responded at once, she'd known that he didn't want to talk to her. And as much as it hurt her to have him separated from her, she wasn't about to force the issue. If he didn't want to be around her, that was his fault. Not hers. She would continue to do the things that she did in her life, be with the people that she was normally with, and see and talk to the people that she normally saw and talked with and eat the same foods and everything just the same, and when Obie decided to come back, she would still be there. Not really waiting on him. But she would still be there, the same person she had been the day that he left.

"If it's not Obie, then I suppose this has come from some sort of understanding with Thomas?"

"You could say that." Clara Rose gave a small wink as she stacked the breakfast dishes and headed for the kitchen.

"I didn't realize there'd be so many people here." Clara Rose allowed her gaze to wander around the fields and all the tractors and cars parked there.

Thomas wrapped his hands around her waist and set her on the ground safely. Then, as the true gentleman he was, he let her go. "This is opening night," Thomas said. "There's always a big turnout on the first day."

True, she thought. But this wasn't turning out to be the intimate night in a wagon with her fiancé she had hoped it would be, especially after her realization the day before. She had another epiphany. She needed to repair the damage to the bond between her and Thomas. Her mother was right: the bond was fragile and she needed to make sure that it was as strong as possible every day. Every minute of every day. And she needed to start yesterday.

"We might have trouble getting a wagon."

"I called in advance and reserved us one. Just in case." Thomas smiled down at her and she returned it, enjoying the twinkle in his brown eyes. It just went to prove how perfect he was. And once again she thanked God for bringing him to her.

"Is that Obie Brenneman over there?" Rachel Detweiler asked.

Clara Rose whirled around to find Obie standing next to Ivy Weaver. Her eyes widened, and she tried her best to make her expression impassive. She really didn't care who Obie went out with. It wasn't her concern. None of her concern at all.

Chapter Five

It's not any of your concern, she told herself as they piled into the back of the wagon. And it didn't matter that Obie was her best friend and had been forever. He could go out with whoever he wanted to. And it surely didn't matter that he had never shown any interest in dating anyone. At least not that she was aware of.

She pushed those thoughts away and sat down in one corner of the wagon, the hay cushioning her back. Thomas settled down next to her.

Of all the luck.

She looked up just in time to see Obie plop into the corner opposite them and pull Ivy down close to him. It was dark, but she thought for a moment that their eyes met and held. But then Obie looked away and the moment was gone, if it had ever been there at all.

"Are you comfortable?" Thomas laid the blanket across their legs to ward off the October chill. Weather in Oklahoma could be very unpredictable, but Clara Rose had checked the newspaper that very morning. This was supposed to be the coolest night they'd had all year.

She smiled gratefully at Thomas. "*Jah*, thanks."

And she wasn't going to look over and see just how close Obie was sitting to Ivy Weaver.

Her gaze wandered toward the opposite corner without any direction from her. They were sitting entirely too close together. Entirely.

She turned her attention back to her corner of the wagon. Thomas was speaking to her and she did her best to pay attention. She was certain he would have no desire to listen to her feelings about a girl like Ivy.

Not that Obie seemed to care. She glanced back over. Were they sitting even closer together than they had been before? It didn't matter. But he was messing up hanging out with Ivy Weaver.

"Clara Rose?"

She turned her attention to Thomas and smiled. She wasn't going to let Obie ruin her night. "Yes?" Even in the dim light Clara Rose could see the frown on his handsome face.

"You were a million miles away."

Not so far. Just across the wagon. "I'm sorry."

Thomas didn't have time to respond as the driver set the horses into motion. They rattled along the path, swaying and bumping shoulders with the motion of the wagon. Obie and Ivy weren't bumping shoulders because their shoulders were already scandalously pressed together.

"Can't be the wedding," Thomas said.

"What?" She turned her full attention back to Thomas, wondering when she had lost the thread of the conversation.

"You're so distracted. It can't be because of the wedding. You said your mother had finished all the sewing. There's nothing left to do but get married."

Clara Rose opened her mouth to respond, but she had nothing to say and shut it again.

Thomas's frown deepened.

"It's a lot of change, getting married," Clara Rose explained, hoping that it would bring Thomas some insight into her feelings on the matter.

His expression remained unchanged. "Or maybe it's just Obie."

Her gaze swung back to him. He was looking at her, as if waiting for her to look away from Obie and back to him.

"Obie's not talking to me right now." She hadn't had an opportunity to tell Thomas, or maybe she just hadn't taken any of the opportunities that had been afforded her. Honestly, she didn't want to talk to Thomas about Obie. Everything lately had been so tense. And then Obie got angry with her. Why couldn't they all get along?

"Because you won't call off the wedding?"

Clara Rose shook her head. "I don't know. I think this is just going to be an adjustment for all of us."

Thomas took one of her hands into his own, tracing the outline of each fingernail as he studied them. "It always is." He folded her fingers into his palm, the warmth of his touch seeping into her bones. It was going to be okay. As soon as she and Thomas got married, or maybe a couple weeks after that, Obie would see that they would still do things together as a youth group and buddy bunch. There weren't that many people in Wells Landing. They all had to stick together. What might seem like more change than they could handle at the present time would turn into a lifetime of friendship in just a few short weeks. She had to be patient until then.

* * *

After thirty minutes of riding in the wagon and doing everything in her power to give all of her attention to Thomas and none of it to Obie, Clara Rose was about to crack. She told herself repeatedly not to look over to see what Obie was doing. Every time she made the mistake of letting her gaze wander to where he sat, she regretted it. And in more ways than one.

"We're stopping for a small break," the driver said as he pulled the horses to one side of the dirt road.

A short distance away, a number of wooden picnic tables sat, clustered around a fire pit. A circle of lawn chairs surrounded the pit. The burning blaze offered heat and a fun place to roast marshmallows, but Clara Rose was not in the mood.

"Can I get you a cup of apple cider?" Thomas asked.

She slid into one side of one of the picnic tables and smiled gratefully back to him. "That would be good, *jah*."

As she watched, Thomas made his way back over to the wagon, where one of the drivers was handing out cookies and warm apple cider.

Clara Rose took the moment to prop her chin in her hand and not have to worry about anything. This time it wasn't about Obie or how he felt about her marrying Thomas. This was all about relaxing and resting and enjoying herself. It might've succeeded too, except the very moment she reached that relaxed state, Obie walked by holding Ivy Weaver's hand.

"Isn't that your little friend?" Ivy asked.

Obie stopped and looked around as if he hadn't seen her sitting there. Then his eyes widened in mock surprise.

"Oh yeah, this is Clara Rose. Clara Rose, Ivy Weaver."

Clara Rose took a moment to push to her feet for a small nod, then she sat back down without offering a hand to shake. She knew exactly who Ivy Weaver was. Everyone in Wells Landing did. She was *that* girl, the one with the reputation. Twenty years old, still in *rumspringa*, not showing any signs of slowing down. This was not the sort of girl Obie needed to be hanging out with. Not at all.

Clara Rose pushed herself to her feet and forced a smile to her lips. "Ivy, I'm sure you wouldn't mind if I talked to Obie for just a moment. *Alone*," she emphasized. Without waiting for a response, she grabbed the sleeve of Obie's black coat and pulled him away from the cluster of picnic tables and toward the dark crop of trees.

"What are you doing?" Clara Rose asked.

Obie gave her an innocent look. A look that was so innocent it had to be guilty. "I was going to get some cider and a cookie, but then someone grabbed my arm and dragged me into the woods."

"This isn't about apple cider and cookies, Obie. And you know it. What are you doing with her?"

He turned and glanced back to where Ivy stood at the picnic table, patiently waiting for him to return. "She's fine."

Clara Rose pinched him on the arm. Even though he had on his thick woolen coat, he let out a small yowl. "What'd you do that for?"

"Pay attention."

He pressed his lips together, his expression suddenly sullen. "I have paid attention my whole life, and it hasn't gotten me anywhere."

"She's trouble, and everyone in town knows it."

Obie shook his head. "Why would you say something like that?"

"Because it's true."

Obie shrugged and shoved his hands into his coat

pockets. His head was down, and she couldn't see his face enough to discern his true feelings on the matter.

"I've heard that she kissed three people, Obie. Three!"

He shrugged again. "Rumors."

But Clara Rose shook her head. "She wears jeans under her dresses and drives a car."

He shot her a bit of a grin. "And a pretty good one. It's a Mustang."

She didn't know the first thing about *Englisch* cars. She supposed they weren't that different from tractors, but she had no idea what a Mustang was. "All the more reason for you to stay away from her."

"I tell you what," Obie started. "You stay away from Thomas, and I'll stay away from Ivy."

Tears rose into her eyes at his hurtful words. "Why are you doing this?" He didn't say a word, just stood there, hands on his hips and eyes flashing green sparks into the night. "You're being totally unfair. I'm marrying Thomas in a few weeks. And unless you can come up with a valid reason why I shouldn't—and I don't think that you can—there's nothing more to say on the matter."

The rest of the hayride was a disaster. Everyone took the same seats as they had before their break, and once again Clara Rose was faced with Obie. Or should she say, Obie and Ivy. Cuddled up like they had known each other forever. Girls like that were trouble. They ran in the fast crowd, drove cars, probably even smoked cigarettes, and did more things than their parents even knew about. Obie had been baptized in the church. He had no business running around with a girl like Ivy. An association like that would only bring trouble.

But even as Clara Rose did her best not to look at Obie and Ivy together or even separately, her gaze seemed to wander in that direction without any say-so from her. It didn't take long for Thomas to realize that the other couple was capturing all her attention. Still. And the longer they were in the wagon, the further he seemed to pull away from her. There was nothing she could do about it. Or nothing that she knew to do about it. She wanted to reach out to Obie and make sure he knew that she only had his best interests at heart. Now, if she could just convince Thomas that she was only looking out for Obie, then everything would be perfect. But as much as she wanted that to happen, she knew it wouldn't. And the two men she loved the most were both angry at her at the same time.

She was careful not to say a word to Obie and Ivy as everyone piled out of the wagon at the end of the ride. But what had started out to be a fun and romantic night, her last hayride with Thomas as an unmarried couple, had turned into a messy ball of tension and nerves.

Lord please give me patience and understanding, Clara Rose prayed. *I surely do need them. Amen.*

Thomas didn't say a word as he led her back toward his tractor. As they approached the big green beast, Clara Rose couldn't help but remember what Obie had said about the Lapps' tractor. And it was true. It was nicer than some *Englisch* cars, and definitely nicer than any of the other tractors in the area. Mainly because it never had seen dirt. Except for maybe the patch of grass where it was parked during the summertime. Nope, the tractor was clean and well-maintained, and definitely different from the necessary farm tractor of the area. But it was more than the tractor that captured her attention. Halfway across the field where they had parked, Clara Rose realized Thomas was walking a good foot away from her.

She sidled in a bit closer, not so forward as to brush up against him, or hook her arm through his, but just a little closer. They had taken no more than three steps when she noticed the distance was back between them. She sidled in a bit closer once more, hoping that the distance Thomas had put between them was simply a coincidence. Three more steps in, it seemed there was even more space between the two of them.

"You're mad." It wasn't a question.

"Why would I be mad?" Thomas asked. He opened the door of the tractor and helped her inside. He might be upset with her, but he was still a gentleman.

A few seconds later, he swung himself up into the cab beside her. "My plan was simple, me and my girl coming out to enjoy the fall weather. Then the next thing I know, I'm staring down her supposed best friend who is all but kissing another girl in front of everyone. Why would I have any cause to be mad about that?"

Was this a trick question? She wasn't sure. Did she tell him the entire truth? Or just enough to ease that pain in his eyes? "Obie's just being ridiculous. He's trying to make me mad."

Thomas snorted, then started the tractor. "He's trying to make you jealous."

A small bark of laughter escaped her, but there was no humor in the sound. "He's trying to make me jealous? Why would he do something like that?"

Thomas gave her a look akin to the one her grandmother had given her the day before. Why was everybody thinking that she knew what was in Obie's mind and heart? She had no idea what he truly felt, only that he didn't want her to marry Thomas.

"Obie has no reason to want to make me jealous." She said the words as emphatically as she could, and they zinged around the cab of the tractor.

Thomas pinned her with another look, but this one was almost as unreadable to her as Greek. "You think so?"

"What reason would Obie have to make me jealous? What purpose would that serve?" she asked.

"I don't know, Clara Rose. Why don't you tell me?"

Chapter Six

"How much longer till you get the kids?" Mariana asked at the next quilting circle. Everyone had been steadily keeping up with Eileen's quest for foster children. Her dream was about to become a reality. Two little girls were coming to live with her. Sisters. They needed a mother now more than ever. Their own had been injured in the same car wreck that killed their father. Because of her injuries, she had become addicted to prescription painkillers, and between that and the depression, the poor woman had made a couple of bad choices and was now serving some time in jail. Who knew if she would ever get her life back in order enough that she would be able to care for her children. In the meantime, someone needed to take care of them, as their extended family was unwilling.

Clara Rose couldn't imagine how anyone's family would be unwilling to take care of two small girls. She had seen the picture that Eileen had brought in the last meeting, and the girls were adorable. Big brown eyes, soft curly blond hair. They looked like little angels. Clara Rose's heart went out to all involved.

"It may be a little while yet. But I'm hoping before Thanksgiving they'll be here. Wouldn't that be wonderful?" Eileen's eyes lit up in a way Clara Rose had never seen. The woman had wanted to have a child for as long as she had known her. Not that it was a great long time. Clara Rose had only been coming to the quilting circle for the last couple of years, but what Amish woman didn't want to have children? A whole passel of kids running around, playing games, helping with chores, and otherwise carrying on the Amish way of life to the next generation. Wasn't that what it was all about?

It was what she wanted. More than anything. To get married and have kids. With Thomas at her side. It was all she had ever wanted.

"That would be good," Mariana said. But she ducked her head over her quilt squares when she spoke, and Clara Rose had wondered if watching Eileen foster children was something of a heartbreak for the other woman. Clara Rose couldn't imagine how either one of them felt, in their forties and not able to have kids. *Lord please . . .* she prayed. But she stopped herself before she could complete the thought. It was selfish to ask for such a blessing. She could only hope that the Lord would see fit to give her the children that she wanted. Even as she wondered why the two gracious and kind women in front of her were barren. It just didn't make sense. She knew everyone around her said it was God's will. And she supposed it was. His will was something she tried so hard to accept each and every day of her life. But if she thought about it hard, maybe even too hard, she came up with more questions than answers. And God's will didn't seem to always satisfy them. Most times, she just chose not to think about it. Not question Him and pray that one day she would understand.

Clara Rose turned her attention back to the quilt squares folded in her lap. This was the stitching-together time, where they took the quilt squares they'd previously made and stitched them into blocks that would eventually be sewn together to form the complete quilt top. She wanted to ask Marianna how Leroy, her husband, was doing, but every week the woman appeared to be more gaunt than the week before, a little less happy, with dark circles forming under her eyes. The doctor had said Leroy probably wouldn't live past December, and everyone knew it was only a matter of time before he succumbed to his illness. Another fact that Clara Rose hoped she never had to face.

"Auntie?"

Her heart skipped a beat as she recognized the voice. Obie.

"In here," Eileen said.

Seconds later, Obie's face appeared at the large door that led to the bonus room. He had an apple in one hand and a grin on his face as he surveyed the room at large. Clara Rose couldn't help but notice that his gaze landed on her for only a split second before he looked away. She still hadn't spoken to him since that night at the hayride. Things were beginning to get more and more awkward between the two of them. Something that she didn't want. If they could just keep things smooth until after the wedding, she knew everything would be okay. But it seemed that Obie had other plans.

"Just another week, and I'll bring that puppy to you," Obie said, his attention back on his aunt.

But Eileen shook her head. "I don't want a dog right now, nephew," she said. The large grandfather clock in the hallway chimed out two dongs, which signified that the time to quilt was over. Most quilting circles ended around two so the women could get home in time to take care of the children coming home from school or get the supper ready for their dairy-farming husbands, who had to milk the herd at four. Since none of them had children walking home or husbands who ran dairy farms, it seemed a little strange that they would quit at the same time. But there was something to be said for tradition.

Everyone got up and started packing up their things, storing the quilt squares, and cleaning up the mess of threads and scraps. In no time at all, everyone was gone except for her, Mammi, Obie, and Eileen.

"Are you coming with me?" Mammi asked, one hand on the doorknob.

Clara Rose looked back to Obie, unsure of how to answer. She wanted to stay and talk to him. But she wasn't sure he wanted to talk to her at all. Especially not after Friday night.

But his gaze snagged hers and held. Those green eyes were unreadable as he studied her face.

"I'll take her home," he said without blinking or breaking the contact between them even once.

"Suit yourself," Mammi said and let herself out of the house.

"Can we talk?"

As much as she wanted to say yes, there was another part of her that wanted to tell him no. "What good is talking at this point? Every time we talk, all we do is fight." Clara Rose shook her head.

"I don't want to fight with you, Rosie. I just want to—" He broke off with a shake of his head, then turned back around, his green eyes pleading. "Please. Just stop and hear me out."

She hesitated, then finally nodded. "Okay. For a bit. It's getting cold outside."

Obie nodded and waited for her to don her sweater before the two of them made their way down the porch steps and around the back of the house. The sky was laden with gray clouds, and the wind held the definite chill of the approaching winter. But Clara Rose knew from experience today could be fifty and tomorrow could be eighty. Oklahoma weather was as unpredictable as her own feelings.

They walked for a few moments in silence, each with their hands in their pockets as they trudged through the brown clumps of grass between Eileen's house and Obie's.

With all the quiet, if the wind blew just right, she could hear the bark of the puppies on Obie's farm. The sound brought a smile to her lips.

"That's the first time I've seen you smile in weeks."

Was it? "You haven't been around a lot."

"Are you saying I'm the reason for your frown?"

Clara Rose stopped and shook her head. "I don't want to do this, Obie. I don't want to fight with you. It's not any fun."

Obie stopped as well, turning to face her, his expression as clouded as the sky above. "I don't want to fight with you either, Rosie. You're the most important person in my life, and I can't imagine it without you."

This. This was what she had been waiting on. She had been praying for this first step in reconciliation between the two of them. The first step toward understanding and a compromise, the bridge between the changes they were making in their lives. She was getting married to Thomas, and Obie needed to understand that. With a little work, they could turn what seemed to be a dead end to their friendship into something much, much more. There was no reason why the two of them couldn't remain friends just because she and Thomas were getting married. And whatever Obie had in his thoughts, it was time for him to let them go, to trust her judgment with Thomas and to know and trust that Thomas was the man he presented himself to be.

"I feel the same way, you know," she said. And she did. The last thing she wanted to do was lose him in order to gain her other dreams. It just didn't seem fair that she couldn't have both.

She said a small prayer of forgiveness at those selfish thoughts. God knew what was in her heart and understood her.

"I know." His words were soft, strained, as he took a step closer. His eyes were unreadable as he tugged her hands from her pockets and held them in his own. His fingers were warm and callused. Hands that did good work. Trusting, loving hands.

"Promise me," he said.

"Anything." She said the word without hesitation. They'd come around the bend on this snag in their friendship. And they were climbing that hill toward understanding. They would get there. They would survive this.

"Promise me things won't be different once you marry him." His voice cracked on those last two words. He cleared his throat. "Promise me."

Clara Rose tilted her head back to stare up at him. He tugged her just a bit closer, the tails of her coat brushing against his. "I promise."

His eyes turned a deep emerald green, a color she'd never seen before, and had an intensity she hadn't known he could feel.

"Thank you," he whispered into the space between them, and then all of a sudden there was no space. And his lips touched hers.

Was this real?

Clara Rose wanted to shake her head. It couldn't be. But she didn't move for fear of losing the contact she now had with Obie. It was sweet, and her lips tingled where his touched hers. Her eyes fluttered and closed as she let the beauty wash over her. It was just the two of them, just a small kiss between friends.

Obie lifted his head and stared into her eyes, searching for something, though she had no idea what. Then he released her hands and cupped her face in his palms, pulling her mouth to his once again.

Clara Rose leaned in to him. His lips were warm, heating the air around them. His kiss was gentle, heady, everything she'd ever dreamed of in a kiss, and it went straight to her head. She wanted to step in closer. Instinctively she wanted to wrap her arms around him and never let go. As first kisses went, it was the best. And he was her best friend. Obie.

Obie!

Her eyes snapped open. She couldn't kiss Obie.

She clasped his hands into her own and pulled them from her face, stepping back and away from him even as she wanted to draw closer than before.

His eyes snapped open and centered on her. Even as close as they stood to each other, she couldn't read his expression. "Clara Rose?"

"We can't do this." She shook her head.

She took another step away even as Obie took one toward her. "No, no, no, no, no."

She was getting married to Thomas in just a few weeks. Yet she'd kissed Obie as if her life depended on it. What made her any better than Ivy Weaver?

"Clara Rose, just listen."

She shook her head again. "No." She turned on her heel and started back toward the house. She had to get away.

She had to get away now. Maybe if she ran fast enough she could catch up with her grandmother. Her legs started to run. And run.

"Clara Rose!" Obie called from behind her.

She ran faster.

She thought she heard him call, "I'm sorry," as she continued up the hill, but it could have been the wind whistling in her ears.

She ran on.

Chapter Seven

Clara Rose could hardly wait for Tuesday's quilting circle to come back around again. There was something about sewing, especially quilting, that captured her mind and calmed her wayward thoughts. And right now she needed all the calming she could get.

All she could think about morning, noon, and night was Obie's kiss. She had been so distracted she ran into the wall in the kitchen and now sported a huge purple bruise on her forehead.

She managed to avoid both Thomas and Obie for the entire weekend. It seemed the more time she spent with either one of them, the more confused she became. And she really needed to be able to avoid running into any more walls. Truth of the matter was, she needed to trust Thomas, love him unconditionally as God had intended, and bind their hearts together so they could go through the rest of their lives as one. But she also had to trust Obie. He was her best friend and had been for as long as she could remember. He always looked out for her, always had her best interests at heart. But after that kiss . . . It'd gone beyond that now. She had heard rumors flying around on

Sunday that Obie had been seen running around with Ivy all weekend, driving in her Mustang car and going here and there and who knew where else. She needed to do something, and she needed to do it quickly before Obie found himself in more trouble than he could get out of. She needed to save him from himself. But how?

She looked up from the quilt squares that she was stitching together. They were almost done with the top. Soon they would add the batting and the backing; then they would edge it and quilt it all together. It would be a beautiful quilt to put up for the Clarita auction come next fall. She was sort of glad that this quilt was going off to help the school, not only because it would help others, but because if it had been her quilt, she didn't know if she could look at it without remembering all this turmoil. This was supposed to be the happiest time of her life, and yet every night she prayed for peace and understanding and understanding and peace.

Lord, just help me be patient as we get through this crisis. Give us support and peace in our thoughts as we get through this time. And Lord, in Your infinite wisdom as we near the wedding day, please help us through to that bright patch on the other side. Amen.

"Verna," Eileen started, "will you be able to sew the rest of these squares together?" Of the group, Mammi was the one with the least responsibilities to family and kin. So she was usually the one who sewed the final quilt squares together. Everyone at this quilting circle sewed as many squares together as they possibly could while there. Then Clara Rose's grandmother took the six or so blocks to piece together into the final quilt top. After that, the true quilting would begin.

"Of course. Of course," Mammi said.

"It'll be so exciting to see it as a quilt top, don't you think, Clara Rose?" Tess asked.

Clara Rose nodded. "*Jah*, that it will be."

Everyone folded up the squares they were working on and gave them to her *mammi* before gathering up their things to go.

"What in the world?" Mariana said, pointing to the golden retriever puppy sitting in the middle of Eileen's living room.

It was about the cutest thing Clara Rose had ever seen. Big brown eyes and fluffy golden fur. Her fingers longed to run themselves through that soft fur, and get a bunch of puppy kisses for her effort.

"Obie, come out here!" Eileen shouted.

Of course it was Obie. He was the only Amish golden retriever breeder in the area. And he had the prettiest and sweetest puppies that anyone could ever want to have.

He ducked out of the kitchen, half of a peanut butter and jelly sandwich in one hand and a glass of milk in the other.

"Don't they feed you at home, boy?" Eileen asked, though her eyes twinkled. It was so obvious she loved her nephew very much. Maybe even more so since his twin had decided to run off to Pinecraft and delay his joining the church by several months.

"Just thought I'd bring him to visit today." He smiled and took a gulp of the milk.

"He better not pee on my clean floor," Eileen said.

Obie shook his head. "Tater would never do that. He's a good pup, and he's already housebroken."

"I am not taking a puppy from you," Eileen said.

"Aw, Auntie, the kids are going to love it."

"It's going to be enough work with two little kids running around the house. We're not accustomed to having children underfoot. The last thing we need is a puppy in here too."

Obie looked crushed, and Clara Rose noticed that he never once turned his gaze to her. Did he feel as awkward as she did about the kiss they'd shared? Was she the only one who'd felt that tingle, that zing? Must be.

"But I saved him just for you. He was the best one of the litter."

"Can I have him?" The words jumped from Clara Rose's lips before she had time to think them through. Her mother would probably pull her hair out if she brought the puppy home, but with all the trouble she and Obie had been having lately, having that pup in the house would be like having a piece of Obie underfoot. A piece that wouldn't tell her that she shouldn't marry Thomas and not give her a good reason why. That was a piece she could definitely deal with.

Obie turned to face her for the first time since he'd come in. "Hi there, Clara Rose."

She gave him a small nod. "He's a great-looking pup."

She hated that things were so awkward between them now. But what was a girl to do? It wasn't every day her best friend tried to kiss her. Not every day at all. Her heart broke that things were so strained between them now. Was that her fault? Had she reacted badly to the kiss? Responded incorrectly? Was she the only one who felt that longing for more?

What she would give to go back to a time before all this happened, maybe even back as far as when Obie first came to the sewing circle and asked her not to marry Thomas. Maybe if she had handled things differently from that day until now, she and Obie would still be friends.

If she asked him, he would probably say that the two

of them were still friends, but everything had definitely changed. It had changed so much that their relationship was hardly recognizable, and she and Thomas weren't even married yet.

They had three more weeks before the actual wedding. Three more weeks of cooking and freezing and ironing and last-minute preparations before they said their vows. She could only pray that things would improve after that. But judging by the distant look in his green eyes, he didn't have a lot of hope.

He gave a small nod. "*Jah*, he's a good pup." He swallowed hard and seemed to think about it a second. "Sure. You can have him. Consider him my wedding present."

Obie ducked back into the kitchen, and Clara Rose picked up Tater the pup. She held him close to her, inhaling that sweet puppy scent even as her tears fell into that soft fur. Nothing would ever be the same again.

"Clara Rose!" Mamm shouted. "Come get this pup!"

Clara Rose hustled down the stairs to rescue Tater from yet another mischievous disaster. Or rather to rescue her *mamm*'s knitting from the ornery canine.

She snatched him up and held him close, quickly noting that she had arrived just in time. The sweater Mamm was knitting was safe once again. At least for a time.

Her mother shook her head and disappeared into the kitchen, her look of disapproval sticking around long after she had left.

Clara Rose kissed the puppy on the top of his head and received a sweet puppy kiss in return.

There were times when he reminded her so much of Obie that her heart hurt. She hadn't seen him since he had given her the puppy. Not even at church. She had heard through the talk at the quilting circle that he had gone over to Clarita to help his cousin, but secretly she feared that he had gone off to Pinecraft with his brother. If that was the case, she wondered if he'd ever come back.

"What does Thomas think about the dog?" Anamaria asked as she came through the house carrying a basket of towels to the upstairs bathroom.

"He uh . . . thinks Tater is staying here."

Once they were married, she and Thomas were moving into the main Lapp house until they built their own house in the lot across the street.

Anamaria looked around to see if their mother was listening in. "Does Mamm know this?"

So far, Tater had chewed up two and a half pairs of shoes, the hallway rug, several baskets, and the lunch-box Clara Rose used when she needed to take food to work with her.

Clara Rose shook her head. "He's not staying here. He's coming with me."

Her sister propped the basket on one hip and eyed her skeptically. "When are you going to tell Thomas?"

She shrugged and placed the pup back on his too-big feet. "Soon, I guess."

Anamaria snorted. "I would hope so. The wedding is in less than five days."

A pain shot through her heart at the thought. In less than five days, she would be a married woman. She and Thomas would go to live in the family house until they got their own place built. Surely Thomas would get used to having Tater underfoot. Sure, the beast was an ornery puppy now, a ball of fur with entirely too much energy for such a small creature. But he wouldn't be so small for long. And when he was a seventy-pound faithful companion and watchdog, Thomas would be thankful to have him.

She shook her head at her own thoughts. Maybe then Thomas wouldn't care that it was her last and final gift from Obie. She didn't know if she would ever see Obie again. Tater was her last piece of her best friend.

"Clara Rose?"

She shifted her attention from the floor to her sister.

"Are you all right?"

Clara Rose nodded. "*Jah*, I'm fine. Just nerves," she said, but she and Anamaria both knew that it was not the truth. Yet she had said it so many times in the last two weeks, she had almost started to believe it.

"Is Thomas coming to pick you up soon?"

"Huh?" she asked.

"Isn't it buddy bunch night?"

"*Jah*, of course." Clara Rose shifted in place and immediately ran through the list of things she needed to do to get ready to play cards with her friends.

Anamaria took a deep breath and immediately Clara Rose knew. "He deserves better, you know."

"I love Thomas," she said. And she did. What was not to love? He was just about perfect in every way, and she was the luckiest girl alive to be marrying him next week.

"He needs someone who won't forget they have a date with him and will give all their attention to him."

"Are you saying I shouldn't marry him?" Clara Rose's throat clogged with unshed tears. She had made her share of mistakes in the last few weeks, but she would do right by Thomas. Always and forever, she would do right by him.

"No, just appreciate him," Anamaria advised before tromping upstairs to finish her chores.

A knock sounded on the door. Clara Rose jumped, and Tater let out a vicious bark. Well, a vicious puppy bark. He growled like a big dog, all the while wagging his tail.

Clara Rose let out a chuckle at the puppy's antics and went to answer the door.

"Hi. Sorry I'm late. Are you ready to go?" Thomas asked.

One hand flew to her prayer *kapp*. "Can I have a few minutes? I got sidetracked with the puppy."

"*Jah, jah.*"

She stepped aside for him to enter. "Make yourself at home and I'll be right back down."

"Try to hurry," Thomas said as he removed his hat. "We're already running behind."

"Okay," she said, then flew up the stairs to change her dress.

"What are you doing?" Anamaria asked as Clara Rose rushed into their bedroom, barely waiting until she had cleared the threshold before unpinning her prayer *kapp* and shucking off her apron.

"Gotta . . ." she started, her words muffled by the fabric of her dress. "Gotta change." In more ways than one. She had been out of sorts lately. She had let Obie's worries get to her. She had let his kiss affect her even more. Too many nights, she had stared at the ceiling, reliving every minute of his lips on hers, when she should have been sleeping.

Well, no more.

She was marrying Thomas in just a few more days. He deserved her entire attention, all of her love, everything. And that was exactly what he'd be getting from her from here on out.

She pulled her favorite purple dress over her head and tied on a clean apron. As quickly as possible, she smoothed her hair down using a dab of baby lotion and the palms of her hands. She didn't have time to brush it out and put it back up so that would have to do. She pinned her hair back into place and gave her reflection a last once-over.

"You look good," Anamaria said.

"I was going for amazing."

"Then you look amazing," Anamaria corrected with a smile.

Clara Rose crossed the room in a heartbeat and wrapped her sister in a tight hug. "Thanks," she whispered.

"What for?" Anamaria asked returning the embrace.

"For helping me see the truth."

Clara Rose released her sister and raced back down the stairs to where Thomas waited.

Chapter Eight

"What's gotten into you tonight, Clara Rose?"

She sighed from her perch next to him on the tractor seat. "Nothing. I'm just happy."

Thomas smiled. "I can see that."

She gave a shrug and a toss of her head. She felt carefree and alive, not weighed down by her doubts and fears of the future. This was what she wanted. To get married, be Thomas's wife, raise kids and corn, and live happily ever after, as the *Englisch* fairytales said. She was still concerned about Obie, and she hoped that he was taking care of himself wherever he was. She said a little prayer for his safety and turned her attention back to the man at her side. "I know I've been out of sorts lately, but I'm getting back to my old self," she said.

"I'm glad." He smiled at her from his place in the driver's seat, and Clara Rose knew in that instant it was all going to be okay. Regardless of stolen kisses and the concerns of her friends, she and Thomas were meant to be together. God had sent Thomas to be her one true love. And she would spend the rest of her life thanking Him for such a wonderful gift. All of her dreams were about to come true.

"Are you ready?" Emily Riehl asked from the doorway of Clara Rose's bedroom.

Clara Rose ran her hands down her white apron one last time and looked in the mirror to straighten her already perfect white cape. Underneath, she wore a dress of soft dusty blue. It wasn't the color she would have chosen herself, but Thomas's mother had gone with her that day to pick out material for the wedding party. Margaret Lapp had suggested the color for its rich undertones and sophisticated appearance. The Lapps were definitely "fancy Amish," and Clara Rose knew that Margaret Lapp had more knowledge about trends and what was popular in other communities as well as the *Englisch* world. If Margaret thought the color becoming for a wedding, then who was she to say otherwise?

But even as Clara Rose tugged on the sleeves of her dress, the aqua-blue material she had been about to buy rose to her mind. It was a loud color, a little flashy, and reminded her of the swimming pool at the rec center.

"Clara Rose?" Emily prompted.

She nodded. "Just about." But in truth there was nothing left to do. She looked around the room. Her sister was dressed, looking as beautiful as ever in the same shade of dusty blue. The color set off her dark hair to perfection and made her gray eyes, so like Clara Rose's own, deepen to the color of smoke.

"You've got a few more minutes if you need some time."

She would have liked a place to sit and quietly pray.

Her good feelings from the weekend had faded as the wedding day drew near with no sign that Obie was returning. She had even gone out to his house the day before and talked to his father a while. Paul Brenneman had assured her that Obie was only in Clarita, that he had not picked up and completely left town. If he had plans to come to the wedding, Paul hadn't known.

There were close to two hundred people in her mother's living room, and the one person who she wanted to be there above all else was nowhere to be found.

"Just give me a minute," she said. Just another minute to collect her thoughts.

Emily gave her a knowing look, then motioned for Anamaria and the other bridesmaids to leave the room. Her cousins, Sophie and Jessica, smiled sympathetically as they passed.

Suddenly, Clara Rose was alone. It seemed as if she hadn't been by herself in a long, long time. Despite the sounds floating up from downstairs, the room was quiet, and Clara Rose closed her eyes and let it wash over her.

A soft knock sounded at the door. "Rosie?"

"Obie?" She spun around to face him, praying the whole while that he wasn't a figment of her imagination. "You came."

He stepped into the room, his gaze darting around as if testing to see if they were really alone. "Of course, I came. You are my best friend."

She rushed to his side and clasped his hands into her own. "I'm so glad you're here."

"Me too," he said, but his voice sounded strained. She was about to ask him what the matter was, but he spoke, cutting off her question before she could ask it. "What are you wearing?"

She looked down at herself. "My wedding dress."

"I know that, but the color." She started to respond, but he continued before she could say the words. "It's a nice color," he amended.

"But?" she asked.

"It doesn't look like something you would pick out."

She looked down at herself. "Margaret helped me."

He gave an understanding nod, but didn't comment further.

"I'm glad you're here," she said again, and realized that the time was drawing nearer. "I guess I should go now." She released his hands and made her way to the door.

"Don't go out there," Obie quietly beseeched her.

She turned to face him, trying to read through his expression to the truth underneath. "I have to. It's almost time."

"Please."

Clara Rose stopped. "Obie, you're my best friend and I would do almost anything for you. But I have to go now."

"I don't want to be your friend."

"Obie Brenneman, what a thing to say. Isn't that what we've always been, the best of friends?"

"Yeah. We've always been friends. And at first I thought that was going to be enough. I can hang out with you, see you every day, touch your hand from time to time, but that would never be enough. And now . . ."

Clara Rose waited patiently for him to continue. When he didn't, she prompted, "And now what?"

"You can't marry Thomas," he said, stopping her. She had one hand on the doorknob and didn't turn around as he said the words.

"I thought we had covered this," she said, exasperation tainting her tone.

"I want you to marry me."

"What?" She spun around to face him.

"You can't marry Thomas because you're supposed to marry me."

His words simply took her breath away. She couldn't marry Thomas because she was supposed to marry Obie?

She burst out laughing, only controlling her mirth long enough to say, "Obie, you had me going there for a minute. Too funny." She continued to laugh but stopped when she realized that he was not laughing with her. She wiped the tears from her eyes and cleared her throat. "Why aren't you laughing?"

Obie shook his head, his jaw tense. "Because I'm not joking. This is not funny. I've let you announce your engagement. I've watched you prepare, thinking that all my feelings for you were something different. But I realize now. I truly love you. And I don't want you to marry Thomas because I want to marry you myself."

She shook her head again. "I don't know what to say."

Obie shoved his hands in his front pockets. "All the way back here from Clarita, I practiced what I was going to say. And this is the part where you tell me that you love me too and you want to marry me and not Thomas Lapp."

Her heart constricted in her chest. Her breath caught, and for a moment she thought she might pass out from it all. "I can't," she whispered as tears rose into her eyes.

Suddenly everything was clear. She loved Obie. She always had. He had been her rock, her best friend, her everything for so long that she hadn't noticed how much he had started to mean to her. She had no idea when she'd fallen in love with him. Or maybe there had been no fall involved. Maybe she'd simply grown into love with him from all the years of being by his side.

"I love you."

Tears spilled down her cheeks. Why was it now, when she was set to marry another, that he came along and declared his feelings for her?

She shook her head and dashed the tears away with the back of one hand. "I wish you had told me this that day behind your aunt's house."

"Would that have changed things between us?"

Clara Rose shook her head. "No," she quietly admitted. He needed to have confessed his love long ago, before Thomas had called for her hand. "I've already promised to marry another man." A man who had declared his love for her long ago.

"I know."

"There are people out there who have come to see—" She broke off, unwilling to say more. "It's not possible," she said, her heart breaking in two.

"Clara Rose?" Anamaria peeked her head through the door. "Everyone is waiting."

"*Jah*, okay." She sniffed, struggling to keep her tears from falling.

"Are you crying?" Her sister looked around to see what could be causing her such distress. "Obie?"

"I was just leaving." He pushed past Anamaria and out the door.

"What's going on?"

"Where's Thomas?" Clara Rose asked.

"In the barn with the other men. Why?" Anamaria shook her head. "You aren't going to—"

"I need to talk to him. Now."

"Now?"

"Right now."

"But," Anamaria started as Clara Rose pushed past her

and down the hallway. "You're not going to do anything stupid, are you?"

"I just want to talk to him for a minute." She continued down the stairs and somehow managed to make it through the crush of people and out the door.

She sprinted across the yard, mindless of the cold and the dust and the dirt. She had to talk to him. Immediately.

She raced to the barn door and went inside, the men all stopping as she entered.

"Has anyone seen Thomas?" Her gaze lighted on an individual face, then on to the next. She had no time for dallying.

"He's in the tack room," one man said. She thought it was Aaron Miller, but she wasn't positive and she didn't have time to find out.

"Thank you." She pushed through the press until she reached the opening of the doorway. There she stopped and took a deep breath, pausing for the first time since she left the house.

She stepped into the room, oblivious to everyone but Thomas.

"Clara Rose?" He stood, looking so handsome in his crisp white shirt and black vest. So fancy.

"Can I talk to you for a minute?"

"Now?" His brows rose in surprise, but she knew if she asked him, he would do whatever she needed.

She wrung her hands, her teeth suddenly chattering. "Yes, please."

He gave a nod and followed her out the door of the tack room, through the barn, and out into the yard. She ignored the looks they got as they pushed through. Now was not the time to stand on ceremony.

A few people milled about outside. The weather was

turning colder, but not so much that a coat and hat wouldn't ward off the chill. Still, her teeth chattered like crazy.

"Are you cold?" Thomas asked. He took off his jacket and slid it around her shoulders. It was warm and smelled like him, like sandalwood and leather. An immediate peace stole over her.

"Thank you," she said, pulling it a little closer around her. Not for extra warmth but for the sensation of being completely surrounded by Thomas. She needed that. She needed to know that he was there for her, that he would protect her and care for her always.

"Are you crying?"

Was she?

He stepped forward and wiped a tear from her cheek. "What's wrong, my love?"

His love? She closed her eyes, trying to get her bearings in the situation. But her head swam and she opened them once again.

"It's Tater," she blurted, ashamed that she had lied to this man, this good and honest man who deserved better than he had gotten from her.

A frown puckered his brow. "What about Tater?"

"He's not staying with Mamm, after we're"—she swallowed hard—"married." Why did she have such a hard time saying that word? Wasn't that what she wanted? Wasn't that what she had always wanted?

But it wasn't just marriage, not anymore. She had spent her entire engagement more in love with the idea of being married than she was in love with her fiancé.

Shame filled her.

"This isn't about Tater." Thomas took a step back. "Are you going to tell me what's really on your mind?"

Could she tell him? Movement flashed out of the corner of her eye, and she turned, distracted by the motion.

Obie glanced toward the two of them as he stalked across the yard to his waiting tractor. It was the only one amid the lines of shiny black buggies. Why hadn't she noticed it before?

"I see." Thomas pressed his lips into a thin line.

Clara Rose shook her head. "It's not what you think." She took a step toward him, grasping his sleeve to keep him from moving farther away.

"I only know what you tell me, Clara Rose."

Now was the time. She could keep quiet no longer. "Obie told me that he loved me and asked me to marry him."

"When? Today?"

She nodded.

"And you told him . . . ?"

"I told him that I was marrying you."

"What about love?"

"Of course, I love him. He's my best friend."

"And me?" Thomas asked. "Do you love me?"

"You are the most wonderful man I have ever met, and I will be the best wife to you that I can be."

"That didn't exactly answer my question."

"Thomas, I—"

"Or maybe it did."

Chapter Nine

Clara Rose hated the clouds that dimmed Thomas's eyes. "I made my promises and I intend to keep them."

He shook his head. "What are you saying?"

"That we have two hundred guests who came to see us get married. I suppose we should stop standing around and get to it."

He studied her for a moment, then gave a stiff nod. Behind him, Obie started his tractor.

The bottom dropped out of Clara Rose's heart. This was the right thing to do. Thomas was a good man, the best. She couldn't drop everything and marry Obie. It wasn't feasible. She couldn't embarrass Thomas that way. She couldn't bring that shame upon her family.

This was it. The right thing to do.

"Go on back in the house. I'll be there in a bit."

Clara Rose gave a quick nod, thankful that her tears had finally stopped. Thankful that God had given her a man like Thomas. Theirs would be a good marriage.

She slipped his jacket from around her shoulders and made her way back inside.

* * *

Somehow she made it through the throng of guests downstairs and back up to her room. She made a quick stop in the bathroom to wet a rag with cold water. If she was lucky, she would have just enough time for the cool cloth to work its magic on her tear-stained cheeks and swollen eyes.

Her bridesmaids were gone, most likely waiting in the kitchen for their cue to take their place at the front of the room.

That was okay with Clara Rose. She used the time alone to pray that she was doing the right thing by them all. She wiped the dust from her shoes and from the hem of her dress. Then took one last look in the mirror and made her way back downstairs.

A hush fell over the room as she entered. All eyes were trained on her. She looked up and caught Thomas's gaze. He gave an encouraging smile.

She tried to return it but settled for a small nod instead. She joined her bridesmaids on the front bench, willing her heart to slow to a normal pace.

Once everyone was seated, Bishop Ebersol stepped forward to start the service.

"Ahem." Thomas stood and went to the front of the room.

This wasn't part of the ceremony. And from the look in the bishop's face, he had no idea what was going on either.

"Friends and family, I want to thank you all for coming here today. We have everything ready to have a wedding— food, cake, paper plates."

Everyone laughed, but Clara Rose's heart tripped in her chest as he continued. "But we are missing one very important item. A groom."

Gasps went up all around.

Unable to stop herself, Clara Rose jumped to her feet.

Thomas motioned her over to stand next to him. On shaking legs, she approached him and turned to look out over the sea of shocked faces.

"We have a bride," he continued, slipping his arm around her waist but not pulling her any closer. "But not a groom. Or maybe I should say we don't have the right groom. But that doesn't mean we shouldn't still enjoy ourselves and the fact that we are here together. In a few minutes, we will cut the cake and serve the food, but for now I have a bit of unfinished business."

"Would you like to explain to me what's going on?" Bishop Ebersol asked. His dark blue eyes searched their faces, but Clara Rose had nothing to say. She was just as confused as he was.

"I found out something very important this morning."

The bishop nodded. "Go on."

"I found out that my bride is in love with someone else. And that this other person loves her in return."

"I see," the bishop said.

Clara Rose tried to wet her lips, but her mouth was so dry her tongue was sticking to her teeth. Where was he going with this?

"Would someone like to tell me what's going on?" Nancy Yutzy came to stand behind Clara Rose. Immediately, she had the love and support of her mother, and she relaxed. But only a little.

"I'd like to know the answer to that myself." Jason and Margaret Lapp came to stand beside their son.

The bishop looked back to Thomas. "We're waiting."

"It's simple, really. Clara Rose loves someone else, and I won't stand in the way of her happiness."

Tears stung her eyes.

"What?" Margaret all but shrieked the one word. "I told you she wasn't the right girl for you, Thomas."

Thomas opened his mouth to speak, then thought better of it and closed it instead.

"There's nothing wrong with my daughter," Mamm huffed, hands on her hips.

"I'll have you know—"

Clara Rose stepped between everyone and held up her hands. "Please, stop. Enough is enough. This is between me and Thomas."

"She's right." Thomas took her arm to lead her away. The bishop followed. Clara Rose figured he had the right to hear the truth seeing as he had had blessed their marriage months ago. But their parents followed.

"We should at least know what's happened here," Mamm said.

"Fine," Thomas said. "But everyone has to keep their feelings in check. This is nothing to get upset over."

His mother opened her mouth to speak, but closed it again after a stern look from Thomas.

"I found out today something I think I have known all along but was too blind to see."

"And that was?" the bishop prompted.

"That Clara Rose and Obie Brenneman are in love with each other. And as much as I know in my heart of hearts that she would be the best wife a man could ask for, I can't stand in the way of true love." He turned to Clara Rose and took her hands into his own. Her fingers trembled in his sure grasp. "I release you from your promise to me."

"Thomas." She knew it was forward, but she pulled him close and wrapped him in a big hug. "Thank you. Thank you so very much."

"Just go and be happy," he said, pulling away from her

to run one hand over the side of her face. "And promise me that the two of you will always love each other."

"I promise," she said. And it was one promise she knew she would be able to keep.

A din of barking welcomed her as she pulled her grandmother's buggy in front of the Brenneman house. Her grandmother was right—the ex-racehorse, Daisy Lane, could still fly like the wind.

She patted the horse on the rump and unhitched her from the rig. She wasn't sure where Obie was, but she knew she needed to get the horse out of the wind before she went in search of him. Once Daisy Lane was in the barn, she went back to the house.

She peered in the window, but the house had that empty look, as if no one was home. Where had they all gone on a Thursday morning? Most likely to their various jobs around town, but she had seen Obie at the wedding and she felt he had to be close.

Then she remembered. His favorite place. Millers' pond.

She knew it was taking a chance that he would actually be there, but that was exactly what this was about: taking chances.

She hitched Daisy Lane back to the buggy, then off she went, so grateful to have such a swift horse on her side. Daisy Lane tossed her head into the wind as Clara Rose pushed her faster and faster. They reached Millers' pond in record time.

She hopped down from the buggy, her heart pounding in her chest as she saw Obie's tractor parked off to one

side. At least she had found him. That had to count for
something.

One down, two to go, as they say.

She tethered her horse, then ducked under the fence,
only then realizing that she wasn't wearing a coat. Not
even her sweater. Up until now, she hadn't needed the
warmth, with adrenaline pushing her. But now that she
had found him, a chill had set in. And it didn't have as
much to do with the weather as it did her own doubts. She
had flown here on the wings of a racehorse, but her steps
slowed as she neared the crop of trees.

What if he told her it was too late? That she'd had her
chance. What if he spurned her as she had him earlier?

Only one way to find out. She clomped through the
trees and into the clearing. Just as she'd known he would
be, he was skipping rocks along the water's surface.

"Hello, Mrs. Lapp."

She shook her head and wrapped her arms around herself, that chill setting in once again. "Don't call me that."

He shrugged. "How'd you find me?"

"I'm your best friend, remember? You love this place."

He gave a quick nod, then skimmed another rock
across the water. "So you are, so I do."

"I know you're upset," she started, but then didn't
know how to finish. *But I love you?* They had already
covered that. *But I'm sorry.* That had been talked about as
well. There was only one thing left to say. "I didn't marry
Thomas."

He stopped and turned to face her, his gaze raking over
her from head to toe. She still wore her wedding dress,
white cape, and apron, though they now looked a fright.
And she was certain her prayer *kapp* had a big snag in it

where she hadn't been careful enough making her way through the trees.

He opened his mouth, then closed it again with another shake of his head. "I want to say something mean and spiteful, but I can't."

"Why would you want to say something like that?"

He shot her a look.

"Oh. Right." She supposed she deserved it. "You can say anything you want to me, as long as you forgive me and tell me again that you love me."

He walked from the water's edge over to the fallen tree trunk and flopped down as if all the energy had been drained from his body. "Do you think my feelings have changed in the last two hours?"

"I don't know." She took the necessary steps to sit down next to him on the log. "I never meant to hurt you, but what kind of person would I be if I didn't go through with my promise to marry Thomas? If I had thrown him over for you, how could you ever trust me?"

"I trust you with my life forever and always." He clasped her hand in his, and a thrill shot through her.

"How was I supposed to know that?"

He gave her a look.

She laughed.

"But I'm glad you held on to what you believe." He sat with her in silence for a moment, just holding her hand in his. "Why aren't you marrying Thomas?"

"He said he didn't want to stand in the way of our true love and released me from the promise."

"I suppose now you want me to marry you."

"It would be nice."

"Nice?" He released her hand, his expression dark.

"Okay, maybe a little more than nice."

"How about so fantastic no one will ever believe us?"

Clara Rose smiled. "That works too."

He leaned in and kissed her, his lips warm, his love clear. How had she not seen it all along? "I love you, Clara Rose Yutzy," he said once he lifted his head.

"I love you, too."

"And tomorrow we go talk to the bishop. I want to get married this wedding season."

She nodded. "We've known each other long enough, I'm sure the bishop would make an exception and approve the union."

He swooped in to kiss her again. Her head swam with the thrill of it all. Married this year. And to her best friend. She could only hope that he never stopped kissing her like he did in that moment.

He pulled away.

She sighed.

"Just one more thing, and this is not negotiable. We name our first son Thomas."

"That sounds like a fine idea," she said and reached up to kiss him again.

MORE THAN
A PROMISE

Chapter One

Finally. The crowd was starting to thin. Mariana had been beginning to believe that they might not ever go home. Between the day she was having and the dull throb starting at the base of her skull, it was past time for a little quiet.

Not that funerals were particularly loud. However, they did have a stress level that couldn't be matched. Even Amish ones.

Mariana shot her bravest smile to her in-laws as they stood by the front door preparing to leave. There were no words left that needed to be said. Leroy was gone. After a long battle with cancer, he was finally gone.

"I'm coming by tomorrow to check on you."

Mariana swung around to find Verna Yutzy standing there. She wanted to tell Verna not to come by. That she would be okay. That she wouldn't need help for a while. But none of that was true, and a person just didn't tell Verna what to do.

"Thank you." Mariana squeezed Verna's hand. "I appreciate that."

The truth was she was going to need more and more

help as the months went on. More than she had ever dreamed.

Verna squeezed right back, then released Mariana's hand and moved away.

Only a few more of the funeral-goers milled around the living room. Just a little bit ago the place had been crowded with people all eating cold roast beef, mashed potatoes, rolls, and prunes and discussing what a great man Leroy was and how it was God's will for him to go at such a young age.

He had been a great man. Until the tumor eating at his brain altered him beyond recognition. Oh, his outside had still looked the same, while his insides were all twisted up, his mind not the same as it had been before. There'd been a time, not so long ago, when he still had his wits about him. When he'd still loved her in his own way. And that night when he'd pulled her close—

"Now, don't you go worrying about anything," Eileen said. Of perhaps all the people around, Eileen was Mariana's best friend. But once Leroy had gotten sick, they'd started to drift apart, only seeing each other at the quilting circle meetings every Tuesday afternoon and occasionally at church. "I've already got with the buddy bunch. We're working out a schedule. One of us will stop by each day to make sure you're doing okay."

Mariana nodded even as tears stung at the back of her eyes. Not tears of sadness so much as tears of joy. She didn't know what she would do without these good people of Wells Landing, Oklahoma. She had moved down soon after she and Leroy had gotten married. But that had been almost fifteen years ago. Now she couldn't imagine calling any other place home.

"Eileen," she started in protest, "you've got so much to do yourself right now."

Eileen shook her head. "Not anything as important as making sure you're okay."

Mariana smiled at the sweet words. Eileen had much more important things to do than look after her. She had two little girls now, sweet things with blond hair and angelic brown eyes. But whether or not they would get to stay still remained to be seen. Eileen had agreed to foster the children from the *Englisch* home in neighboring Pryor with hopes of adopting them herself one day. Making sure two little girls had everything they needed and were adjusting well to the different lifestyle was more important than Mariana's well-being. She had known this day had been coming for almost a year now. And definitely within the last month. She trusted God to get her through it. That was always the best way: trusting God.

"And I'll be fine," she said.

Eileen gave her "that look," then squeezed her hand and moved away.

Mariana straightened her spine and resisted the urge to sigh as she rubbed the pounding at the back of her neck. She just needed a little more time. Not to get used to the reality of Leroy's death. But there were . . . other things. She pressed her hands to her stomach and hoped no one noticed. It wouldn't do for her news to get around this soon. Leroy hadn't been buried more than an hour.

"Mariana?"

She pasted on her bright smile and whirled around to face Reuben Weisel, Leroy's best friend and business partner. "Reuben." Her face relaxed as her smile turned genuine. "I thought you'd gone on home."

He shook his head and jerked a thumb over his shoulder. "I've been out in the barn. Feeding the horses and stuff. I figured you could use a hand with that."

She'd been feeding the horses for a couple of months

now, but today she hadn't thought about it. Not even once. *How am I going to take care of a baby when I can't even remember to feed the horses?*

"Thank you, Reuben. That means a lot to me."

"I thought I might stop by tomorrow." He twirled his hat in his hands. He seemed nervous, though Mariana couldn't figure out why. He had known as long as she had that Leroy's time was growing short. "To check on things, you know? Make sure you're doing okay."

"That's not necessary," Mariana said. She had enough food to last all of this week and half of the next. And Reuben had been coming by steady since Leroy went down. Everything was caught up. Nothing needed to be done.

Well, that wasn't exactly true. She had to figure out what she was going to do with the rest of her life and how she was going to support herself and this baby. After fifteen years of waiting and praying and wishing for a baby and being envious and jealous of all the new mothers in the community, then praying about that as well, she was finally pregnant. Four months, to be exact.

Thank heaven she carried a little bit of extra weight anyway. No one really noticed the belly that had started under her mourning black. She only wished she had realized that she was having Leroy's baby before he died and was able to tell him when he was still coherent enough to understand. She could only hope now that he was up with Jesus, smiling down, knowing that their dreams had come true even if their time together had been cut short.

"I would feel better if I stopped by."

He was a good man, Reuben Weisel, and Mariana couldn't figure out why he had never married. He was caring and kind, hardworking and handsome. Not that she had thought about his looks much over the years, but it was true. Reuben was a fine-looking man. His dark, curly hair only held a touch or two of gray and seemed not to want to lie in the typical Amish "chili bowl" style. His green eyes sparkled as if he had a secret that no one else knew. He hadn't reached his fortieth birthday, at which time unmarried Amish men grew a beard regardless of their lack of a wife. So there were no whiskers to detract from the dimples framing his smiling mouth or the one that bisected his chin.

"Mariana?"

She pulled herself from her own thoughts and centered her attention back to the man in front of her. "*Jah?*"

Concern puckered his brow. "Are you sure you're going to be okay? I can get one of the ladies to stay with you. Verna maybe. Or your sister."

Mariana shook her head. "My sister has her own family to take care of. She can't stay with me forever." She had to get used to the fact that Leroy was gone. And that was all there was to it.

"You just seem . . . distracted or . . ." He stumbled, unable to find the word.

"I'm fine." She shot him her best smile just to prove it. She might not be fine now, but she would be. Leroy was in a better place. He was no longer in pain. He was healed and hopefully with God. She had to be happy for him, even as she was sad for herself.

"If you're sure," he said, though he didn't look convinced.

"Positive." She walked with him to the door, only then realizing that he was the last one to leave. "Good-bye, Reuben."

He donned his hat on the way out the door, then

turned to face her as he stood on the porch. "I'll see you tomorrow."

Mariana bit back her protests. He was only being kind. And she had the feeling the more she protested, the more he would dig in his heels over coming to check on her.

In typical Reuben style, he loped down the steps and over to his tractor. He climbed aboard and gave her one last wave before starting it up and heading back down her drive.

It was better to let his concern run its course. She would have plenty of time to be alone now that Leroy was gone. Five more months, to be exact. Then she would have the baby.

She rubbed a hand over her slight pooch as tears filled her eyes. "Oh, little one, what are we going to do?"

Reuben came by every day for the rest of that week, just as he had promised. Truthfully, she was glad he had. It gave her something else to look forward to each day besides feeding the chickens and trying to figure out how she was going to support herself and the baby.

"Have you given it any thought?" Reuben asked. He took a sip of his coffee and steadily eyed her over the rim of the mug.

She had given it more than "thought." Not much else had been on her mind in the few days since they had buried Leroy. "Some."

"And what do you think you'll do?"

It was a valid question. How was she going to support herself? That was what Reuben wanted to know. What he didn't know was that it was not just her anymore. That she had to have a job so she could support herself and the baby. Honestly, she didn't know how those *Englisch* women did it. Just the thought of juggling a baby and a job so she could keep her house was almost more than she could comprehend. Maybe she should talk to Caroline Fitch. She had raised Emma for over a year before she ended up married to Andrew. And she had worked at Esther Fitch's bakery. That was back before Esther married Abe Fitch and Caroline had married his nephew.

"Mariana?"

She swiveled her attention back to Reuben. "*Jah?*"

"You were off in dreamland."

Hardly. "I'm okay."

A frown puckered Reuben's normally line-free brow. "You've been doing that a lot lately. You sure you're all right?"

She would be. "I'm fine."

"I'm worried about you."

She shook her head. "There's no need to concern yourself. I'll sell baked goods or jelly or—"

"Or what?"

She had no idea. Esther had lost her husband and started the bakery, though with the *Englisch* grocery store selling cookies, cakes, and pies of all sorts, she wasn't sure that Wells Landing was large enough to support another store of that kind. It might be, but she wasn't willing to take that chance. Old Katie Glick took in sewing and had for as long as Mariana could remember. She had been in the same situation when her husband had died and she needed a way to support herself. She did darning and mending for the bachelors, sewing projects that became too much for the parents come Christmas pageant time, and made quilts to sell to *Englisch* tourists.

Mariana supposed she could sell jelly in a stand at the front of her house like a lot of Amish people did. But she couldn't say that her jelly was any better than anyone else's. Tolerable, she thought her father would've said. It tasted all right, but it wasn't spectacular. She needed spectacular if she was going to be able to support herself and this baby she carried.

She sat back in her seat and crossed her arms protectively over her stomach. "I don't know. I just don't know." She couldn't imagine trying to raise a baby on the amount of money she would make from selling only to whoever happened by her drive.

"Don't worry," Reuben said. "You will find a way. God always provides."

It was the one thing she was certain of. God would provide for her. And He would provide for her baby. But she also knew that she had to be an active participant in her life. She didn't have time to settle in with her grief, get to know it and get comfortable with it. She had to fight back, get on her feet, and make a living. She had no other choice; she would soon have a baby depending on her. Leroy's baby. The last piece of him. And a child that special needed special care.

"I'm here to help, you know." His eyes turned serious, and the corners of his mouth went down.

Suddenly his concern was almost more than she could take. Tears rose into her eyes as emotions burned the back of her throat. She covered her face with her hands as tears shook her.

She barely registered the scrape of his chair before he was next to her, crooning softly. "It's going to be okay, Mariana. Somehow. Some way. No one here is going to let you starve." He patted her on the arm, though the action seemed awkward. She needed to pull herself together. This sort of behavior wasn't helping anyone. She sniffed and sat up in her chair.

Reuben handed her a handkerchief.

She dutifully wiped her eyes as she struggled to get her runaway emotions under control.

He patted her arm once again, then moved to sit in the chair next to her. He had been seated across the table. Now he was close enough so she could see every line of worry, every fleck of gold in his eyes.

"You really are a good man, Reuben Weisel." She sniffed again and handed him back his handkerchief.

He tucked it into his pocket without responding. "Maybe you should go and stay with your sister."

Mariana shook her head. She and Elizabeth had never been close, most likely because of the difference in their ages. By the time Mariana had gotten old enough to remember spending time with her sister, Elizabeth had been preparing to get married and move into her own house.

The truth of the matter was Reuben was more of a friend to her than her own kin had been. She had family scattered all over. It was unusual for an Amish family to be so dispersed, but she had heard whispers about differences in beliefs that had led her *mamm* and *dat* to move from Indiana all the way to Oklahoma. They had settled in Clarita, leaving behind everyone they had known to start over in the tiny settlement. So there were no cousins to speak of, no aunts or family to take her in as she faced this time of need. Just her sister.

"She lives all the way over in Clarita," Mariana said. "I don't want to go all the way over there." She wanted to stay here, in her own house, with the neighbors she knew and in the church district she loved.

"I'm worried about you."

Those tears welled again, and Mariana bit her lip to keep them from falling.

The concern so clearly written on Reuben's face increased. "You can't stay here like this." His lips pressed together and his chin took on a stubborn slant. "You need to be around people."

She shook her head. He didn't understand.

"I'm not talking about months or even weeks. Just give yourself a few days to come to terms with this, then you can come back."

"No."

"Mariana, you can't go around sobbing like this whenever someone mentions Leroy's name."

"I'm not crying because of Leroy. I'm crying because I'm pregnant."

"You're what?" he whispered.

But Mariana had said it once. She wasn't about to repeat it. Men and women didn't talk about such things. But Reuben wasn't just any man. He was her husband's business partner and best friend. A wonderful friend to them both.

"A baby?" His gaze flickered from her face to her thickening waistline.

She nodded.

"Leroy's baby." He seemed to be having as much trouble as she had understanding the situation.

"Yes."

"This is . . ." He stopped, and for a moment she wasn't sure what he was going to say. "Wonderful! This is wonderful!" A smile brighter than the sun spread across his face.

"You think so?" she asked. She was still a bit numb from discovering she was pregnant and burying her husband so soon after the news.

"I know so." He scooted his chair a bit closer, his gaze flickering from her face to her belly, then back again. "Did Leroy know?"

She shook her head and her eyes filled with tears.

"He would have been so proud."

She smiled through her tears. "Pride is a sin."

Reuben grinned in return. "Any man who isn't proud of his children is a fool."

"Then he would be proud," Mariana returned. If there was one thing Leroy Miller wasn't, it was a fool. His wife, on the other hand . . . well, she wasn't so sure. How was she going to support herself and this baby? She had to figure out something, and quick.

"A baby," Reuben murmured. "Now, this changes everything."

Chapter Two

Mariana let herself into Eileen Brenneman's house, the screen door bumping into her behind as she stopped just inside the doorway.

A little girl about four years old stood next to the food table, thumb firmly in her mouth as she gazed at Mariana with serious brown eyes.

"Hi, there," Mariana said, moving toward her. For a moment she thought the girl might dart away, but she stood her ground.

She had to be one of the foster girls that Eileen had taken in. Mariana had heard that Eileen had finally gotten them, but that had been a couple of weeks ago, just before Leroy's death and funeral. Mariana had missed three meetings of the quilting circle and it felt good to be back.

Mariana set the plate of cookies and the plastic container of cheese dip on the table next to what could only be Verna Yutzy's mini pecan pies and Tess Smiley's experimental goat cheese pizza. At least she thought that was what it was.

"Hi, I'm Mariana," she said, extending her hand toward the young girl.

She looked at it, then back into Mariana's eyes. She seemed so sad, so misplaced. Then Mariana remembered that these foster children were *Englisch*, though she made a cute Amish figure in her aqua blue dress and twin braids.

Joy burst within her chest. A girl. If Leroy were still alive, she would naturally want a boy for him. But he wasn't, and she wanted a girl. A baby girl who would grow up to be a good Amish woman. A girl that she could teach the proper way to fix her hair, a girl to help her feed the chickens and give water to the horse. A girl she could teach everything to. The heady thought went straight to her heart. She swayed in place as she continued to look at this wonderful creature before her.

"She doesn't talk much." Mariana whirled around as another small face appeared from the kitchen. "Or any," she continued.

"Well then, it's good she has you to speak for her."

The young girl nodded. "I s'pose. I'm Crystal. Her sister."

"I'm Mariana." She took a step toward the girl, extending her hand as she had done to her sister. "What's her name?"

"Brittany."

She took Mariana's hand into her small one and shook vigorously. There was a maturity about her that belied her young age. If Mariana had to guess, she would say the girl was no more than seven. Yet she had an old air about her as if she'd seen way too much in her seven short years.

"It's nice to meet you, Crystal. And you too, Brittany."

Brittany continued to suck her thumb and warily eyed Mariana.

"Are you here to do the quilt?"

"I am."

"You weren't here last week."

"I had some family business to take care of." That sounded much better than *I was burying my husband, and I was a little busy*.

"What kind of family business?"

"Crystal!" Eileen admonished as she came out of the kitchen with another tray of little pizzas. "What have I told you about asking personal questions?"

"Not to. But how am I supposed to find out anything if I don't ask questions?"

Mariana stifled her laugh.

"You have to trust that I'll tell you the things you need to know. Now, if you want to stay here while we have our quilting meeting, then you may. But if you do, you may not ask a bunch of personal questions."

A small frown wrinkled Crystal's brow. She scrunched up her face, showing Mariana the gap where her two front teeth had been. Mariana's heart melted a little more. A baby girl. She couldn't ask for anything more than a healthy baby girl. "How do I know if the question is personal or not?" Crystal finally asked.

Eileen sighed. Mariana had the feeling that Crystal's spunky attitude was beginning to wear on the poor woman. Mariana supposed that was why God gave children to families as babies. He gave them a chance to become accustomed to them before they started walking and talking and otherwise getting their own personalities.

But this was a special situation. Like Mariana, Eileen had never been blessed with children of her own. Unlike Mariana, she had decided to adopt, starting with foster children to get into the system quickly. She had hoped to have the young girls by Thanksgiving last year, but here it was just after Easter and they had finally come to live with the Brennemans.

"If it's not about quilting, or making clothes, or last week's church service, then it's too personal to ask. Does that clear things up for you?" Eileen asked.

Crystal seemed to think about it for a moment. "I guess." Then she turned back to Mariana. "Why is your dress black?"

Eileen slammed the tray down and whirled around to face her foster child. "Crystal! That is too personal a question."

"But—but it's about clothes." Her brown eyes filled with tears and Mariana's heart went out to the girl. She dropped to her knees in front of her. "It's okay. My dress is black because my husband recently passed away."

She sniffed. "You mean like he died?"

Mariana nodded. "That's right."

"My dad died."

"I'm sorry."

Crystal nodded. "I'm sorry about your husband too." Then she turned back to Eileen. "Should I have a black dress since my dad died?"

Eileen shot her an indulgent smile. For all of Crystal's pert and sass, Mariana could tell right away that Eileen was already head over heels in love with the child, and she said a quick prayer that it all worked out. She would hate to see her friend fall completely in love only to lose the children again.

Crystal looked from Mariana back to Eileen. "I don't understand. If we all have to wear dresses that are the same, and her husband died and my dad died, I don't see why my dress is blue."

Eileen sighed once more. "I'll explain it to you later." She moved behind the girls and urged Crystal and Brittany to go into her bonus room, where Mariana knew the rest of their quilting circle waited along with the quilt they were currently working on. They had just started piecing the quilt squares together when Leroy had taken a turn for the worse. After missing three weeks, Mariana could only guess at how far they'd gotten. It was probably just about ready to quilt.

"They're adorable," Mariana said as the girls disappeared into the room.

"They're a lot of work," Eileen said, then shook her head. She closed her eyes for a moment, and Mariana wondered if she was praying. Then she opened them once again. "Brittany seems to be adapting okay. At least she doesn't ask as many questions as Crystal."

"She's something else," Mariana said.

"That's putting it mildly. She has such an inquisitive nature she's forever asking question after question. I'm sorry if any of hers upset you."

"It's all right." Once again Mariana shot her friend a quick smile to back up her words. It was all right and she was fine. As fine as she could be not knowing how she was going to support herself and her baby. But she would think of something. God would give her the idea. He always came through. He always took care. This time would be no different.

"Are you ready to go quilt?" Eileen asked.

"After three weeks away? I surely am."

They made their way into the bonus room, where Mariana was greeted by each and every one of the quilting circle's members. There was Verna Yutzy and her granddaughter Clara Rose, who recently had gotten married to Obie Brenneman, Eileen's nephew. Tess Smiley was there along with Helen Ebersol, the bishop's wife, and Helen's daughter, Emily. It had only been a couple of years since Emily had gotten married as well. Everyone in the county had thought that she would one day marry

Luke Lambright, but instead he'd run off to race *Englisch* cars and Emily had married Elam Riehl.

"Where's the baby?" Mariana asked.

Emily stepped to the side so Mariana could see the car seat where tiny Sallie Mae peacefully slept. No doubt about it. The child was truly a gift from above.

"She's beautiful," Mariana murmured, wishing the baby was awake so she could hold her for a bit. How long had it been since she had held a baby? Years and years. Soon she would hold her own baby in her arms. The thought made her light-headed.

"Mariana, are you all right?" Emily's voice seemed to come from far away.

Mariana managed to pull herself from the place she'd gone and back to the present. "*Jah*," she lied. She wasn't feeling well. Not well at all.

"Are you certain?" Helen asked.

Somehow, Mariana managed to nod.

"Why don't you sit down?" Eileen said. "You look a little pale."

Mariana nodded and allowed her friend to lead her over to a nearby chair. She could almost hear everyone's thoughts. All this was too much for her. Maybe she shouldn't have come today.

But she had felt fine when she left the house. Only when she had gotten inside and started visiting had the waves of exhaustion overcome her. That must be it. The last few days had been trying. And she was pregnant, after all. She just needed some rest.

She waved everyone away and did her best to put on a brave and less tired face. She didn't want anyone worrying about her. They had all done enough, bringing food to the house and checking on her daily since the funeral.

"Are you sure you're okay?" Clara Rose leaned in close

as they stitched side by side. This quilt was a beautiful combination of greens mixed with calico flower prints to make a pattern of vines and leaves.

"Of course."

Clara Rose looked pointedly down at the slow stitches Mariana was making.

"Your hands are shaking. Maybe it's too soon for you to come back," Clara Rose said.

But Mariana shook her head. "I'm just tired."

As they talked, Verna leaned in closer. "Maybe we should eat. You look a little peaked."

"I'm fine." Mariana gave her a small smile, but it felt forced on her lips. "Maybe a bite or two would be good."

Verna patted her knee and stood. "Let's break custom and eat now. Everyone okay with that?"

Mariana looked up as everyone murmured their agreement and started putting their work aside.

The rustle of fabric seemed to come to her from far away. *Jah*, that was what she needed. Something to eat. She just needed to feed herself, feed the baby. She set her squares to one side and cautiously stood.

Carefully she made her way to the food table, hoping that the graying at the edges of her vision would hold off until she got her plate and sat back down.

"Here." Mariana stopped as Eileen pressed a glass of apple juice into her hands. "Drink this."

As if in slow motion, Mariana raised the glass to her lips, but before she could take even one sip, everything went black.

"Somebody call nine-one-one!"

Someone was shouting.

Mariana blinked, trying to bring her focus back in.

"Wait. I think she's coming around."

Why was somebody shouting? Had something happened? She took a moment to assess the room around her as so many concerned faces hovered above her. Tess, Verna, Clara Rose, even Helen and Emily all stood around looking down at her.

Down at her? She pushed herself up onto her elbows, only then realizing that she was flat on her back on the linoleum floor.

"What—what happened?" Several pairs of helping hands reached out to assist her, and Mariana was grateful. She still felt wobbly. "How did I get on the floor?"

Helen's mouth pressed into a thin line. "You passed out," she said. "Did you hit your head?"

Mariana took a quick inventory and rubbed her shoulders a little. She supposed she must've fallen and hit them somewhere on the way down, and the back of her prayer *kapp* was crushed. She would have to get a new one now. But other than those two things, she seemed to be okay. "I'm fine." *If I only had a dime for every time I said that in the last eight days.*

"Are you sure you're okay?" Emily asked.

Mariana only nodded.

Someone pressed a glass of water into her hands and she drank it thirstily.

"I think this has all been a little much for you," Helen said.

A chorus of murmuring agreement went up around the quilting circle.

"I'm fine, really." She tried to push herself up, but only got halfway before she swayed like a tree in a hurricane. Again those helping hands reached out to steady her.

"Something's up." Verna pinned her with that sharp blue gaze. "You want to tell us what it is?"

All attention swiveled to the oldest member of the circle.

Mariana supposed now was as good a time as any to break the news to her friends. She still wasn't sure how she felt about it herself. Happy, of course. But there were many more emotions mixed in.

"I'm going to have a baby." Gasps went up all around, and Mariana was very aware of them as Clara Rose clapped her hands and jumped in place.

"How exciting!"

But the looks on Emily and Helen's faces were not so joyous. "Have you seen a doctor?" Helen asked.

Mariana shook her head. "I'm fine."

"Would you stop saying that?" Verna groused. "If you're passing out at the quilting meeting, you are most definitely not 'fine.'"

"It's just a baby." Mariana said the words even if she didn't believe them. She'd never been pregnant before and didn't know if it had anything to do with the baby or not. But somehow, something just felt . . . wrong. Just not right.

"You didn't answer my question," Helen pressed.

"No," Mariana admitted. "I haven't been to the doctor."

With everyone's help, she managed to get back on her feet, though she was immediately whisked into a chair and another glass of juice was handed to her. She looked down at her dress. It was covered in sticky wet, and she could only assume that she had spilled the first glass of juice on her way to the floor.

"Why haven't you been to the doctor yet?" Helen asked. "It's not been too soon."

Of all the people surrounding her, Helen Ebersol knew more than anyone about Leroy's illness. She alone had known how bad those last few days were, those last few weeks, those last couple of months. Helen had been with Mariana almost every day. She knew how sick Leroy had been, and she knew, Mariana could see it in her eyes, that Mariana was at least three months pregnant. Plenty enough time for a checkup.

How could she explain that she had not gone to the doctor because going made it real, and she couldn't do that just yet. Her husband had been dying, her life falling apart, and the one thing she wanted most in the world was finally going to be hers. The emotions were varied and conflicting, and it had simply been easier to ignore them and take care of her husband in those final days than it had been to admit the truth. She was going to be a mom and a widow, though not in that order.

"I'll make an appointment next week."

Helen's frown deepened. "I think you should go sooner. Maybe to a specialist."

Mariana shook her head. "I don't know a doctor like that."

"I know one," Eileen said. "I'll get his number." She bustled off, returning a few minutes later with a scrap of paper. She held it out to Mariana, but Helen snatched it away.

"I'll make your appointment."

"But—"

"No buts. I'll make the appointment and get us a driver."

"You're going with me?" Tears stung her eyes. It seemed that was all she could do these days. Crying had become her new pastime.

"Of course." Helen smiled. "We mothers have to stick together."

* * *

Mother. She was going to be a mother. The thought was becoming more and more real to her. Even more so as she sat in the doctor's office surrounded by women in varying degrees of pregnancy.

She liked the doctor well enough, and the exam hadn't been as bad as she had anticipated, but the wait . . . that was making her batty.

After she had peed in a cup, given more blood than she even knew her body contained, undressed, pretended to be somewhere else, and dressed again, she was now waiting with Helen in the doctor's office. Her nerves were shot and her palms sweaty. Her heart pounded in her chest. What if he came back and said that something was wrong? How would she handle that?

Helen squeezed her hand. "Give it to God."

Such wise words. Mariana bowed her head and said a quick prayer, barely finishing before the door opened behind them and the handsome doctor breezed in.

"Well, now, Mrs. Miller. We have the results of your tests back." He set the folder he carried on the desk, then instead of going behind it and resting in the chair, he propped one hip against the edge and crossed his arms. "You're pregnant," he said. "But you already knew that."

Mariana nodded dumbly.

"And that's why she passed out?" Helen asked. "Because she's pregnant? That's the only reason?"

The doctor nodded sagely. "Good question. A pregnant woman can pass out for several reasons during pregnancy, it's not uncommon at all. Unfortunately, I do believe that Mrs. Miller's problem stems from the fact that her blood pressure is way too high right now."

Is that really bad?

"What can you do for that?" Mariana asked.

"We have medications you can take, of course. But in your case I'm going to prescribe immediate and extensive bed rest as well."

Bed rest? "You mean like I have to stay in bed all day long?"

"That's exactly what I'm saying. You need to rest, and you need to get your blood pressure back in line. We're going to give you some medication to help, but I want you to relax as much as possible. That means no cleaning house, no cooking meals, no getting up. If absolutely necessary you may go to the bathroom on your own, and you may wash every day, but no baths, just showers. I'll see you back here in two weeks. Once your blood pressure is down, you can come once a month and we'll talk about giving you a little more time to exercise. Do you have any questions?"

"That seems very strict," Helen said. Mariana thought the same thing, but she didn't have the nerve to ask. And once again she was so grateful that Helen was with her.

"Oh, well, that's the good news. See, in cases of multiple births it's always best to rest as much as possible, and given your age, Mariana, I think that in your case it's of the utmost importance. I know you've been under a lot of stress lately, and this is going to be best for you and the babies."

Wait. What? "Babies?" Surely she had heard him wrong. It was a baby. Right? One. Baby.

The doctor grinned as if somehow he was solely responsible for the phenomenon. "That's right. You're going to have twins."

Chapter Three

Mariana had been in bed approximately four hours longer than normal, and she already thought she was losing her mind. She wasn't sure she could stand five more months of this. But the doctor had told her yesterday that chances were that she would have the babies much sooner than that. That was why it was so important she stay in bed. She had to let the babies grow, give them everything she could. Rest, relax, relieve the stress, and get her blood pressure back to a manageable level.

Twins. She was having twins. Not one baby girl, but two. Or perhaps a boy and a girl. Maybe even two boys. The thought made her smile. Leroy would have been so proud. She had to do everything in her power to keep those babies safe, though she had no idea how she could support herself while she lay flat on her back for the remainder of her pregnancy. With any luck her doctor would let her out of bed. But she wasn't sure she'd be able to work and keep these babies healthy.

She sighed and shuffled the deck of Uno cards once more, flipping over the first one and trying to guess its color before she saw it.

"Mariana?"

"In here," she called in return. The screen door slammed and she listened for the footsteps as Reuben made his way to the back of the house where the guest bedroom was. She had taken to sleeping downstairs in order to be closer to the bathroom and all the company as they came to visit.

He stopped in the doorway, almost hesitant to take a step into the room. "How are you feeling?"

Tired. Lonely. Bored out of my mind. But she pushed those thoughts away, refusing to give them a voice. Negative statements wouldn't make anything better.

"I'm good."

He shook his head. "I know better than that. What can I get for you?"

Mariana looked at the nightstand next to her. Yesterday afternoon after they returned from the doctor's office, Helen had laid out everything she might need. Mariana had a pitcher of water, a hairbrush and a hand mirror, a pack of gum, a can of peanuts, her Bible, a book about the Oklahoma land runs, and a pen and paper.

"Nothing, I guess."

"I could get you some candy."

Mariana shook her head. "I've got to watch my weight. Especially since I'm not going to be able to move around much." Though candy would be nice. She was just bored. "How about some pickles?"

A small frown puckered his brow. But he nodded anyway. "Pickles. Got it."

In a flash he disappeared out the door, leaving Mariana alone again.

After what seemed like half an hour but could've only been five minutes or less, Reuben still hadn't returned. That in itself wasn't bad, but she could hear him opening and closing every cabinet door she had. Not once, but twice. Finally, Reuben appeared in the doorway. "Where are the pickles?"

"Bottom shelf of the pantry."

He frowned. "I looked there."

Mariana smiled. "Bottom shelf. I promise."

Reuben shook his head but disappeared once again, though his steps weren't quite as peppy as they had been before. She heard the pantry door open but no other sounds for quite some time.

"Bring the spicy ones," she called.

Reuben appeared in the doorway once more. "What was that?"

Mariana smiled. "The spicy pickles. Bring those, please."

Reuben nodded. "*Jah*. Okay." He disappeared again, and Mariana listened for sounds that he might actually be finding the spicy pickles without any more trouble.

"Here you go," he said as he entered the room a few moments later. He had the pickles in one hand and a spoon in the other.

Mariana scooted back with her spine against the headboard of the bed and pulled the covers up around her lap. She had known that she would have a lot of company in the days to come, so instead of a nightgown she had put on a house dress with no apron. And though she had bought a new prayer *kapp*, she opted for a bandana to cover her head. She reached out as Reuben drew near. He came only close enough to hand off the pickles and the spoon before retreating back to the doorway.

"Thank you." Mariana gripped the ring lid of the Mason jar and turned it to no avail. She tried a second time as Reuben watched. She held it out toward him. "Can you open this for me?"

Something strange flickered across his expression.

He eased into the room and loosened the ring before scampering back to the doorway.

Mariana eyed him quietly as she used the spoon to pop the sealed lid from the jar. She pulled out a pickle, then set the rest on the nightstand next to the book about Oklahoma history. She turned back to Reuben. "Are you embarrassed to be in the same room with me since I'm . . ." She sputtered. "I mean, I know it's strange. But I don't want you to feel uncomfortable." Not that he was going to come by that often, but still. When he did, she wanted him to come in and visit with her a little.

Reuben shook his head. "No. Of course not." But he turned red as he said the words. She supposed it was odd, but this was the situation they found themselves in, and she was going to make the best of it.

"There's no need, you know. You were my husband's best friend. And a good friend of mine as well. I want you to feel that you can come by and visit anytime you want."

He nodded, and his color returned to normal. "Good. Because I'm coming by every day."

Mariana shook her head. "You can't come by every day. You have a business to run."

"*Jah*, and I need to watch out for you as well."

"No, you don't."

"I do."

Mariana shook her head again. "The women from the quilting circle are taking turns, coming by to feed the chickens and gather the eggs. The horses have gone to stay at Obie and Clara Rose's house. There's nothing else to do here."

"There's plenty to do here."

Mariana finished her pickle and reached for another. It was perhaps the first craving she'd had since she had gotten pregnant. Or maybe all the stress and trauma just before Leroy had died had hidden those things from view. "Like what?"

"The gutters need to be cleaned, the barn could use some paint, and I noticed the front porch railing was a little loose when I came in."

"The porch railing is fine. You don't need to be doing those things here. You need to get jobs that pay."

He tilted his head thoughtfully to one side. "It's really twins?" His gaze flickered to her belly, then back to her face.

Mariana smoothed a hand over the growing mound and smiled. "That's what they tell me." She shrugged. "I don't know. I don't know what any of this is supposed to feel like."

Reuben took two more steps into the room, easing closer and closer until he could perch on the foot of the bed. "Leroy would be . . . He would be beside himself with joy."

Mariana blinked back her tears. Leroy would have been so very happy. But all things happened for a reason. At least, that's what she'd been told her entire life. And she had to believe that there was some reason why all this was happening now, after he was gone.

"What are you going to do?" Reuben asked, his voice solemn and soft.

"I guess I'm going to have two babies."

He shook his head. "What are you going to do for money?"

She knew what he'd meant. Between the two of them, Leroy and Reuben had brought in just enough to take care of the three of them. But now there was only one person to do that work. It wasn't like she had land she could lease or cows she could allow somebody to milk. And she couldn't do any of the work herself. All of her ideas from a couple of weeks ago had been completely scrapped. She couldn't very well sell jelly—however mediocre—if she had to lie on her back in her bed day after day.

"God will provide." She kept telling herself that, but every time the thought crept into her mind, her mouth went dry and her stomach fluttered with nerves. God would provide. He always did. But something maternal in her kept rising up and reinforcing her need to ensure that everything was going to be okay.

Reuben nodded. "Have you had many visitors?" he asked.

Mariana smiled. "I've only been here one day."

"Right." He looked out the window, then turned his attention back to her. "I guess what I want to know is how are you eating breakfast, lunch, and dinner?"

"Whoever feeds the chickens is helping me with breakfast. Then they're packing me a sack lunch that I can have right here. Somebody will stop by in the evening and get my supper. I know they've got a schedule worked out." She hated to be such a bother. She wasn't worthy of such intense care and beautiful friendship, but it was there all the same, and she was so incredibly grateful for it.

"I could bring you lunch."

Mariana shook her head. "That's not necessary."

"It is. Besides, I have to eat too."

She couldn't very well protest. It wasn't like it was out of his way. He never knew where he would be, in Wells Landing or Taylor Creek, when the next call came out and someone needed something repaired. He could be next door to her house or all the way across town. And if he wanted to waste his gas and drive his tractor all the way over here just to have lunch with her, then who was she to tell him no? Plus, it would be nice to have some company between seven o'clock in the morning and five o'clock at night. "Thank you, Reuben Weisel. That's mighty good of you."

He smiled as if he'd just won the greatest prize on earth. "No problem, Mariana Miller. That's what friends are for."

After six days of doing absolutely nothing, Mariana was sure she was going to go completely out of her mind at any time. Someone from the quilt circle came in every morning just as they'd promised and fed the chickens, fixed her breakfast, and left her with a sack lunch.

In those six days, Reuben had managed to be there every day at lunch just as he promised. At least she had something to look forward to, but the stretches in between those visits seemed to get longer and longer. She had taken to reading her Bible after Reuben left, to fill in the space until someone came by to prepare her supper. In the morning she read the Oklahoma history book, finding it fascinating and nearly unbelievable at the same time.

Day in, day out, every day the same. Come tomorrow she would have been in this bed a solid week, and she had so many more to go she was unsure how she was going to keep her sanity until these babies were ready to be born.

Reuben stood and started to clean up the scraps from their meal. He had brought a chair from the dining room into her bedroom early last week, and now when he came in he didn't seem quite as bashful. Maybe because he had some place to rest as he talked to her. Or maybe he was just getting used to the idea. The idea of being in her room alone. Not that anything would ever happen between her and Reuben. Aside from the fact that she was newly widowed and pregnant, the idea just seemed absurd. Sure, Reuben was a great man. He was honest and forthright, and giving to a fault. Despite all those wonderful traits, he had been her husband's best friend.

"You're leaving?" Mariana said as he continued to gather up wrappers and scraps.

"I've got an appointment at one fifteen."

Mariana nodded and bit back her questions about who the appointment was with. Why was he going there? Was he fixing something, painting something? She wanted to know anything and everything about what was going on outside her four walls, but she knew it was just boredom talking. Reuben didn't deserve a grilling just because she was on bed rest.

"You be careful."

He stopped gathering trash and gave her a solemn nod. "Of course." He seemed about to say more, but pressed his lips together as he finished his task. "Can I get you anything else before I leave?"

"No," Mariana said. There was nothing she needed except for company. Somebody had stopped by nearly every day sometime during that week, but once they left, the house grew heavy and silent. Being confined to her bed in such a quiet place made her realize all the more that Leroy was sure and truly gone. "I've got my Bible. I'll just read." She gave him her best smile and hoped it was convincing. As much as she wanted people to visit and stay and come by and see her, she knew that everyone had chores to do, errands to run, jobs of one kind or another. Her job right now was taking care of these babies. It was a wonderful job. She just wished it wasn't so . . . solitary.

She pulled her Bible into her lap as if to prove her enthusiasm.

Reuben nodded and seemed convinced. "I'll see you tomorrow, then."

"Tomorrow," she said, not even bothering to pretend that she didn't want him to stop by.

He left the room and she sat there with her heart heavy as she listened to his footfalls on the linoleum floor, the slam of the screen door, the growl of his tractor engine as he started it, and its steady chug as it made its way down the driveway.

That sound was joined with others. More tractors, or perhaps a bigger-engined vehicle on the roadway. They seemed so close. Then she heard engines cut off, doors shut, and female voices.

Her heart lifted in her chest. She had company!

"Mariana?" The inquiry was followed by the slam of her screen door.

"In here," she called.

The voice sounded very much like Eileen, but it was Tuesday just before one o'clock. Eileen would be at the quilting circle meeting at her own house. But it was Eileen's face that appeared in the doorway.

"Surprise." She carried what looked to be a pineapple upside-down cake in her hands.

Mariana loved pineapple upside-down cake and attributed to it any extra weight she carried around her middle. It was the last thing she needed and the best thing she could ask for.

"What are you doing here?" she asked.

Eileen smiled. "It's time for the quilting circle. You can quilt, right?" She deposited the cake in Reuben's recently vacated chair. "But we will need some more chairs in here."

"Eileen?"

"In here," she called in return.

"Is that Tess?"

Eileen turned back to Mariana. "Of course. How can we have the quilting circle without Tess?" She whirled around toward the door once more. "Grab a dining room chair on your way in. There's no place to sit in here."

"Got it," Tess called back.

"But—" Mariana sputtered to a stop. She really had no protest. Her friends had come calling on this special day. They didn't want to leave her out. God was truly good and had given her the best friends anyone could possibly have. She sat there, smiling like a fool as her quilting circle group filed in one by one, each only carrying one dish of food that they then carried back into the kitchen for later. Verna arrived with a large plastic container on wheels that Mariana soon discovered contained all the pieces of the quilt. Clara Rose had a similar container that held all the other materials, the batting, and extra fabrics.

Eileen surveyed the room and tapped her chin thoughtfully. "I wasn't sure about bringing the quilting frame. It's just so bulky, but I've got an idea." Her eyes sparkled. "We drape the quilt over the bed and sit around it."

"That's a great idea," Verna said. And that was exactly what they did.

Mariana felt somewhat akin to a princess with the quilt draped over her legs as her friends sat around her and stitched.

"Where are the girls?" Mariana asked.

A shadow crossed Eileen's face. But it was quickly gone. "I left them at home. I wasn't sure how well-behaved they would be. And how much we could get done with them underfoot."

"I'm sure it would have been fine," Mariana said. But she had a feeling that Eileen's decision not to bring the girls was buried in something deeper. She hoped that things worked out for her friend. Mariana was getting her chance at being a mother, and she wished for Eileen to have the same. Unlike Eileen, Mariana and Leroy hadn't done any fertility tests with special doctors. They had just figured it was God's will. And as much as Mariana would've loved to know exactly what the problem was and why they hadn't gotten pregnant all those years, she didn't press the issue with Leroy. Unfortunately, Eileen knew the exact reasons why she couldn't have children, though she had never shared them outright. And for years Eileen had accepted it, only lately deciding that if she couldn't have a baby of her own, she would find a child in need. Mariana considered it most noble.

"Did you hear that Reuben was seen at Shelley Glick's house two days ago?" Clara Rose asked.

The words made Mariana's heart thump a little harder in her chest. He hadn't told her that he had gone to Shelley Glick's house. And every day he explained where he was going and where he had been, sharing his day with her since she was trapped inside. But that was one of the tales he'd left out. Because there was something going on between the two of them?

"Oh, posh," Verna said. "Don't act like they're courting. Everybody knows that older couples are extremely secretive when they start courting."

"But this is Reuben's first relationship," Tess pointed out. She made her tiny little stitches, looking up only so often to join in the conversation. Of the younger girls in the quilting circle, Tess was perhaps the shyest. Though today, to Mariana, she seemed almost withdrawn and a little pale. Or maybe Mariana just needed to get out a little more. She might be reading things into situations that weren't there. Like what Reuben was doing at Shelley Glick's house two days ago.

Like it mattered to her. It didn't matter what Reuben did. He was her husband's best friend and his business partner. Right now, he was perhaps her best friend as well, but that was all. Nothing more.

"I have a feeling y'all wouldn't be gossiping so much if Helen and Emily were here."

Clara Rose giggled. "Ouch." She stuck her finger in her mouth. "I poked myself."

"Maybe we wouldn't," Eileen said. "Or maybe we would."

The women laughed, and Mariana chuckled along, though she still couldn't help but wonder if Reuben had decided to finally get married.

Chapter Four

"Are you sure nothing's bothering you?" Reuben asked the following afternoon.

"I'm good," Mariana said.

He tilted his head to one side and studied her. "You just seem sort of . . . Well, not yourself."

They had started a game of Uno just after they ate, intending to play just one hand. But since Reuben didn't have a job until later, one hand had turned into four.

"Everything's great," Mariana repeated.

Reuben threw a green seven on top of her red five. "That sounded convincing."

"You can't play that."

He picked up the card and studied the pile before tossing a red Draw Two down. "Quit avoiding my question and get two cards."

Mariana picked two and frowned. The last thing she wanted to do was tell Reuben what was on her mind.

"Discard," he nudged.

She tossed down a card and studied her hand. "This game is no fun with two people."

He studied the top card, then pulled one from his hand.

"Skip you," he said, placing a red Skip card on the pile. Then he pulled four more in succession. "Reverse, skip you again, skip you again, and draw four." He looked up and grinned. "It's fun for me."

"You can't play a green Draw Four on top of all those red cards. What's wrong with you?"

He grinned. "You promise you won't tell?"

"Tell what?"

"I'm color-blind."

Mariana stopped. "Really? I didn't know that about you." They had been friends so long and she didn't know something so basic about him?

He shrugged. "It doesn't come up much."

Mariana pulled a card from her hand and tossed it onto the discard pile. "I guess."

"See? Why did you do that?"

"What are you talking about?" Though her heart pumped hard in her chest as if he had discovered some big secret she held. A secret she didn't even know herself.

"For a little while you seemed like yourself, now you're back to being all . . . grumpy."

"I am most certainly not grumpy."

"Again, convincing."

"Are you seeing Shelley Glick?" Nothing like blurting out personal questions without a second thought.

Reuben stopped. She could almost see the wheels turning in his mind. Then he burst out laughing. "Quilting circle, right?"

"What?" she asked.

"The quilting circle. That's where you heard such a thing."

"Maybe." Though Mariana couldn't meet his gaze.

Instead she picked at a loose thread on the quilt covering her bed.

"Those girls will talk about anything."

"You still didn't answer my question."

He turned back toward her, his eyes sparkling yet somehow serious. "Neither did you answer mine."

"It's hard. Being in bed here all day. Everything's going on out there, and I'm stuck in here."

His face softened and his expression took on an almost dreamy look. "But you're growing babies." Even as he said the words, his color deepened to a dark rose. She found the involuntary reaction charming.

"It's not real to me yet."

He frowned. "Not at all?" His hand twitched as if he wanted to reach out and touch her belly, but thought differently of it. Amish couples were reserved when showing affection. Such a move would surely be odd coming from him, her husband's best friend.

"It's strange. I don't know how to describe it. It's almost like I've wanted this for so long that I'm afraid to let it be real because—" She couldn't finish that thought.

"Because you're afraid it will end?"

"*Jah*," she whispered.

He dragged his gaze from hers and stared out the window. Outside the wind blew, rustling the leaves in the trees. The only sound between them was the click of the clock as the seconds ticked by. "I'm not courting Shelley Glick. I went over to repair a spot in her flooring. It turned out to be a bigger job than I anticipated. I ended up having to be there for a day or so. Funny how people jump to conclusions."

"And that's all?"

"That's all."

Her heart suddenly felt so light. "*Jah*," she said. "Funny."

* * *

"I brought you something."

Mariana tried hard not to allow her grin free rein as Reuben stepped into the room the next day. But she was just so glad to see him. It was nice having the girls from the quilting circle come by, and they had promised to try to hold the meeting at her house again the following week. But between now and then, there were a lot of hours in the day to be filled with nothing more than her own company.

"A present?" She sat up a little straighter and clapped her hands.

Reuben stepped close to the bed, extending a small, flat package toward her. It was wrapped in newspaper and tied with a piece of ribbon that looked as if it had been a part of an *Englisch* hair decoration at some point in its life.

Mariana didn't care where it came from. It was the most beautiful thing she'd ever seen. She took the present from him and set it in her lap, staring at it in wonderment.

"Aren't you going to open it?" Reuben asked as he settled on the end of the bed.

"*Jah*. Of course." She picked up the box and started to tear the paper, her excitement growing. Inside was a hard-bound book. The cover showed a pair of tiny baby feet, muted and softened to give it a dreamlike feel. The verse on the front read, "Children are a gift from the Lord; They are a reward from Him. Psalms 127:3."

Tears sprang into her eyes as she opened the book. But she didn't need perfect vision as she flipped through the pages, noting only for a second that they were blank. Just lined, like notebook paper.

"It's a journal." Reuben smiled, obviously so very happy with his gift. "You can write each day to the baby, and then later when he's bigger, you can give it to him. That way he can know what you are feeling now."

"Her," she whispered. "Them," she corrected herself. "Reuben, it's beautiful. Thank you so much."

His smile widened. "It'll give you something to do when I can't stay."

Mariana did her best to hide her disappointment. She knew eventually this would start to happen. Everybody had been coming by and she'd had quite a bit of company to keep her days from being completely and utterly boring. But she knew that after a while, the novelty of visiting with her would wear off and people would start to have other chores and things to do that would prevent them from coming by as often. She just wished it would have lasted longer than a couple of weeks. "I understand."

"But you still have your lunch, right?"

She nodded, pointing to the paper sack sitting on her nightstand.

"Okay," he said. "Sorry I can't stay." His smile was so sweet she couldn't be too angry with him. Like she had any right to be upset. She was just being selfish, and she promised herself that after Reuben left she would say a little prayer to keep her thoughts in order. "Will you come back tomorrow?"

"Of course." He started for the door and then turned just this side of leaving. "Did you think I wasn't coming back?"

"Well, I know how it is. People get busy and . . ." She shrugged. "I know that. It's not feasible for somebody to come and stay with me every day. As much as I would like it, it's getting to be summertime and people are busier and busier." Which brought up another problem. She would spend most of the summer, if not all of it, confined to her bed. How could she put up any food for the winter?

"I can't get too busy for you," Reuben said with a smile.

He left not much longer after that, though his sweet words carried Mariana straight through until evening. She spent most of the day writing in her journal, thinking of Reuben and all the things she wanted to tell the babies. She wanted to tell them about their dad. Make sure they knew what a special man he was. How much he would've loved to have known them and how much she missed him.

But she had been missing him for months instead of just the weeks since his death. His illness had changed him, turned him into a different person, until he was nothing more than a shell of the man that she had once loved, nowhere near the man he had once been. Sometimes it was hard for her to remember those before times, and she wanted to get it down on paper before she forgot them completely. They were his children and deserved that much, that memory of their father.

"I'm going to head out now," Eileen said, coming into the room and surveying it with a critical eye. Of all her friends, Eileen was perhaps the most persnickety. She was constantly looking for something to dust, something to clean, to air out, sweep, or smooth the wrinkles from. But Mariana had known Eileen practically their entire lives. She might be a clean freak, but Mariana knew the actions hid the restlessness of a nervous soul.

Mariana patted the bed next to her. "Want to come sit down for a minute?" she asked. "Just visit for a while."

For a moment Mariana thought that Eileen might protest, but instead she moved to the bed and perched on the spot next to Mariana.

"I have a feeling that something's wrong." Nothing like getting right to the point.

Eileen shook her head. "What could be wrong? I have two beautiful girls and a wonderful husband. God is good, *jah?*"

"Of course. But something can be wrong, and God can still be good."

Tears welled in Eileen's eyes but she shook her head, pressed her lips together, and looked away. "It's just an adjustment. We've been without children for so long it's hard now."

Mariana could totally agree. She was going to have a hard enough time adjusting to having one baby, much less two. She could only imagine what it was like to get children who had already been influenced by the outside world. And then not to know if she was going to get to keep them at all . . . "Any word on the adoption?"

Eileen shook her head. "There's just so much to it. They have to get the grandparents involved and see where the mom might be when she finally gets out of jail." She looked out the window, then back to Mariana. "I'm not even sure it's such a good idea anymore."

Mariana reached out and squeezed her friend's hand. "Don't say that. Trust in God and everything will come out the way He intended."

Eileen nodded and sniffed, her tears disappearing into a watery smile. "You're right, of course. Has being confined to your room made you wise beyond your years, Mariana Miller?"

Mariana smiled and shrugged. "I guess so." But she

needed to remember those words herself and apply them to her own life as often as possible.

The screen door slammed just before lunch the following day. Mariana pushed herself up a little straighter in the bed and smoothed down the sides of her handkerchief. Maybe she should have put on her prayer *kapp*. She didn't have time to worry about that now. She pressed her fingers down the front of her dress and the quilt that covered her legs, then folded her hands and waited for him to enter.

But instead of Reuben, a tiny ball of fur scampered through her doorway. The minute the dog stopped, looked at her, and barked, his little legs raising off the floor with the effort.

"Hey there," Mariana said. "Where'd you come from?"

"Don't mind her," Reuben said, scooping up the tiny puppy and depositing her on the bed. "She's with me."

Mariana couldn't stop the laugh from escaping her. "Are you sure you can handle her? I mean, she looks pretty vicious."

Reuben scratched the puppy behind one ear and shot Mariana an indignant look. "What's wrong with her?"

"She doesn't look to be . . . well, like a guy dog."

Reuben scoffed. "That's because it's a girl dog. I told you that. You need to listen."

Mariana shook her head. "That's not what I'm talking about. I'm talking about the fact that most men don't have a dog that . . ." She struggled to find the words. "Sissy," she finally said.

"There's nothing wrong with this baby." Reuben moved his efforts to the dog's chin. "But she's not really my dog."

"She's not?"

"No. She's yours."

As if in agreement, the tiny dog barked.

Mariana stared at the dog as if it might morph into something unrecognizable. "Mine? My dog? Reuben, I can't have a dog."

"Why not? She's little. A Yorkie terrier, I think the woman said. She won't take up much room."

"I'm confined to the bed indefinitely. And whenever I am allowed up, I'll have two newborn babies to take care of."

His joyous expression disappeared in an instant. "I didn't want you to be alone. I thought that if you had a dog, you would always have company."

It was perhaps the sweetest thing anyone had ever done for her. "She's adorable," Mariana finally said, "but I'm not going to be able to take care of her."

"What if I take care of her?"

"How are you going to do that?"

"I'm over here every day. I'll feed her when I come and take her outside for a bit. Then the rest of the day, she can stay here with you and keep you company."

When he said it, it sounded like the perfect plan. But she knew it was riddled with holes. "She's going to have to get up in the middle of the night and go outside. They will barely let me go to the bathroom on my own. I can't let her out at night."

"I'll put in a doggie door."

"And teach her to use it?"

"*Jah.*"

"And clean up any accidents she has until she learns to use it?"

"*Jah.*" He smiled, and she knew he thought he had broken her down.

The puppy climbed across her legs and up, settling herself on the slight mound of Mariana's stomach. Mariana looked at that tiny black face, into those sweet brown eyes. Then the puppy rested her chin on her paws and closed her eyes for a nap. This tiny ball of black and tan fur no bigger than one of her shoes.

How could she say no?

Chapter Five

For the remainder of the afternoon, the puppy stayed right by her side. Mariana wasn't sure if it was because the little dog knew she was her new owner or because she was afraid of all the noise Reuben was making. He pounded and sawed and otherwise created a huge ruckus as he installed the doggie escape hatch in the door off the kitchen.

Once the noise stopped, Mariana eased from the bed and made her way into the other room. "Are you sure this is going to work?" she asked with a pointed nod toward the new installment.

Reuben was on his feet in a heartbeat. "What are you doing out of bed?"

"I needed to use the bathroom." That wasn't entirely true. She wanted to see the dog door and thought she could do that under the guise of taking care of her necessities.

"Then why are you in here?"

"I just wanted to see it."

"You've seen it. Now get back in bed." He smiled, taking the sting from his words. Then he stood and herded her back toward her room. "Besides, you shouldn't leave the puppy unattended. What if she falls off the bed?"

Mariana rushed back into her bedroom and scooped the pooch into her arms.

"She's okay." The puppy licked Mariana's face, showering her with sweet doggie kisses.

Reuben chuckled. "What are you going to name her?"

Mariana tilted her head and studied the tiny face before her. "I don't know."

"What about Candy? Because she's so sweet," he suggested.

She smiled. "Candy. I like that."

Reuben grinned in return. "Then Candy it is."

Candy proved to be more company than Mariana could have ever imagined. She proved to be easy to train as well, and by the time Tuesday rolled back around, Candy would stand at the edge of the bed and whine when she needed to go out, then race back to Mariana's side when her business was taken care of.

Mariana wasn't sure who she was the proudest of: Candy, herself, or Reuben.

He gave the tiny dog a pat on the head and a scratch behind the ears. "I guess I should be going," he said. They had just finished their lunch and a hand of Uno. She had tried her best to distract him enough to make him put the wrong cards down, but he never had. He did tell her that since the cards were always the same shade of red and green, he could see a difference in the shades of gray that they looked like to him. But she had also discovered that once he was distracted, he didn't pay close enough attention and often played the wrong card. For some reason, she found this entirely too entertaining.

"You're leaving so soon?" She loved spending time with him, loved when he came to have lunch and play cards. She hated when he had to go. But she understood.

"*Jah*. I have an estimate I need to do in Taylor Creek. A man there wants a brand-new sun porch."

Mariana nodded. "Oh, that would be a good job, *jah?*"

He nodded. "I guess I better get on over there. It may take me a little while."

"Did you hire a driver?"

Reuben shrugged. "It's not too far. I thought I'd just take my tractor."

Mariana tried to tell herself that it didn't matter. Reuben was a grown man. And if he wanted to drive his tractor all the way to Taylor Creek, who was she to say anything otherwise? But it seemed awfully dangerous, the miles of highway he would have to travel on a slow-moving vehicle. Granted, most people in the area were used to their tractors and buggies. But she worried for him just the same.

"You'll be careful, okay?"

He smiled and donned his hat, then winked at her, his eyes twinkling. "Of course I will." He seemed about to say something more, then turned on his heel and left the bedroom. Mariana listened, his footsteps both comforting and sad. She hadn't asked if the quilting circle was definitely coming to her house again, but she was hopeful. If not she would be spending the remainder of the afternoon all alone.

"Yoo-hoo, Mariana?" The screen door slammed, then Mariana heard, "Reuben. What are you doing here?"

She could almost hear his blush. "I . . . I was just leaving."

"*Jah*. Okay then." Eileen Brenneman had arrived.

The screen door slammed again, and Mariana could

only assume that it was Reuben leaving. Her theory was confirmed when Eileen popped into the doorway. "Hi. How are you?"

Mariana nodded and smiled reassuringly. "I'm good." These days it was closer and closer to the truth.

"What is that?" Eileen stopped in her tracks and pointed to Candy.

"It's a dog."

Then Eileen was in motion, slipping into the room and scooping Candy into her arms. "Well, I can see that. And she's precious. But where'd she come from?"

Mariana smiled. "Reuben brought her to me. He said he didn't want me being alone all day."

Eileen turned and gave Mariana an inquisitive look. "Oh, he did?"

Mariana shook her head. "It's not what you think."

"Who said I was thinking anything?" Eileen stroked Candy's head and pasted an innocent look on her face. "It seems to me that you came to that conclusion awfully quick."

"Don't put words in my mouth," Mariana said. "I wasn't the one who brought it up."

"You sure were."

"Brought what up?"

Somehow in their discussion, Mariana had missed Clara Rose's entrance.

Eileen turned to their young friend. "Reuben brought Mariana this sweet puppy so she wouldn't be alone all day. What do you think about that?"

Clara Rose gave a small squeal and took Candy into her arms. "I would say that's adorable."

"The puppy or his reason?"

Clara Rose stopped hugging the dog just long enough to think about it for a heartbeat. "Both."

Eileen gave a self-satisfied nod. "That's all I'm saying. It just seems really sweet and really adorable that Reuben brought you a present."

Mariana shook her head. "He was my husband's best friend and is a good friend to me too. He's come by every day at lunch and kept me company for a while so I wouldn't be alone. And to help train the puppy."

Eileen's mouth fell open. "Every day? He's come by *every day* to eat lunch with you?"

"Yes. And we played a couple of games of Uno or something. Sometimes we just sit and talk."

Eileen and Clara Rose exchanged a look.

"What?" Mariana asked.

"I think he has a crush on you," Clara Rose said.

"Who has a crush on who?" Verna asked.

"Reuben Weisel has a crush on Mariana," Clara Rose answered.

"Is that so?" Verna turned her sassy blue gaze to Mariana.

"No. It's not. Eileen and Clara Rose have it in their heads that since he brought me a dog so I wouldn't be by myself, he has some kind of secret crush on me."

"It does seem mighty sweet."

"Ah, a puppy," Tess exclaimed. "Can I hold it?"

"Sure." Clara Rose handed Candy to Tess.

"Whose is he?" Tess bounced the puppy like a baby in her arms.

"He's mine. But he's a she. Candy," Mariana said.

"Reuben Weisel gave her to Mariana. What do you think about that?"

Tess planted a small kiss on the top of the puppy's head. "I'd say that's a nice thing to do for someone. Except you're confined to bed and it'd be really hard for you to train a puppy if you can hardly get around."

"Exactly," Eileen said. "Ask her how the puppy got trained."

Tess swung her attention back to Mariana.

"Is your life so boring that you have to make up stories about mine?" Mariana asked.

"Crush," Clara Rose said in a singsong tone with a smile on her face.

"My life is just fine," Tess said.

But her words were so stiff and adamant that Mariana had a flickering thought that perhaps things weren't as good at home as Tess wanted them to think.

She pushed that thought away as Clara Rose asked, "How did the puppy get trained?"

"Reuben trained her," Mariana said on a sigh. "That was part of the deal when he brought her over. I said he had to train her since I couldn't get up."

"So he brought you a puppy *and* he housebroke it?" Clara Rose's eyes grew wide. "That man's got it bad."

Mariana shook her head. "Y'all are just making up stories where there are none."

Eileen propped her hands on her hips and turned to face Mariana once more. When she spoke, her tone had lost its teasing edge. "Listen, I know how hard it must have been for you to lose Leroy the way you did. But all joking aside, Reuben Weisel is a good man."

Mariana shook her head even as she said, "I know that."

"It's not been very long since we buried Leroy, but keep an open mind, okay?" Eileen said. "You're fixing to have two babies to care for and no job. How are you going to support them?"

It was a question she had asked herself countless times, but there had never been an answer.

"You think she should get married again?" Clara Rose asked. "So soon after she lost her husband?"

Verna shrugged. "I don't see why not. Lots of women do. And even more men. We weren't meant to walk this world alone."

Mariana thought that was interesting, seeing as how Verna had been widowed for a year and had made no secret of the fact that she was enjoying single life again.

Eileen sat on the edge of Mariana's bed and took her hand. "I'm not saying you have to make any decisions. I'm just saying it's time for you to start living again."

It was true. She had spent the last few months taking care of Leroy. Those final days were brutal. But she couldn't imagine marrying someone else now. But if there was someone that she wanted to marry . . .

"Well, I guess this is as good a time as any to bring it up. We're getting a benefit auction together for you, Mariana," Verna said. "I guess it's not supposed to be a secret or anything, but we know that you're going to need some money coming up, and now that you don't have Leroy here . . ."

Tears stung Mariana's eyes. "I'm sorry," she said as the tears started to fall. She managed to hide one sigh, making it a hiccup instead. But the emotion was still there. "I don't know what I would do without you." She looked at each of them in turn, this mismatched group of friends she had.

They said everything happened for a reason, and that she had to believe. So there was a reason why all these ladies were her friends. And for that she was eternally grateful.

But the conversation stayed with her all through the night and into the next morning. It was Verna's turn to come feed the chickens and get her lunch and breakfast ready, but the older woman didn't bring up Reuben or the dog or Mariana getting married again. Verna simply acted as if the conversation from the day before had never even happened.

Not long after she left, Reuben stopped by. He came in as he usually did, whistling tunelessly as he gathered up the puppy's food and water, then set the little beast on the floor.

"What's that?" he asked, pointing to the shoe box she had sitting next to her on the bed.

"Candy sleeps in it. I was worried that I'd roll over and squish her. I figured if she was in the shoe box, she might be safer at night."

He nodded. "Good plan. Wait right here," he continued. "I have something else." He disappeared from her room and returned a couple of minutes later with a small staircase. At least it looked like a staircase to her, four little steps with no back.

"What are you doing with that?"

"Watch this." He set the staircase at the foot of her bed, the tallest step next to the mattress. "Come here, Candy." He clicked his tongue and called the puppy away from her empty food bowl. She'd taken to licking it across the floor as she made sure she got every morsel. "Come here."

Candy did as she was asked, scampering across the floor with her little pink tongue hanging out.

"Come on, puppy," Reuben said, holding his fingers out as if he was holding a treat. Candy dutifully climbed the little stairs and onto the bed.

"Did you make that for her?" Mariana had never seen such a thing. Who would've thought to build a staircase so that her dog could climb up onto the bed unassisted?

"Yeah." He shrugged. "It was nothing. But I thought it

might make it easier on you and her when Candy needs to get in and out of your bed."

"That was really sweet. Thank you, Reuben." But Clara Rose's words that Reuben had a crush on Mariana resurfaced again and again, mixing in with Eileen's and Verna's suggestion that perhaps she should get married again.

"What's wrong?" Reuben asked.

"Nothing. I'm fine." But this time she couldn't even convince herself.

"I don't believe you." Reuben came up beside her bed on the opposite end.

"The quilting circle's getting a benefit auction together for me."

Reuben nodded. "I heard something of that nature."

"That made me start to wonder. I mean, what am I going to do?" She didn't have to explain that she meant what was she going to do with no job and two babies but no husband to help support her.

"I guess you could get married again." She started to speak, but Reuben held both hands up to stay her response. "Now, just hear me out. I know how much you cared for Leroy and I know how much he cared for you, but . . ." He stopped, took a deep breath, then plunged forward. "I think we should get married."

"Married?" It was all Mariana could say. "Married?"

"Just listen," Reuben continued. "It doesn't have to be a real marriage. I mean, I know how close you and Leroy were. I would never be so bold as to assume I could ever take his place. But I think we get along well enough. You need someone to look after you and the babies and even little Candy here. I seem to be the logical person. Don't you think?"

"None of this is logical," Mariana said. Her mind reeled. Married?

"You don't have to say anything now. You don't even have to make up your mind now. But give it some thought."

Mariana was certain it would be hard to keep his marriage proposal out of her thoughts. But how could she marry Reuben? Now he was her husband's best friend and yes, they did get along. She knew for certain that many marriages had started with less. But what if one day he wanted more?

"I don't need to give it any thought, Reuben. I can't cheat you out of the life that should be yours."

He frowned. "What are you talking about, cheat me? How would you cheat me out of anything?"

"What if you meet somebody and fall in love? What then? You'll be married to me forever. I don't want that to happen."

"If I haven't fallen in love by now, I'm probably not going to."

"You don't know that for certain."

A strange look crossed his face, then Reuben pushed to his feet and stalked over to the window. He looked outside, though with his faraway stare Mariana had to wonder if he saw anything at all. "Do you know why I never got married?" he asked.

"I guess you just never found the right girl."

"Something like that." Reuben turned back, his gaze falling on her once again. "I always wanted what you and Leroy had." He shook his head as a sad smile flickered across his face. "Always wanted someone to look at me the way you looked at him. As time went on, I realized more and more that it wasn't someone else that I wanted, but maybe you."

Mariana's heart gave a hard thump in her chest. Was he saying . . . ? "I don't think I understand."

"The more time I spent with the two of you, the more I realized that it wasn't someone like you I wanted, but just you."

Mariana was dumbstruck.

"I was planning on giving you enough time to mourn, to go through the process, then you came to me and told me that you are having a baby. Now you're having two babies, and they need a father. You need a husband. It only seems logical that I fill those shoes."

"But . . . But . . ." She had no idea what she thought she would say. Her thoughts were like scrambled eggs.

"I know you don't care about me that way. And I wouldn't expect you to. It will just be for convenience sake. So I could take care of you and the babies."

"And what would you get?"

"I get to be close to you."

Mariana shook her head. "I don't know, Reuben."

He came back to the bed, standing near, but farther away than he had been all week. "I scared you, didn't I?"

"Oh no," she lied. He did more than scare her. He terrified her. All these years and she had never known that he thought more of her than just as his best friend's wife.

"I don't know what to say," she said.

He gave her a rueful smile. "I was hoping you would say yes."

"Yes," she repeated, turning the word over in her brain, trying to figure out exactly what it meant for her and the babies. Someone to take care of them. Someone to work, to bring in an income so she could take care of these two little unexpected bundles. "What would people say?"

Reuben shook his head. "People are going to say what people are going to say. If we talk to the bishop, get special permission, maybe we can get married sometime this fall. Your mourning time wouldn't be over, but we could get married after the babies come. I think folks would understand. If not . . ." He shrugged. "Our relationship is our business. As long as the bishop approves, who can say anything different?"

He was right, she supposed. And as strange as the decision seemed, how could she not take him up on his offer? "Where will we live?"

"Wherever you want to. You want to live here? Fine."

"And you wouldn't care about that?" she asked.

"Not at all. I just want to take care of the three of you. Where we do that doesn't matter."

"Can I have some time to think about this?"

"Of course," he said. "But please . . . don't take too long."

Chapter Six

Mariana lay in the darkness and stared up at the ceiling. They had told her at the doctor's office that she might be more comfortable lying on her left side with the pillow beneath her knees and maybe one at her back. But then they had followed that up with as she got bigger. Right now the babies were just a bulge, not much bigger than her stomach when she ate too much. Was she the only person they didn't seem real to? Everyone else seemed to embrace the idea, but to her, they seemed as far away as the moon and as much of a fantasy as an *Englisch* fairy tale. She couldn't wrap her mind around the fact that she was having one baby, much less two, that Leroy was gone, she was confined to her bed, and Reuben had just proposed to her. Maybe she should pinch herself to see if she was dreaming.

Beside her, in the tiny shoe box, Candy whimpered in her sleep as if she was chasing rabbits. It was too much of a detail not to be real. So what was a girl to do?

"Oh, Leroy," she whispered to the darkness. "I don't know what you would have me do." How could she determine the right thing to do when she was so entrenched in it?

Marry Reuben. Was that the answer? It would certainly give her a partner in this new adventure of parenthood. And she couldn't think of anyone better to marry than him. But how could she marry him knowing how he felt about her even when she was married to someone else?

Though he had been mighty good at hiding his feelings, she had never once suspected that he felt anything stronger for her than merely friendship. Although he claimed otherwise, she couldn't help but believe that one day he might find someone he truly loved.

Maybe that was the problem. Maybe she was afraid that he only *thought* he loved her, and when real love came along he would be tied to her forever. Not just her, but her babies as well. Never ever could she steal his life and freedom from him that way. It just wasn't possible. Not for her own selfish reasons.

She eased onto her side, wishing she knew the right thing to do. It would be so much easier to accept Reuben's proposal, allow him to take care of her and the babies. Have him move in and support them while she took care of him as a wife should.

And though he said otherwise, what would they do if the day came when he was no longer happy with their arrangement? Losing Leroy had been hard enough, but to lose Reuben too . . .

She pressed a hand to her belly, wishing for something, some kind of sign. Anything to let her know what to do.

Dear Lord, help me, Lord. Help me know what's best. There's more than just me to think about. And more than just Reuben. My thoughts are a mess and my judgment seems inadequate. So help me, Lord, find the answer I need. Help me. Direct me to do Your will. Direct me to what I'm supposed to do. Amen.

Just then it happened. A small flutter, like butterfly wings beating against the walls of her belly. She had never felt anything like it before. Joy overcame her and tears rose into her eyes. Her babies were moving. The first sign that life was really there. And she was all alone except for Candy. She lay there in the dark, wishing someone was with her. Her mother and father, they were both gone. Leroy, gone. Her sister, halfway across the state. There was no one to share it with. No one to share one of life's great moments. No one there to share the miracle of God's love.

She could just imagine the joy and wonderment on Reuben's face if he had been there to place his hand next to hers and feel that soft flutter.

And instinctively she knew. It was the sign she had been looking for.

"I've been thinking about what you said yesterday," Mariana started, gathering up the pieces from their game, more for something to do with her hands than anything else.

Reuben perked up. "I didn't want to ask," he said haltingly.

She nodded. "I think maybe it is a good idea that we get married." She looked at the game pieces in her hand, the floor, the box where Candy slept, and out the window. Any place but in Reuben's searching green eyes. "Later, of course. The babies are due in September, but the doctor thinks they'll probably come in August. He said twins usually come early. So maybe December?"

"What's wrong with November or October? Those are good months to get married."

"*Jah*, I suppose." She chanced a look back in his direction.

He was staring intently at her as if he could see straight through her lie of an expression to her very soul. "I think this may be a bad idea," he said. His expression saddened until it was as dark as a storm cloud and twice as miserable.

"It's not that. It's just that . . ." But she didn't know how to finish.

"I understand," Reuben said. "I know what you and Leroy had was special. And I don't want you to think that you have to marry me. I just wanted to take care of you, that's all. It wasn't right of me to make you uncomfortable."

"I'm not uncomfortable."

He pushed to his feet and stalked across the room. "You are. You're so uncomfortable you can't even look into my face."

Candy whined as he raised his voice. Then he seemed to pull himself back together. "It was a bad idea. I should have thought about it more before I said anything."

"I wish you would stop saying that. I just agreed to marry you."

He stared out the window, not bothering to move his gaze to her as he spoke. "I'm not trying to belittle what you shared with Leroy. I'm not trying to make that less than what it was."

"I know. And . . . And my life with Leroy wasn't perfect." She couldn't believe the words had come out of her mouth. But once they started, she couldn't stop them. "You didn't see him at the very end. You didn't see how bad he progressed. Every day it grew harder and harder. He was different when company was here, when the bishop would come over or a neighbor. Then he seemed more like himself, but somehow with me—" She shook her head. "It was as if he didn't know me, as if I was somehow at fault. He changed until he became a person I didn't know anymore. You didn't belittle anything we had. The cancer did. And I lost my husband twice. Once when he stopped being himself and the second time when I buried him."

"I'm sorry," he said. "Why didn't you tell me?" His voice returned to a normal tone, even lower, softer, more concerned.

"What difference would it have made?"

He thought about it a second. "I don't know."

"It would have only changed how he felt about me and I felt about him. It wouldn't have changed anything, not what the disease did to him. I loved him with all my heart, but when he died he set us both free."

Reuben crossed the room in an instant. He knelt by the bed and clasped her hands in his. "I'm sorry. So very sorry."

"It's not your fault," she whispered in return. He tugged on her hands until they were eye to eye and nose to nose. Then he tenderly kissed her forehead.

Mariana closed her eyes, relishing the small token of affection. It had been so long since she'd had even the gentlest of touches.

"I promise you," Reuben said. "We'll only remember the good times. The bad ones will be forgotten. And then we'll make more good memories. You'll keep your journal and we'll tell the babies all about their father and all the wonderful things he did. And that's all anyone ever needs to remember of Leroy Miller."

* * *

"Are you sure this is okay?" Reuben cast a quick glance in her direction.

"I told you, the doctor said it would be fine."

Even as she said the words, Reuben slowed the buggy. They were barely going at a crawl. "If we go much slower than this, we're never going to make it to church."

A wrinkled frown creased his forehead. "Better make it late than not in one piece." He pulled back on the reins again. If they went much slower, they might just be at a stop. "I should have asked the bishop to let me bring the tractor."

Mariana laughed. "Like a tractor rides any smoother than a buggy and horse."

"I think so."

All in all, it really didn't matter to her. She was outside. She had been released from total bed rest. At her last doctor's appointment, her blood pressure had been lower and everything looked good. The doctor said the babies' heartbeats were strong, and he told her that she could go to church but with stipulations.

She adjusted the pillow at her back and shifted on top of the one she sat on. It felt strange to have such a cushion in an Amish buggy. She supposed that if she kept this up, she might not ever want to go back to the old way.

"I called the bishop and left a message to make sure. He said that Eli Miller would have a nice cushion chair for you in the back room during the service. I don't want you to sit for three hours on one of those hard benches."

"I already called. Are you forgetting they're my in-laws?"

"In-laws or not, I wanted to make sure you had a chair."

Mariana smiled, still loving the feel of the breeze on

her face. She only wished the buggy was topless so she could actually have the sun on her shoulders. She was just so happy to be out of the house for the first time in over a month.

"There's no telling what they think. I called them, then you called, and then the bishop." She laughed.

Reuben pulled down the Millers' driveway, lining up his buggy with the several already parked there. Before he even set the parking brake, Aaron Miller was there to put the horse in the pasture.

Mariana slid the door open and Aaron gave her a hand down. "*Danki*," she said.

He nodded in her direction. "You look well."

She smiled. "I feel well."

"*Mamm* has a chair all set up for you. We wanted to make sure you were as comfortable as possible." His brown gaze flickered from Mariana to Reuben and then back. But he said nothing.

"Thank you, Aaron."

He gave a quick nod as she and Reuben made their way across the yard to the house.

She wasn't sure if it was because she hadn't been to church in so long, or because she showed up with Reuben, or maybe because it was becoming more and more apparent that she was going to have a baby—correction, babies—but it seemed as if all eyes had turned to them.

She glanced at Reuben, but if he had noticed, he made no remark. He simply walked next to her, his steps slow as if not to tire her, his eyes straight ahead.

"Let's get you settled down before everyone else comes in."

She nodded and he clasped her elbow and assisted her up the steps, across the porch, and into the Miller house.

She had been there too many times to count, seeing as

how she was married to Eli Miller's brother, and she knew her way around.

She steered Reuben toward the living area of the Miller house. Like many Amish homes, it had sliding walls that pushed back to allow for extra room. The church benches were already in place, along with padded seats in the back for the infirm. She'd never before thought she would be among them, sitting in the back like some sort of queen. But she had a feeling that if she went against the doctor's orders and sat on the regular benches, Reuben would have a heart attack before the service was over from worrying about her so much.

"Do you think you will be comfortable enough here?" Reuben asked.

"Of course," Mariana said. "I'm not broken, just . . . You know."

"I don't want the doctor to regret allowing you to come here."

"He's not going to, though I'm starting to wonder if this is a good idea. Now leave me be and go do what men do before church."

He seemed as if he was about to protest, then changed his mind. With his lips pressed firmly together, he nodded once, then reluctantly walked away.

Mariana sank down into one of the padded chairs lined up across the back of the room. She wasn't sure how long she would be able to attend church services in the upcoming months, and she was grateful to have this time today.

"I'm so glad you made it." Gertie Miller stopped by Mariana's chair and squeezed her hand. She had been by the house a couple of times since Mariana had gone on bed rest, but with Jonah having as many problems as he was and a house full of teenagers in *rumspringa*, Mariana knew Gertie had already more than she could handle.

"I'm so glad to be here." Of course it would be better to be outside, but even the change in room was a blessing to Mariana. She hoped that if she could take it easy today, make it through this without getting herself overtired or making her blood pressure rise too much, she might be able to make short trips to town. How wonderful would it be to go into Wells Landing and grab a piece of pie and a cup of coffee at Kauffman's. Oh, the things a person took for granted when all was right in the world.

"Did I see you come in with Reuben Weisel?" Gertie asked.

"Yes, he's been a great help to me since Leroy passed."

Gertie nodded, but Mariana noticed that her eyes were guarded. "That's good. That's good."

The tone of her voice alone was enough to let Mariana know that Gertie Miller, for whatever reason, did not approve of her being seen out with Reuben Weisel. Mariana supposed it was because it had only been a couple of months since Leroy had died, but there was no way that Gertie could know the tragedy that Mariana had suffered at Leroy's hands. However unintentional, the hurt still remained. And the fact that she was now alone and pregnant and unable to care for herself played a big part in the decisions she made.

She wanted to tell Gertie that Reuben had asked her to marry him and she was going to do so, but she bit her tongue and smiled. Some people she was friends with because she loved them and they loved her in return, and other people she had to be friends with because she had to be friends with them. For Mariana, Gertie Miller was one of this last group of people. Oh, she seemed nice enough, and Mariana supposed that she was. But their personalities were different and they seemed to clash whenever they were in the same room. Mariana had hoped now that Leroy was gone it would be different. Wishful thinking at its finest.

"Thank you for getting me a chair out today and the pillows too."

"Yes," Gertie said. It was apparent to Mariana that extra cushions were not on Gertie's list of top priorities for a church service.

"Well, I must go now. Lots of things to do to finish up."

Mariana nodded and murmured something that must've passed as a farewell, for Gertie moved away, leaving her thankfully alone. But not for long.

James Riehl came in, his sunglasses firmly in place. He had started wearing them a year so ago to help block out the sunlight and help him focus. With his traumatic head injury, it was hard for him to tolerate bright lights and loud noises. But after witnessing his grin, Mariana thought that perhaps he just liked wearing the glasses.

He sat down next to her, though he perched on the edge of his seat. She knew in a few moments, before church started, he would move to the opposite side, where chairs had been lined up behind where the men sat.

"It's good to see you here, Mariana Miller," he said. His eyes skimmed over her dress and she hoped that he remembered she was in mourning. He gave a small nod. "It's good to be at church, *jah*?"

Mariana smiled. "It is."

"I like church," James said. "Except for the shirt." He plucked at his white shirt, so crisp and clean underneath his black vest. "I don't see why we can't wear purple."

Mariana did her best to stop her smile. She wouldn't want James to think that she was laughing at him. But since his head injury, he had become obsessed with the color purple and wondered why everyone didn't wear it every day. She'd seen him in town and he was always

wearing some shade of the royal color. In fact, other than
church when he had to wear white, she didn't think she'd
seen him in anything else.

"I suppose they feel white is purer," Mariana suggested.

James seemed to think about it a moment. "I guess.
But purple sure is prettier."

Mariana smiled, so glad that she got to come out today.
"That it is, James. That it is."

He moved away as everyone began to file in from
outside. First the men came in and seated themselves,
followed by the women, who took to the opposite side.
Mariana couldn't help but watch for Reuben to come in.
The men looked so handsome in their church attire. And
she wondered what Reuben would look like with a beard.
He would start growing one just after they got married.
Her heart gave a funny pound in her chest. She was really
going to do this. She was getting married again, and as
much as she wanted to pretend that it was just to take care
of the babies . . . Well, that's what it was, just pretending.

As if sensing her gaze on him, he turned, his green
eyes catching hers. He gave a small smile and turned back
to face the preacher.

Mariana's breath caught in her chest. Yes, it was just
pretending. She had done the unthinkable. She had fallen
in love with Reuben Weisel. The thought nearly took her
breath away. How had this happened? She had buried her
husband only a few weeks before. But that wasn't entirely
true, she thought as she continued to stare at Reuben's
profile. She had said good-bye to Leroy months ago,
sitting in a doctor's office with a bleak prognosis. An in-
operable tumor that would take away his self, his memory,
and eventually his life.

His cancer was such that it'd been hard to find, even harder to diagnose, and by the time they knew what treatment was needed, it was too late. Not that she suspected Leroy would have done anything differently. He was that kind of man, willing to accept God's will for what it was. That was how she knew that he would not go in for any treatment, he would not fight it. He had something wrong with his brain, and that something had to be part of God's will. So she had said her good-byes to him long before he had become something different, long before he turned into someone she didn't recognize.

She dragged her gaze from Reuben only to have it clash with that of Gertie Miller. Her sister-in-law's eyes narrowed as she traced the line of Mariana's stare. Gertie couldn't understand. She couldn't know everything that Mariana had gone through. She didn't know what it was like to have to deal with the loss of a spouse, the loss of love, and the loss of a best friend.

Mariana looked away. Reuben had asked her to marry him, and that was all there was to it. And with the bishop's permission they would get married while Mariana was still in mourning. It was a unique situation. They had babies to take care of, and she needed Reuben so much more than he claimed he needed her. She could only pray that he never found anyone else he truly loved. Not that she doubted that he loved her. She felt more that he loved the *idea* of her, the idea of having something similar to what she and Leroy once had. She just prayed that she could give him that and more. It might take a while, but eventually perhaps their marriage could be real, a loving and caring partnership as they raised children and grew old together.

She wasn't under the impression that she was young

enough to have any more children. The babies she carried now were a gift that she hadn't expected. It would probably be best for her not to get pregnant again, but that didn't mean they couldn't enjoy the babies that they would share now. But as she pulled her gaze from Gertie's disapproving one, she knew not everybody in Wells Landing would be happy concerning their decision.

Chapter Seven

Somehow Mariana talked Reuben into letting her stay at least through the meal. She wouldn't serve the meal, and simply rested with the other infirm and elderly. But she wanted to stay out as much as possible. She knew Reuben had wanted to agree, otherwise he wouldn't have given in to her pleas for normalcy.

She supposed she was worried that it wouldn't be long before she was right back where she was last week, completely confined to the bed once again without a once-a-week outing to break it up. She wanted this to last as long as possible.

"Did I see you arrive with Reuben Weisel?" Linda Miller Stoltzfoos came up to her from behind.

"*Jah*," Mariana said before she could think the answer through. Linda was sister to Leroy and Jonah's dad, Eli. Unfortunately, Linda had about as much approval for Mariana as Gertie did. She wasn't sure what she had done to earn these women's scorn, but it was there all the same. Oh, they were nice enough to her on the outside, but she was constantly left out of sister days and other such activities, and she had been for years. Once Leroy got sick, their excuses not to invite her became valid and inarguable. Not that she cared. She would rather hang around the quilting circle gang than anyone else. They might all be part of the same community, but that didn't mean they all needed to be friends.

"Interesting," Linda said. "Seeing as how Leroy has only been gone a short time."

"Leroy's been gone a lot longer than that," Mariana said. She wanted to continue with, "If you had visited more, then you would realize that." But she managed to keep those words out of her mouth.

"*Jah*, well, I just think it's odd for you to be taking up with a man when you're pregnant." Linda's pale blue eyes flashed with something that Mariana didn't recognize. "You are pregnant? Right?"

Of all the things to be worried about. "I am. The babies are due in September."

"I'm still not sure how my brother could father a child in his condition."

Mariana stiffened her spine and her resolve. She would never win with this woman, and she should never try. "A lot of times when people are terminally ill, they have a stretch of really good days. The doctor told us it's like God giving them a second chance to say good-bye and love all things they love. To enjoy life for just a little bit longer. Leroy had one of those times. And that's all I'm willing to say about it."

Linda nodded, but Mariana could see the disbelief in her gaze. *Let them think what they want.*

"Well, it seems I'm the biggest sensation today, even over Titus Lambert coming back to town, *jah?*"

"Titus doesn't concern me as much as you do. Those are my brother's children you are carrying. Or some say."

"Linda!" Verna Yutzy picked that time to come up behind the woman.

Linda whirled around to face the older woman. Verna might be little, but she packed an awful lot of power and gumption in her small frame. "You need to keep your ugly thoughts to yourself. I don't want to have to say something to the bishop."

Linda's gaze scraped over Mariana, then landed on Verna. "I'm sorry if I offended anyone."

Mariana seriously questioned the sincerity of her words.

Without a good-bye, Linda turned on one heel and sauntered away.

"Thank you," Mariana said, looping one arm through Verna's.

Verna shook her head. "That woman. She's just jealous, you know. Since she could never have kids either."

Mariana had forgotten about that. Linda had been in the childless couple buddy bunch with Mariana and Eileen. Now Eileen was adopting and Mariana was pregnant. That left only three members to that group. And it seemed as if it was getting the better of Linda Stoltzfoos.

"Oh well," Mariana said. "I guess there goes my invitation to the family reunion."

Verna smiled. "You're welcome at mine any time."

"Are you sure this is a good idea?" Mariana asked as they drove home from church. Her weeks of being inactive had left her a little weak. She was tired and so ready to be back at home, though she had enjoyed her time out.

"I told you we shouldn't have gone," Reuben said. He cast a concerned look in her direction.

"That's not what I'm talking about," Mariana said.

"Are you sure it's a good idea for the two of us to get married?"

He frowned. "Why would I think otherwise?"

"It just seems like some people are less than enthusiastic about the idea."

Reuben gave her another look and pulled the horse and buggy into the nearest turnoff. It led to an *Englisch* man's house. Mariana wasn't exactly sure who lived there, though she thought he owned some type of sporting goods store just this side of Taylor Creek.

Reuben set the brake and turned to face her. "You can't let those people get to you. This is your life, your babies, and I want to do everything in my power to help you. There's nothing wrong with that."

"I know, but it just seems like—"

Reuben placed a hand on either side of her face, holding her gaze steady as he looked into her eyes. "I don't care what anyone else says. I don't care what anyone else thinks. I just know that I care for you. I love you, and I want nothing more than to help you raise these children. I think Leroy would be okay with that. Don't you?"

Mariana stared into his soft green eyes, absorbing his words like a balm to her soul. He cared about her. He loved her. She wasn't in this alone. She had felt so abandoned, being pregnant and burying Leroy. But Reuben had given her a new hope and a new start, a new chance, a new life after the one she had with Leroy had been destroyed. Was it wrong to want that?

"No," Reuben answered.

Had she asked the question out loud?

"Mariana . . . I'm going to kiss you now." He said the words softly and slowly, as if he was giving her time to change her mind. Time for her to tell him no. But Mariana could do neither.

"Okay," she said. Her gaze still locked with his, their eyes steady. A breath of anticipation hung suspended between them as he moved slowly toward her. Did she need time to change her mind? Should she change her mind? No. She was marrying this man, and one day they would pledge their lives to each other. Just like all the other promises that she had made once upon a time to another. These vows would be different. Somehow she just knew.

Mariana's eyes fluttered shut as Reuben's breath brushed across her lips. Then his mouth touched hers, softly, gently, sweetly.

His lips were warm and coaxing. It only took an instant for her to realize that she had never kissed anyone but Leroy Miller. And even then it had been nothing like this. Any doubts she had melted, her concerns evaporated, and all that was left was the honesty and truth of their decision.

His lips moved across hers. Tiny, teasing kisses, then deeper until her breath was stolen from her lungs.

He lifted his head, his green eyes dark with some emotion she couldn't name, but she hoped and prayed it was the love he'd spoken about.

"Have no doubts, my sweet Mariana. In our marriage, there will be no room for doubt."

"No doubt," she said. "*Jah*. No doubt."

Chapter Eight

The tingle from his kiss remained with Mariana even after he released her and pulled his buggy back onto the road. If this marriage to Reuben meant kisses like that, she was certain she could ignore anything Gertie Miller and Linda Stoltzfoos could dish out.

She studied Reuben's face as he drove. Such a handsome man. She was so blessed to have him as a friend. Those blessings would increase when he became her husband and father to the children she carried. So many blessings she had to be thankful for.

"Do you mind if we run by my house real quick? I mean, it's on the way, so you won't have to be in the buggy for much longer." He turned and caught her staring at him. "What?"

"Nothing." She ducked her head to hide her smile. She felt like a teenager again.

"Okay then." He cast another look in her direction. His expression was anything but convinced.

Thankfully he let the matter drop as he pulled his horse down the familiar drive.

"I'll only be a few minutes," he said as he set the brake on the buggy.

Mariana slid the door open.

"You don't have to get out," Reuben said.

"I need to use the restroom."

The buggy rocked as Reuben jumped to the ground. He came around and helped her down as well.

"Why didn't you go before we left the Millers'?"

"I did."

Reuben shook his head. "Come on then." He helped her up the steps, and once again Mariana was reminded what a wonderful father he was going to be. All at once those countless blessings surfaced again.

They entered the house and Reuben started for the staircase just to the left of the front door. "I won't be but a moment. I just need to run upstairs for something."

Mariana nodded and turned toward the back of the house where she knew the downstairs bathroom to be. She took care of her business quickly and was back in the kitchen before Reuben. She figured he would have beaten her back, but instead she wandered around his living space.

It wasn't a bad house. Smaller than the one that she had shared with Leroy and not quite as fancy. Still, it was a good house with a beautiful front window that stretched nearly from the floor to the ceiling. It let in the bright Western sun.

Mariana could only imagine what it would be like to sit at the little table that Reuben had placed in front of it and read a book. Or her Bible. And it seemed that was exactly what he thought as well. His Bible, a notepad, and a pen rested there, waiting for his return. She would have to make sure when they were married that Reuben had a place where he could enjoy reading and the wondrous light of the sun.

She ran her fingers over the cover of his Bible, tracing

the gold letters on the front. This was his English Bible. She knew somewhere in the house was the German Bible and his copy of *Martyrs Mirror*, but it seemed nowadays learning to read and speak in German was becoming a lost tradition.

She picked up his Bible and flipped through it, enjoying the flutter of the pages as they went from one side to the other. But it stopped as it fell open to a paper tucked between the pages.

It wasn't any of her concern and certainly none of her business, but she extracted the paper and unfolded it. It was a letter, in Leroy's handwriting. A letter to Reuben. Moreover, it was the list of things that Leroy wanted his best friend to do once Leroy was gone. Of course Leroy had left his tools to Reuben, but the letter contained more than that.

Please, please, please, I can't ask you enough. Please take care of Mariana. She is a good woman and deserves a whole and complete life with a husband who loves her. I can't be that for her, and I don't know if she will ever have that again. She'll need someone to watch after her. Someone to make sure that things at the house are taken care of. That she doesn't want for anything. I trust for you to do this for me. I know that you will do everything in your power to make sure she's seen about. I leave this world knowing that she is in your capable hands. She will not suffer loss or neglect as long as you are there to watch after her. Thank you.

> *Your loving friend,*
> *Leroy*

"Mariana, I . . ." Reuben's words died as he came down the stairs and found her standing there, the letter in hand.

She had thought that Reuben had cared about her. That he wanted to marry her and take care of her babies, but it was all just a promise that he had made to Leroy.

"How could you?" She folded the paper even though her hands trembled. Then she placed it back between the pages of the Bible and put the Bible back on the table, giving him ample time to find an answer.

She turned to face him.

"It's not what you think."

Not the right answer. He'd had plenty of time to change his mind, change his thoughts, change something about the situation they found themselves in. And that was all he could say? That it wasn't what she thought? How could it be anything else? "I want you to take me home now, Reuben."

He shook his head. "I'm not taking you anywhere until we talk about this. There are things that you don't understand."

"I understand perfectly. Leroy asked you to take care of me and so you offered to marry me. It's pretty obvious."

"No. It's not. If you let me explain—"

"I want you to take me home," she said a second time. She had made a fool of herself in front of her in-laws and the church. But she would be a fool no more. The sentiment was there. And it had been nice to feel loved once again. But it had all been a lie.

"I'll take you home if you let me explain."

"I'm walking home." She started for the door, but Reuben's words stopped her.

"You can't walk home in your condition."

She stopped just short of the front door. "Then I'll sit

in your buggy until you decide to take me home." She wasn't yelling; she was simply stating a fact. She wanted to go home, and if she had to wait, then she would wait. But there would be no more discussion on the matter today. If ever.

She slipped out the front door and down the porch steps. Somehow she would keep herself together until she got home. Then, in the privacy of her bedroom, she would let her tears loose. She would cry for the loss she had suffered. A loss of something that was never really hers, but that she had wanted so badly all the same.

"Mariana, wait!"

She heard his footsteps behind her, but she wasn't waiting, not until she got to the buggy. Then she would wait till he realized that she was serious. She reached up to pull herself into the buggy, her added girth a little awkward. She shifted and something in her side popped. A flash of red pain zinged before her eyes. She gasped.

"What's wrong?" Reuben was immediately at her side.

"Nothing." But she was stopped in position. She couldn't get into the buggy and she couldn't get back down. Every move caused her pain. More pain than she had ever experienced in her life. Her breath was stuck somewhere between her lungs and her lips. Her foot was still up on the buggy step, her trembling arms holding her in place.

"You keep saying that to me, and one of these days I'm going to believe you."

"Reuben," she started, trying her best to lower her foot to the ground. She felt as if she was being torn in half. Every move, every breath was excruciating. The pain took over as she slipped into his arms and out of consciousness.

* * *

"Well now, you gave us quite a scare."

Mariana looked up as the doctor came into the tiny cubicle. "But everything's okay?"

He smiled that kindly smile doctors had been giving to overly cautious pregnant women for generations. "Everything's fine. You pulled a muscle in your side. Probably because you've been so inactive. It's a double-edged sword, as they say. It's easy to injure muscles that are inactive and suddenly put to use. But in your case, if you're too active, then you run the risk of other complications. You're just going to have to be really, really careful from here on out. Complete bed rest. You have at least two more months before the babies get here. You're going to need that rest, so take it."

Mariana nodded. As much as she hated the thought of being confined to her bed once again, she knew it was necessary for her and the babies.

"I spoke to your husband."

The joy Mariana felt in knowing that the babies were fine, that she was going to be fine, was completely overshadowed when he mentioned Reuben.

"He's not my husband."

The doctor stared at her, a quizzical frown on his brow. "Somebody needs to tell him that."

"Once we get you home," Helen Ebersol said, "It's right to bed."

Mariana faked a smile. "Of course. Story of my life these days."

Helen patted her hand. "You're very lucky, you know. It could've been so much worse than a pulled muscle."

"*Jah*, I suppose."

But it was worse than Helen knew. She might have a pulled muscle physically, but her heart was broken. How could Reuben do that to her? She had believed him and trusted him. She had thought that he really wanted to spend his life with her. But all he was doing was upholding a promise he'd made to Leroy.

"Are you sure you're okay?"

Mariana sighed. "I wish people would stop asking me that. I'm as okay as I can be."

Helen studied her, those kindly eyes seeing straight through all of Mariana's defenses. "It's good to be loved, you know."

It was. She knew that. So why had love been taken from her yet again? She simply didn't know the answer.

"So is Reuben coming by?" Helen asked.

Mariana turned and looked out the window as the miles passed. Helen had rented a van to bring her home from Pryor. She had wanted to think that maybe Reuben taking such good care of her had changed things. Once he knew that she was hurt, he had run to his *Englisch* neighbor's house and had the neighbor drive her to Pryor in his car.

Yet how did that prove his love? Who wouldn't do that for a fellow human being? No, that didn't prove anything other than he had a heart. It didn't mean that it belonged to her.

"No," she finally answered. "I don't think Reuben will be coming by."

"That's a shame since he already talked to Cephas about getting married to you this fall."

Mariana's heart flip-flopped in her chest. She ignored it. "That was before. Everything's different now."

"It didn't seem like he had changed his mind in the hospital."

"Things aren't always what they seem." Mariana laid her head against the window and closed her eyes. How she wished that wasn't true. How she wished everything was like it seemed. She had trusted too much, loved too much, maybe even loved too soon. And now it had all fallen apart.

"If you want to talk about this," Helen started, but Mariana shook her head.

"There's nothing left to talk about."

Helen gave a quick nod. "If you change your mind, you know where I am."

"*Danki*." There was no way she was changing her mind. She couldn't open herself up for that kind of heartbreak again.

"I don't understand what the big deal is," Clara Rose said at the quilting meeting two weeks later. "They know you're going to take good care of the girls, don't they?"

A pale and drawn Eileen nodded. "The grandparents don't want the children, but they want to make sure that we're not brainwashing them."

"Brainwashing them!" Verna exclaimed. She shook her head with a tsk. "That's the craziest thing I've ever heard."

Almost the craziest, as far as Mariana was concerned. The craziest had happened two weeks before just after church. But she wasn't letting herself think about that these days. She was going to be fine without Reuben. At least financially. For a while, anyway.

The benefit auction was coming up and she would have some money from that. She had paid into Amish Aid, and they would help pay for the babies to be born, the hospital bills, and anything else that happened to arise. She was Amish and they pulled together. It was just how it worked. But it would've been so much easier, so much nicer, if Reuben's intentions had been pure.

"I'm sure the children will get to come back," Tess said.

To Mariana the younger girl looked sadder than usual. But who was she to say? She had her own misery wrapped around her like a scratchy blanket.

She didn't want any of her friends to know how Reuben had broken her heart. She had scoffed that there was nothing between them. Never had been. This just proved it.

He had come back twice since that afternoon after church, but she had locked the door and wouldn't let him in. It was bad of her, she knew. But she needed time to heal—not physically, but emotionally—before she faced him again. She needed to be strong. She needed to hold her ground. And she didn't need to be swayed by a pair of flashing dimples and soft green eyes.

Still, it was much easier to worry about the problems of others than her own.

Eileen murmured something unintelligible, then turned to Mariana. "So what about you and Reuben?" she asked brightly.

"There is no me and Reuben. I tried to tell you that a few weeks ago."

"It surely didn't seem that way at church."

"Things aren't always what they seem," Mariana said.

Then she realized how harsh the words sounded and she flashed her friend a smile.

"I suppose not," Eileen said. "It just looked like the two of you were so happy."

Mariana shook her head. "We're just friends."

A look passed between the other members of the quilting circle, and suddenly Mariana felt like she was on the outside of a story she should've known the ending to. "What's going on?"

"Nothing," Clara Rose said. "*Mammi*, how do you get your stitches that tiny?"

"It takes patience, granddaughter," Verna said.

Clara Rose laughed and looked around at the others. "Why do elders always say that?"

A murmur of agreement and other comments rose up all around the quilting circle, but no one said much more. Mariana had the weird sensation that the whole exchange was nothing more than a not-so-clever tactic to change the subject. That was fine with her as long as they weren't talking about Reuben.

"Are you ready?" Verna asked. She set her needle and thread down and looked around at the other members of the group. They all nodded.

"Ready for what?" Mariana asked.

Clara Rose flashed her a quick smile. "We have a little surprise for you."

"A surprise?" she asked, but Eileen was already up and out of the room.

She returned a few moments later with a wheelchair. "Now, don't think you get to keep this. We borrowed it from the First Baptist senior center and we have to have it back tomorrow. So don't get any ideas about zooming around Wells Landing in it."

Mariana laughed even as tears welled in her eyes. They had brought her a wheelchair? Even just for the afternoon, being able to get out of bed and do more than shuffle to the bathroom would be fantastic.

"Where are we going?" she asked as Tess helped her into the chair.

"To a party, of course," Clara Rose said.

Eileen got behind her, and together they pushed Mariana into her kitchen. Pink balloons had been blown up and allowed to rest against the ceiling, creating a forest of pink ribbon. Crepe-paper streamers of pink and white swayed from side to side along the cabinets and the window. A cake iced with pale pink frosting and darker pink roses sat in the middle of the table. CONGRATULATIONS had been written across the top. There were pink plates, pink forks, and pink napkins. Pink everything.

Mariana laughed at the sight of it all. "Do you know something I don't know?"

"No," Clara Rose said. "But we figured it was the best way to celebrate. I mean, you want girls, right?"

Once upon a time, she had wanted nothing more than two baby girls. Now everything had changed. "I just want two healthy babies."

"With any luck you'll have two healthy babies who love the color pink," Verna said.

Mariana wiped the tears from her face. She had the best friends anyone could ask for. "I can't believe you did this for me."

"This is what the *Englisch* do. They have showers. So we figured since you couldn't get out and go shopping, we would try to get the things that you need," Tess said.

"Come and open your presents." Clara Rose motioned for her to draw near the table. Boxes were stacked one on top of the other, all wrapped in pastel paper with the pink ribbons.

"Babies need a lot of things," Tess added.

Mariana dashed the tears from her cheeks again. She knew that she had everything that she needed right there. Almost everything. The whole picture would have been complete had Reuben been there.

"Do you smell paint?"

Clara Rose looked up from sweeping the bedroom floor and lifted her nose. "I don't smell anything."

Mariana had been reading a book about what to expect when having twins, and nothing had ever been brought up about smelling things that weren't there. "I'm sure I smell paint."

Clara Rose shrugged and went back to her sweeping. "I don't know what to say."

Mariana lay back on her pillows, wondering if the strong odor was just her imagination. "I really do appreciate the party yesterday. No one's ever done anything that sweet for me."

Clara Rose stopped sweeping again and turned back, a smile on her cherub face. "It was great fun. And so what if now we're behind in getting the quilt done, right? We still have time to do plenty more before the auction in September."

The Wells Landing quilting circle was one of the very few year-round quilting circles in the area. They sewed their quilts all during the calendar year, then donated their wares to the Clarita School Auction in September. From time to time they branched out and made comfort patches and things for disaster relief, but they were most known for their quilts.

"Oh, *jah*," Mariana agreed. "We'll have plenty of time to make quilts between now and then."

Clara Rose tilted her head thoughtfully to one side. "Do you think so? I mean, the babies are going to keep you really busy. Do you think you'll be able to come back to the quilting circle?"

Mariana hadn't thought about that. But after the babies were born she was going to be so incredibly busy. She hadn't even figured out how she was going to support herself. That jelly idea was looking better and better. Maybe if she practiced a little she could make something fancier than the normal fare and she could make a little bit of money. But how would that help? Probably not much, considering her jelly-making skills.

"I don't know. I guess I'll just have to see how it goes. Maybe when the babies get a little bigger."

Clara Rose nodded. "Maybe," she said. "And anytime you need a sitter, I'll be more than happy to come over. Or you could bring them over, and Obie and I could watch them together. That'd be fun."

Mariana laughed. She wasn't sure who would have the most fun, Clara Rose watching the babies or Clara Rose watching Obie try to care for the babies. Either way it was sure to be full of laughs.

"I appreciate that." Mariana helped Candy from the bed so she could run out to the doggie door. Despite the tiny staircase that Reuben had built, the puppy seemed to prefer Mariana's assistance. She turned back to Clara Rose. "Are you sure you don't smell paint?"

Clara Rose bent her head over the task of sweeping up the debris into the dustpan. "Nope. I don't smell a thing."

* * *

The first two weeks turned into another month. The hardest times for Mariana were in the morning when Clara Rose and Verna left and she was all alone until evening. The other members of the quilting circle had stopped coming by since Mariana had wanted to lock the doors. She had told them all a fib, that she was worried about a recent rash of break-ins happening in and around Wells Landing. The excuse seemed plausible enough. She didn't need to tell them that she wanted to keep Reuben from coming in and trying to convince her to forgive him. Her heart wasn't sane where he was concerned. So she locked her doors and kept to herself.

Verna and Clara Rose took turns. Sometimes they came together to make sure she had her food for the day, the chickens were fed, and Candy had food and water as well.

The first couple of days after that fateful afternoon, Reuben had come by and tried to talk to her, but she wouldn't let him in. Thankfully he had respected her wishes and hadn't tried to convince Verna or Clara Rose to let him come in. There was nothing left to say. He had promised Leroy that he would watch after her and that he would do anything it took. He hadn't shirked his responsibility. He'd just been found out.

"Do you need anything else?" Verna asked. "I need to get back to the house."

Just some more company. Or maybe all she needed was to be able to go back in time before she had discovered Reuben's deceit. She missed him so much.

Or you could forgive him.

She pushed that thought away. "I'm fine." The words

had become her mantra. And maybe if she kept thinking them, she would somehow start to believe them.

"All righty then. I guess I'll see you tomorrow. And . . . I'm sorry." With that Verna disappeared from view.

"What do you mean, you're sorry?"

But Verna kept walking, her footsteps fading and finally ending with the slam of the screen door.

Mariana watched out the window to see if Verna was actually leaving. Her horse and buggy were still parked out front.

Most everyone in Wells Landing drove a tractor during the week. All except Verna Yutzy. Ever since she had gotten that new horse, she drove her buggy everywhere.

She came into view striding toward her carriage. Then she turned and looked back at the house one last time before climbing in and driving away.

"Hi."

Mariana whirled around, her hand pressed to her heart. "Reuben! What are you doing here?"

Candy barked, rising from her nap to wag her stumpy tail at this familiar face.

"You shouldn't be here." Wait. That wasn't what she wanted to say.

"I need to talk to you."

She wanted to tell him to go away, but her gaze drank in the sight of him. He looked good, the same as he had a month ago. Had it been only a month since she had read the letter written by Leroy? It seemed like yesterday and forever ago all at the same time.

"I don't think we have anything to talk about."

"But we do." He stepped from the room and returned a few seconds later, pushing a wooden cradle in front of him. The cherry wood gleamed in the sunlight that streamed in from the windows. It was the most magnificent thing Mariana had ever seen.

She gasped as he pushed it closer to the bed. It was the perfect height for nighttime sleeping. The babies would be within reach and she wouldn't have to get out of bed when they needed her.

"Reuben," she whispered. "It's beautiful."

He beamed with pleasure. "I made it myself."

She ran trembling fingers over the polished wood. It must have taken weeks and weeks.

"It's one of a kind," he told her, pointing toward the center divider of the cradle. "Both babies can sleep together, but they are separate as well. They can see each other, but they can't tumble on top of one another."

"It's perfect." Tears rose into her eyes. The closer she got to her eight-month mark the more fragile she seemed to be. And it had nothing to do with the fact that it was the most wonderful gift anyone could have ever given her.

"I have something else for you too. Do you think you can make it up the stairs?"

She nodded and started to rise from the bed.

He was there in an instant to help her to her feet.

She slapped his hands away. "I'm not an invalid." Then she sighed and shook her head. "I mean, thanks. I appreciate your help."

He nodded in return, and together they made their way up to the second floor.

"I smell paint," she said as they started down the small hallway. The door at the end was the one she had determined would be the babies' room. It was the perfect size and close to the room she had once upon a time shared with her husband.

Reuben walked ahead of her and opened the door.

Mariana caught one look inside and stopped dead in her tracks. The room was painted the exact shade of raspberry sherbet. Deep, bright pink on all four walls. A plain white shade covered the window. The twin white cribs sat opposite and took up most of the space.

She wasn't sure what to ask about first, the color or the furniture. There was a changing table, a chest of drawers, and several toys ready to welcome the babies home. A large rag rug of pinks, oranges, and white covered most of the dark wood floor, and an oak rocker waited patiently in one corner.

"The beds are the kind that convert into other beds. One for when they're too big for a crib and not big enough for a regular bed. I forget what they call them."

"A toddler bed," Mariana whispered.

"*Jah*. Then when they outgrow those, the bed becomes a regular bed. All we'll need to do is get them mattresses. I mean, you. You'll need to get them mattresses."

"And you did all of this?"

He blushed. "Most of it. The girls helped me pick out the furniture and the rug."

"I don't know what to say."

"You can say that you like it."

"I love it." She wiped her tears away with the back of one hand. "I can't believe you did all this for me. For us."

"I made a promise to Leroy that I would take care of you. I didn't know when I did that you were pregnant. I didn't know that you were having twins."

Her heart squeezed in her chest. "I think you have more than kept your promise to Leroy."

"You think so?"

She nodded.

"Good." He got down on his knees in front of her.

"Reuben! What are you doing?"

"It's an *Englisch* custom," he said. "But I think I may need some help up."

She propped her hands on her hips and gave him her most skeptical look.

"*Jah*, right. You're pregnant and can't help me. I'm on my own. Got it."

"What sort of *Englisch* custom is this?"

He took her hand into his. "I'm asking you to marry me. My promise to Leroy is already complete. This is about more than that."

"More than a promise?" she whispered.

"I can take care of you and the babies even when you try to shut me out. I will find a way to care for you and the twins. Always. But I want you to marry me because I love you. I think perhaps I always have. But you were married to Leroy and I never let myself believe it.

"Now please say you'll marry me so I can get up off this floor."

How could she say no to such a romantic *Englisch* proposal?

"*Jah*," she said, the word part laugh, part sob.

Reuben pushed to his feet and sealed their new promise with a kiss.

A few moments later, after he'd kissed her light-headed, he lifted his lips from hers. "And if you ever doubt my love," he started, "just come in here and take one look at this room."

"At all the wonderful things you bought for these babies?"

Reuben shook his head. "I painted a room bright pink for you. I'm not sure the bishop would approve."

She laughed. She was fairly certain Cephas Ebersol wouldn't care one way or another as long as they continued to love each other and be the family God had intended for them to be.

"About that . . . what are we going to do if this turns out to be a girl and a boy? Or even two boys?"

Reuben smiled and pulled her close. "Those boys will have the prettiest pink bedroom in all of Wells Landing. Or we could paint the room blue."

She smiled into the eyes of the man she would soon marry. "Not a chance."

MORE THAN
A MARRIAGE

Chapter One

"Tomorrow would be a perfect day to go visit my parents in Clarita, *jah*?"

"What?" Jacob Smiley, Tess's husband of almost three years, looked up from the screen of his smartphone. His expression said it all. He'd been too engrossed in what he had been reading on the tiny screen to pay her very much mind.

Tess tried not to frown and injected as much patience and understanding into her voice as she could muster. "I said I want to go see my parents tomorrow." The next day was Sunday, but for their district, there was no church. Instead families spent time with each other, visiting in fellowship with one another and enjoying the company around them.

Tess wanted to go see her family. It had been far too long since she had spent any time with her parents and her sister. Clarita might only be three hours away by car, but when your primary mode of transportation was a tractor or a horse and buggy, three hours might as well be ten.

It was the one thing she hated most about moving to Wells Landing, but by far it wasn't the only thing. She cast a quick glance at the cell phone her husband held. She hated the small electronic device almost as much as Jacob seemed to enjoy it.

"I don't know. We'll have to get a driver and . . ." Jacob's voice trailed off as he glanced back at the phone.

Tess bit back a frustrated sigh. "I've already called Bruce Brown," she said, referring to one of the favored drivers in Wells Landing. A retired Air Force medic, Bruce was always in great demand, but she'd hoped that he might have time tomorrow to take them to Clarita. "He's not available, but he said his cousin can take us."

"His cousin?" That got Jacob's attention. "I don't know him."

"Bruce said he was hoping to get into the driving business, and you have to admit that if he's kin to Bruce, chances are he's a great guy."

Jacob shook his head. "That's not necessarily true."

"You could call and talk to him."

"It's eight o'clock at night. On a Saturday night. It's too late to call him."

"It's hardly that late."

"It's late enough."

"But, Jacob—"

"If you had wanted to go to your parents' house, you should have told me sooner so I could make arrangements."

"I did." Her voice rose until she was almost yelling at him. "I did," she repeated, quietly this time.

"You did?" Jacob frowned. "I don't remember that."

Of course he didn't. He couldn't remember anything these days. Not unless it had something to do with that blessed phone. To make matters worse, he even had a Facebook account! He said he needed it and the phone for his job at A-1 Roofing, but Tess couldn't see the necessity at all. He could use the phone; she would give him that much. But a Facebook account?

"Besides, it's Sunday and we wouldn't be able to pay him."

They could have paid him in advance if he had planned better. If he had been listening to her. But he had been messing with his phone.

And the worst part of all was the time it took away from the two of them. Everything that happened on that tiny little device seemed so much more important than what was really going on in their lives. And this was no exception. It was Saturday night and they were at home, which wasn't a problem at all. But she was looking through a book on better ways to make goat cheese while he was playing with his phone doing heaven knew what on his Facebook account. She didn't have one of her own, nor did she have a cell phone. How could she monitor what he was doing? Did she even want to?

She placed her marker inside the book she was reading and set it to one side. "Play a game with me." They used to play games all the time, card games, guessing games, even silly things like truth or dare. Just the two of them. But that had been before. Before they moved to Wells Landing. Before he took a job with the English roofing company. Before the cell phone and the Facebook account.

"What?" Jacob looked up, his expression blank.

Tess jumped to her feet. "Were you even listening to me?"

"Of course I was." Jacob frowned. "I just didn't hear what you said."

Tess shook her head. "Isn't that what listening is?"

"Are you going to tell me or not?"

"Play a game with me," Tess asked again, but this time

the words sounded more like a demand than a request for his time and attention.

Jacob stood and stretched, slipping his phone to the side pocket of his pants. "I don't know. It's getting kind of late."

"It's barely eight o'clock." This was the biggest problem of all. And he couldn't even see it.

"I get up early, Tess. You know that."

"You don't have to get up early tomorrow. Just for an hour. Play a hand or two of Uno with me."

He gave her a look that was both condescending and chastising. "Uno is not any fun with two people."

But she remembered a time when they had fun playing Uno, just the two of them. It had been less about the game and more about spending time together, bonding, enjoying each other's company without another soul around. It'd only been a few years since that time. Where had it disappeared to?

"We can play something else, then." Tess hated the desperate sound in her voice. But she felt as if things were slipping out of her grasp. She and Jacob had been so close once, and now it seemed as if they were miles apart even when they were in the same room.

"Maybe tomorrow." Jacob eased his hand into his pocket as if assuring himself that his cell phone was still there. Tess wanted nothing more than to grab the vile thing and smash it against the wall. That would not be very becoming. And it didn't actually belong to Jacob. It belonged to the company he worked for. One day he would have to give it back. Just another reason why she hoped and prayed every day that they would finally save enough money to buy the farm of their dreams and move.

They wanted to be out of town a bit. They wanted to live off the land like God intended.

"I think I'll go to bed."

Tess didn't know how to respond. She wanted to call him back, try to work through it, figure out some way they could spend some more time together. He said he wanted to go to bed but she was antsy, agitated. "I think I'll go check on the goats."

Jacob stopped with one hand on the stair rail. "That's another thing."

"*Jah?*"

"Mr. Bennett came by today. He brought back your little brown goat."

"Millie?"

Jacob shrugged. "I don't know her name. Just the little brown one."

"What do you mean he brought her back?"

"Evidently she got out and he found her in his garden eating all his squash plants."

"Oh, no." Millie was the wiliest of all her goats. She was the smallest and could somehow manage to wriggle through the tiniest spots in the fence. "But I had her tied up as well." She hated to loop the rope around the sweet little goat's neck. But this was not the first time she had gotten out. And unfortunately not the first time she had eaten Mr. Bennett's garden fare.

"Apparently she ate through the rope, managed to get out of the pen, then headed over to his house."

"Did she eat very much?"

Jacob frowned. "Enough that I owe him some squash."

"I'm sorry."

Jacob sighed. "Sorry isn't going to work this time, Tess. The man was ranting about how much squash he is losing over the summer. And this was not the first time she's eaten his plants. Those goats are more trouble than they're worth."

"That's not right. They're very useful."

Jacob held up one finger as if to warn her that his next words held great meaning. "I don't like having the neighbors angry because your goats got out. If they get out again, we just may have to get rid of them."

"You can't do that."

Jacob gave a quick nod. "Oh, *jah*. I can." He turned and headed back up the stairs.

Tess watched him disappear, wanting to ask him why he picked now to tell her. But she knew. He had been too involved with his cell phone to remember it until now. And as far as she was concerned, that was a much bigger problem than her goats eating Mr. Bennett's squash.

"Tess, why aren't you ready to go?"

She looked up from the catalog she had been reading. She had wanted to check and see if perhaps she could find Mr. Bennett some late-blooming squash plants in the seed catalog, but so far she hadn't found any she thought would suffice. "Go where?"

"To my parents' house." His tone clearly stated that she should have remembered this. But Tess had no idea what he was talking about.

"I didn't know we were going to your parents' house today."

Jacob shook his head as if she were more than he could handle sometimes. "You did. I told you yesterday that we were going to my parents' house."

"You did not. You told me we weren't going to *my* parents' house." *His* parents had never been mentioned at all.

"I'm sure I told you."

"I'm sure you didn't."

"Don't be difficult, Tess. And go change your apron."

Something in his tone didn't set well with her. Or maybe it was the fact that after he delivered his command, he reached into his pocket and pulled out that infernal cell phone and glanced at the tiny little screen. He smiled a little to himself, hit something on the screen, and re-pocketed it.

"I don't think you're supposed to use that on Sunday."

Jacob shrugged as if it was no big deal. "It was a text from work."

He said that, but she found herself doubting his words. She didn't know who was contacting him through that tiny little phone, and it wasn't like a phone shanty or a phone in the barn attached to an answering machine that recorded everybody's call. She felt strangely left out of a part of Jacob's life that she had never considered before. When a couple worked at home and farmed the land, they were always near to one another. But Jacob left for work every day. He drove the tractor into town, parked it in the empty lot across from the post office, and waited for his English boss to come by in his truck and get him. Tess knew that several Amish men worked for the same company, but she didn't know if they all had cell phones. And she didn't know if they got text messages all the time, even on Sunday. She wondered if any of their wives hated the fact that their husbands had Facebook pages. Didn't that depend on knowing a bunch of other people on Facebook? Who would he know on Facebook? Maybe just the men he worked with. But didn't he get enough of them during the week? The whole thing was completely confusing to her. She didn't know how it worked and had never wanted to know how it worked. Until now, when it was directly affecting her relationship with her husband.

"I don't know why I have to change my apron." It was the closest to rebellion she had ever come.

Jacob seemed to hold his breath as he stared at her. "What's gotten into you, Tess?"

"Nothing. What's gotten into you, Jacob?"

He studied her intently. And suddenly she felt as if she was having an argument with a stranger. Oh, he looked the same as Jacob Smiley always did, thick chestnut hair and full beard, also rusty in color. He had the same beautiful eyes and strong build. He looked exactly like the man she had married. But somehow he felt like a stranger.

She stared back at him, but there were no answers in his expression, only a stiff jaw as he waited for her to comply. She wanted to tell him no, tell him that she wasn't going to his parents' house if they couldn't go to her parents' house. She missed them terribly. And it seemed as if Jacob found plenty of time to go visit his family while she never saw hers anymore. She couldn't say that it had been the easiest thing to move from Clarita over to Wells Landing, but she had been hopeful for new opportunities. Jacob had followed his father and stepmother to this larger community hoping that they both would find new and better, maybe even exciting opportunities there. But so far all she had found was mild heartache and a stranger in her house.

"I guess you can stay here if you want."

Tess was spurred into action, though as she made her way upstairs to change her apron and make sure she looked presentable for a Sunday afternoon visit, she had to wonder which was worse, visiting with his *mamm* and *dat* or being at home by herself.

* * *

Jacob stole a quick glance at his wife as they ambled along. Sundays were all about taking it a bit slower, so while most of the good citizens of Wells Landing drove tractors during the week, come Sunday everybody got out their horse and buggy and traveled at a slower pace. Part of him enjoyed the slower step of the horses and another part of him wished they could speed along in the tractor, maybe even a car. It would sure get them there a lot quicker. He knew that most believed it was the journey that was the most important thing, but sometimes he disagreed and thought that the most important thing was the visit. Getting there quicker would mean more time to visit.

Of course now would be a good time to try and talk with his wife, see what was bugging her. She hadn't been the same lately, and he didn't know what was going on. He hadn't changed. But he conceded that Tess had. She walked around with an expectant air, as if any minute something big was about to happen and she didn't want to miss it. But there wasn't anything big. The next big thing for them, unless the Lord saw fit to bless them with a child sooner rather than later, was for them to buy a piece of land, a farm, and work the land. He had hoped they would already have that checked off and be working toward the next item on their goal list, but it seemed that wasn't in God's plan for them. And with all the hours he'd been taking on at the roofing company, it had become harder and harder to look for those plots of land and other opportunities for farming. Why, just last week he had heard of a farm that was quite possibly well within their budget, but he had only heard about the land after it had been sold. Why hadn't he heard about it before? He could only assume that God had other plans for them, but he was starting to get a little impatient. He was ready to go back to working the land, farming, growing crops, getting back to a simpler life. At least a simpler one than what he had now.

When they had moved to Wells Landing, there hadn't been a great many opportunities available. And he had jumped on the chance to build roofs. It was good money in Oklahoma with all the winds and storms. Hail damaged any roof it came in contact with. So he couldn't say the money wasn't good. But the hours were terrible and the work was very hard. Not as satisfying as farming, for certain. The harsh summer temperatures drained him both physically and mentally. He wasn't the boss by any means, but he was a supervisor on the job site, overseeing four to six men as they worked diligently to tear off the old roof and put another one on as quickly as possible. The worst part of all was that the more roofs they put on, the more money they would make, so the more roofs the company wanted them to put on. He felt as if he worked night and day, well before sunup to well past sundown. It was a never-ending work cycle: get up, roof, move to the next job site, roof another house, come home until he was dead tired on his feet from everything that he had done in a day. When that happened, all he wanted to do was sit down and escape. He knew that wasn't the Amish way, but it was how he felt all the same. His job was hard, physically and mentally, and it never seemed to end. He supposed that was a good thing. He wasn't afraid of hard work, but he felt like he was working so hard for someone else. Someone who might or might not appreciate all the effort he put in.

So his escape came in the form of his cell phone. He knew that it irritated Tess a bit, but she didn't understand.

She had the dream life, raising her goats and staying at home, cooking and cleaning and all the other things that Amish women had been raised to do. The problem was he hadn't been raised to build roofs. He'd been raised to be a good Amish man, a father and provider. Well, he had provided, but now the stress of working outside his home was sometimes more than he could bear. Was it too much to ask to be allowed to enjoy the time that was his? He didn't think so, but he had a feeling his wife did.

Chapter Two

"Are you going to tell me what's wrong?"

Tess turned toward Jacob. "Nothing's wrong." But it was a lie. Yet to say the words out loud sounded petty and childish. So the lie would have to do, until she figured out what to do with her sadness. It had found its way into her thoughts and hung around like a dark cloud overshadowing her every thought. Why couldn't she and Jacob go see her family? Why did this marriage seem unfair?

"It doesn't seem that way to me."

And if she told him, would it change anything? Probably not. It was simply something she had to learn to live with. This was her life now. And whether she was unhappy with it or not, it seemed to be what God had planned for her.

But does God really want me unhappy?

Or maybe she was looking for happiness in the wrong places. She and Jacob had a nice home, food on the table, everything they needed. She had her goats and the quilting circle, a wonderful group of friends who loved and supported her. It wasn't that she didn't like living in Wells Landing, but she hated being so far away from her family.

"Maybe when we get home we could play a game."

Jacob didn't look at her as he spoke the words. And he said them so softly she was uncertain if she had heard them at all. Then he turned, eyebrows raised as if waiting for her answer.

"After I'm done milking the goats." Cleaning out their pens and all the other stuff she had to do on a daily basis where the creatures were concerned.

Jacob faced the front again. His lips were pressed together. He looked almost . . . mad. What did he have to be upset about?

He was the one who wanted to go visiting. Was it her fault that the goats needed to be taken care of? If they had stayed home they would have had plenty of time to visit with each other and play games.

Jacob turned the buggy down the drive and pulled up next to the barn. He sat there for a second as if contemplating the merits of speaking his mind. But Tess wasn't in the mood for it. She had done everything he had asked of her today, and now she had work to do. He had to understand that.

She slid open the buggy door and stepped out without a word. She had chores to do, and she surely didn't have time for an argument with her husband.

After changing into her chore dress and replacing her prayer *kapp* with a faded handkerchief, Tess made her way over to the small pen that held her goats.

As far as she was concerned, they were beautiful creatures. She loved their round bodies and coarse fur. She loved how their lips moved when they chewed on something. In all, she loved just about everything about them.

She had started milking the goats twice daily instead of once in order to increase the milk production. Their property was small and his family had no room to keep the goats. But soon, she prayed, she and Jacob would find a farm on the edge of town. They would move out and she could expand her production. She was starting to sell the goat's milk raw in addition to making cheese, soaps, and lotions. Helen Ebersol, the bishop's wife, made a few products herself, but Tess knew that she did it only for friends and family. Tess enjoyed the work, though it was to help their household. She dreamed of a day when Jacob didn't have to work so hard at his roofing company and she would be able to spend more time with him. Or maybe he could quit the place altogether, and that would mean the end of the cell phone and the Facebook account. Wouldn't it be fantastic if she and her goats could make all that possible? It was merely a dream, she knew, but if a dream was all she had, she would take it. It gave her hope that one day things would be different for her and Jacob.

But until then . . . She hooked the first goat to the milking leash, grabbed her stool, and got down to work.

Sunday was a day of rest not work, and Jacob hated to see his wife out milking those goats. In fact, he hated the goats altogether. To him they were a sign of his failure. Tess's mother had given her the beasts, arranged for her to take over the small herd from an elderly aunt. When she first brought them home she had been beyond excited, chattering nonstop about the money that she would make, money that he evidently wasn't supplying. But it was hard to save every dime, near impossible to get ahead when paying rent on a house. A house he hated too. He wanted to farm, and though farms were widespread in northeast Oklahoma, farms for sale were a little harder to come by.

As he stood at the window and watched, Tess unhooked one goat and grabbed another by the collar. She looked hot and tired. Part of him wanted to go out and help. Because he loved her. She was his wife, his life mate. But another, more stubborn part of him wanted her to realize how much work the goats were and how unnecessary it was. He wanted her to give it up on her own. But it had been almost a year and she showed no signs of letting up.

He turned away from the window. As much as he hated it, it was no skin off his nose, as they say. Somehow she managed to balance all the work she did. The house was always clean, supper was always ready, his clothes washed and hung neatly in the closet. He could find no fault in that. So why did the thought of her keeping the goats make him so angry? He shook his head and took his phone out of his pocket.

Jah, that was one of the stipulations for having a phone in Bishop Ebersol's district. One wasn't supposed to use it on Sunday. It was a reasonable rule considering that no work was to take place on Sunday other than only what was absolutely necessary. But more and more, Jacob had a hard time adhering to that rule. What was the harm in scrolling around on Facebook? He rarely commented on anybody's posts, instead preferring to see what was going on in the world and what everyone around him was doing. He had a few English friends that he liked to keep in contact with and there were the few ex-Amish who had left Wells Landing, Lorie Kauffman and Luke Lambright. It was fun to see their pictures. As far as he was concerned it was like the *Die Botschaft*, a place for news and connecting. What was the harm in that?

He thumbed open Facebook and sat back in his recliner.

* * *

Monday came and brought with it stormy skies. The rain fell off and on, and still Jacob went to work. Oklahoma storms were hard and severe, but rarely lasted long before moving on.

Tess knew they needed the rain. It would water their gardens, help the farmers, and cool the earth from being scorched in the summer heat. But the rain always made her sad. She could tell herself again and again the rain was necessary, but it didn't stop the melancholy feelings that stole over her at the sight of the gray skies. Her only hope had been that Jacob would take one look at the sky and call his boss to see if they were working. He would tell Jacob no, then the two of them could spend the day together like they should have on Sunday. But it seemed that wasn't to happen either.

She took the pan of blueberry muffins from the oven and set them on the stove top to cool. Her blueberry plants were producing like crazy and she knew she would have to can pie filling before long—there were that many of them. Good thing Jacob liked blueberries or they would both be in trouble.

The phone rang out in the barn. Rarely did she go out and answer it, waiting instead till the end of the day to check the messages, but what did she have to do today?

Despite the light drizzle that fell from the sky, she ran out the back door and toward the barn. She managed to catch the phone on the third ring, raising the receiver to her ear. "Hello?"

"Tess?"

"Hi, Lavina." It was her sister. Never before had she been more grateful that she'd rushed out to answer the ringing phone.

"Are you busy?"

"Not at all." It was so good to hear her sister's voice.

They didn't talk very often on the phone. Tess preferred to go to Clarita and see her sister and family face-to-face. She sorely missed them.

"I have some news." Lavina's voice dropped to almost a whisper.

"Oh, *jah*?" She had to believe that the news was good news. Surely her sister wouldn't call on the phone to tell her something bad.

"I'm having a baby."

Tess nearly dropped the phone, but somehow managed to recover. "A baby? But Joseph . . ." She couldn't finish.

"We've moved the wedding up a bit." It was July now, and Lavina and Joseph had planned their wedding for the first of October.

It wasn't unheard of for a couple in love to give in to the temptations presented to them. Now that they had, they would have to stand before the church and confess their sins. They would ask to be forgiven. It was a sensitive matter in the church, but none of that was what sent jealousy and remorse burning through Tess.

"I'm so happy for you." And she was. How could she not be happy for her sister? But she was jealous. Oh so jealous. There was a reason that envy was one of the seven deadly sins, and she would do well to remember that. She prayed about it every day, but perhaps now she should move that up to twice a day. Or maybe she should write it on a piece of paper and pin it inside her dress over her heart so she never forgot.

She was happy for her sister, but Tess had been married for almost three years. She had followed God's plan and done everything she was supposed to. So why wasn't she the one calling Lavina with news instead? She just didn't understand.

"I knew you would be happy for me." She could almost

hear her sister smile. "Of course *Mamm* and *Dat* are a little shocked, and I think his parents are as well, but it's just one of those things."

One of those things. Just like God's plan.

"So when is the wedding now?"

"Two weeks. I hope you can come."

Two weeks. It was a short turnaround, but a necessary one all the same. All the plans that Lavina had made for her October wedding were tossed to the side. There would be no bridesmaids, no long guest list, no big supper. It was sort of a punishment for her transgressions past, but as far as Tess was concerned the trade-off was worth it. Her sister was having a baby. A baby!

"Are you excited?"

"Of course I am. It's what we've always dreamed of, *jah*?"

Tess and Lavina were barely a year apart in age. They had grown up playing wedding games and house, doing all the things that other little Amish girls did: dreaming of who they would marry, how many children they would have, how big their farm would be. But Tess hadn't gotten her farm. She hadn't gotten her children, and that was something she wanted more than anything.

Tears sprang to her eyes and she blinked them back, thankful her sister had called instead of coming to Wells Landing to deliver the news. She wouldn't want to put a damper on Lavina's exciting news with her own sadness. Of course it didn't help that the rain had now begun to steadily pound against the roof of the barn.

"Tess?" Lavina's voice was soft and filled with concern.

"I'm okay." Of all people, her sister knew how hard this move had been on her and all the things she wanted from life.

"I almost didn't tell you. But how could I not? I hope you will come to the wedding."

They both knew that the wedding was less about celebration and more about correcting mistakes, but it didn't seem to dampen Lavina's spirits any. Why should it? She was having a baby. The church would forgive her, and she was marrying the man she loved. Joseph Miller had a big farm on the edge of Clarita. Sometimes he worked as an auctioneer. He was an all-around good guy from a great family in the area. Lavina had the good life, as they say.

"Of course I'll come to the wedding. I wouldn't miss it for anything." And that was the truth. But what did a girl do when the life she thought she was going to have wasn't exactly the life that was handed her? Pray, she supposed. She was almost out of prayer. It seemed she said one so often these days that her words were running thin.

She said her good-byes to Lavina, promising that she was okay and vowing to be at the wedding. Tess hung up the phone and stared at the receiver for a full minute, unable to move from her seat. What was a girl to do?

She looked around her at the immaculate barn, the beautiful wood, the good strong horse they had to pull their buggy. Her house was nice, her husband provided, to the outsider she was sure it looked as if she had everything. She felt heavy and small wishing for more. And there was only one thing to do when thoughts like that arose. It was to pray. But she wasn't certain God was listening anymore.

Chapter Three

Tess Smiley set the tray of sausage balls on the table set up just outside Eileen Brenneman's kitchen. She was surprised that Eileen wanted to have the quilting circle meeting today. She had been through so much lately.

Just then Eileen came out of the kitchen. She held a tray of oatmeal cookies in one hand, her mouth pinched with an emotion Tess couldn't name. Disappointment maybe. Hurt, dejection. Maybe a combination of all three. Eileen had wanted a baby for so long. Tess had only been in Wells Landing for a few months, less than a year really, and even she knew of Eileen's heart's desire.

"Hi, Eileen." Tess tried to make her voice as cheerful as possible, when she herself had a host of issues and concerns. The Lord said love your neighbor as you love yourself, and she did her best to abide by that each day.

"Good to see you, Tess."

Tess nodded, unsure of what to say next. The week before Eileen's house had been filled with the sound of little girls' laughter. The sound of family, of promise. But now the rooms were unusually quiet. Crystal and Brittany, the foster children that Eileen had taken in, had gone to live with their grandparents. Their father had died and their mother had slipped into drug addiction. With no one willing to care for the spunky girls, they had been fostered out. Eileen had been hoping to officially adopt them, then all these weeks later, the grandparents decided that they didn't want the girls to be raised outside of the family. They had taken Brittany and Crystal back to Glenpool, on the other side of Tulsa. It wasn't too far for Eileen to visit, but Tess was sure she had been discouraged from doing so.

For lack of words, Tess reached out a hand and squeezed Eileen's fingers. To her dismay, Eileen's eyes filled with tears. Tess released her fingers as Eileen blinked to clear her vision.

"Have you been to see Mariana?" Tess asked. She wasn't sure that Mariana and her twin girls were a better topic, but it was all she could come up with.

"I saw them yesterday." Eileen gave a sad nod.

Tess was hoping to get to see them this weekend, before they left the hospital. But with Jacob's job, they just didn't seem to have the time. He left in the morning exhausted and came home even more so.

But it's more than that.

She pushed the nagging voice aside and concentrated on placing her platter in an artful arrangement.

"Are those sausage balls?"

Clara Rose Brenneman bustled out of the sewing room, plate in one hand and leash in the other. A golden retriever puppy trotted happily behind her, his pink tongue lolling out of one side of his mouth.

"I made them myself."

Clara Rose stopped mid-reach. "Are they made with goat cheese?"

"Of course."

"I see." Clara Rose pulled her hand back slowly, as if the finger food was a snake about to strike.

"You know, goat cheese is a lot better for you than regular cheese."

Clara Rose shook her head, her strings dancing with the motion. "That's what you keep telling me."

"It's true." But she knew her words fell on deaf ears. "One day you'll believe me."

Clara Rose filled her plate with ham and cheese pinwheels and the pickles Mariana had left for them.

"Are you hungry?"

Clara Rose turned a sweet shade of pink. "*Jah*. Hungry."

But Tess had a feeling her friend had a secret. It was written there in the color of her cheeks and the smile that graced her lips. And Tess had a feeling what it was too. But she couldn't ask Clara Rose if she was having a baby. Not with Eileen's loss so fresh in their minds.

Clara Rose hummed a little song as she filled her plate, then she headed back into the sewing room, the puppy trotting happily in her wake.

"Did you two come to quilt, or are you going to stand out here all day and chin-wag?" Verna stood at the large double-door opening of the bonus room Eileen used more for the quilting circle than she did for church.

Tess turned to Eileen and mouthed, *chin-wag?*

Eileen just shrugged. "We'll be right there."

"So are we eating first?" Tess asked. Her hand hovered over the stack of paper plates as she waited for Eileen's answer. Verna had already disappeared back into the sewing room.

"Clara Rose came in starving and grabbed a plate first thing. Everyone else is waiting until we take a break. Though I don't know how anyone can eat that much in this heat."

The weather outside was typical for Oklahoma in July. Temps were well into the nineties with heat indexes stretching above one hundred.

Tess murmured something she hoped sounded like agreement. It wasn't the heat that had her appetite down, just as she was sure it wasn't for Eileen. And she didn't want to complain.

Together she and Eileen walked into the sewing room. It was their usual crowd minus Mariana Miller, who'd given birth to identical twin girls the week before, and Helen Ebersol, the bishop's wife. Tess was pleased to see Emily Riehl there. Emily didn't always make it, and her life had grown ever busier since she'd married Elam Riehl. His father had been kicked in the head by a milk cow a few years back and hadn't been the same since.

Tess never heard them complain about the hardships they had come through. Emily always had a smile on her face and Elam seemed to be a caring, loving husband. She could see it in his eyes every time he looked at Emily.

Jacob used to look at her that way. Back before they got married. Back before they moved to Wells Landing. Back before a lot of things.

"Tess?" Fannie Stoll laid one hand on her knee, drawing Tess's attention out of her own thoughts. "Are you ready to sew?"

"*Jah*. Of course." She reached for her bag with the squares she had pieced together at home. Everyone except her and Clara Rose had theirs out and ready to begin stitching.

Tess hurried to get herself together and began. They were making a Star Dahlia quilt. Not necessarily more difficult, but it did require a great deal of ornamental quilting. And Tess didn't mind. She needed something to keep her mind off . . .

Jacob.

"So tell me again why you have the puppy with you?" Emily asked.

"It's for Gabe Allen Lambert."

"Titus's brother?"

Clara Rose nodded. "He's been building doghouses for the English. Obie wanted to gift him a dog since they're working together. That way if someone comes to look at doghouses and they want another pet . . ." Her words trailed off.

"Has anyone heard from Zeb?" Eileen asked. Even in her time of sorrow, she was thinking of others.

Tess looked up just in time to see a shadow of sadness pass across Clara Rose's face. Tess knew that Obie had been hoping that his twin brother would come back from Pinecraft to attend their wedding, but he hadn't showed. Zeb and Obie were as close as brothers could be. And she made a mental note to say a prayer for Zeb tonight. Something was happening down in Florida, but no one could say exactly what. The spring and summer months were far too busy to abandon their farm chores and head south. But she couldn't say that early fall was any better.

"Paul says he'll come home when it's time for him to come home, but I know that Obie worries."

"Worry comes to nothing," Verna said shortly.

That was true and several heads bobbed in agreement, but how did a person stop worrying? Tess worried all the time. She worried about her family and living so far away from them. She worried about Jacob. He didn't seem very happy these days. She looked around at the faces of her friends. They all seemed as happy as women could be. With the exception of Eileen.

"You're awful quiet, Tess." Verna pinned her with her sharp blue stare. That was the thing about Verna. She could see straight through a person and had no hesitation about voicing her observations.

"Tess is always quiet," Clara Rose countered.

"I believe I said awful quiet. There's a difference."

"There's nothing wrong, if that's what you're asking." Could she have sounded any guiltier? "I mean, nothing's wrong."

And that was the crux of the matter. What truly was wrong in her life? She had a roof over her head and a husband who worked night and day to care for her, but her life still didn't seem to be turning out the way she had thought it would.

"Uh-huh." Verna peered at Tess over the top of her wire-rimmed glasses, then looked back to her stitches.

The puppy, having decided that no one was going to give him any more attention, curled up at Clara Rose's feet and laid his head on the toes of her shoes.

"I'll be glad when Mariana can come again," Fannie mused. Her needle stilled as she surveyed the group. "You think she'll come back, don't you?"

Eileen shrugged. "It's hard to say. I mean, she will have a lot to do with two babies at her age. And it's not like Reuben will be at home all day to help her."

Mariana had discovered she was pregnant just before her husband died from cancer. His best friend Reuben Wiesel had promised to take care of Mariana, a promise that almost ruined their own budding romance. Now the two were planning to get married sometime in the fall. Still, Reuben checked on Mariana every day. Such a sweet ending for what could have been a tragic story.

"I'm happy for her," Clara Rose said. She had finally finished her early snack and had settled down to quilt.

"Are you going to tell us what has you glowing like

a firefly?" Verna turned her all-knowing stare to her granddaughter.

Clara Rose blushed again, dropping her hands into her lap. "I'm going to have a baby."

Murmurs of good wishes and joy went up around the room. Normally they didn't talk so much about having babies and such, but Tess knew that the quilting circle had become so close in the years they had been sewing together. The group had become more like sisters than Tess even felt toward her own siblings.

She reached out and captured Clara Rose's fingers, giving them a little squeeze. "I'm so happy for you." And she was, but there was a part of her that was also so incredibly sad.

Like her sisters before her, and her friends and neighbors, she had been raised to be a wife and mother. She had gotten the wife thing down. She could cook with the best of them. She kept a fine house and did everything in her power to have her laundry on the line bright and early. She raised a couple of goats in her tiny backyard and made goat cheese along with soaps and lotions and such to help bring in a little more money. Everything she earned went into the cookie jar over the stove, destined for the down payment they so desperately needed.

A baby right now would only take money away from that fund. And she knew that her sisters would chastise her for her English way of thinking, but she had to have a reason for their lack of a child. Clara Rose and Obie had only been married a few months, and already she was with child. Tess and Jacob had been married for going on three years. She knew that God had a plan for everything, but she wished she knew when He planned for her to have a family. She wanted to ask Jacob how he felt about it, but he had become so stern lately, working all sorts of weird hours. He seemed to pour himself into his job, leaving no room for anything else, including her. What happened to the dream of moving to Wells Landing and buying some farmland?

But she knew. They needed money, which meant living in a house without much property and Jacob working for an English company until they could save up enough to buy a piece of land of their own. But sometimes even that dream, much like her dream of family, seemed as far away as the stars.

"Tess? Is that you?"

She walked into the house just after three. "You're home?" What was Jacob doing at the house during work hours?

He came around the corner and into the kitchen as she shut the door behind her. All at once she was slammed with just how handsome he was. Rusty chestnut hair and eyes so blue as to rival the summer sky. His beard was neat and full and she loved the sight of it. To her it represented the pledge they had made to love one another. Yet it was the frown on his face that commanded her attention.

"The neighbor called me at work. Your goats got out again."

Her stomach sank. Just the disappointed tone of his voice was enough to turn her heart over in her chest. "And you had to come put them back up."

He nodded. She could tell that he was angry. "Those goats are more trouble than they're worth."

"But the money from the cheese—"

"Doesn't come close to the wages I lose when I have

to come home from work early and put them back in their pen."

"They haven't gotten out that many times." She nearly slapped her hand over her mouth, but it was too late; she had already said the words.

"They've gotten out plenty. They take your time away from the chores you need to be doing and they eat up more than their milk brings in money to replace."

Something snapped inside Tess. She worked hard. She did everything she had been asked to do. She lived her life in a godly manner, and yet, He seemed to pass her over. She might not be able to do anything about God's plan, but she surely could alter her husband's. "What are you saying, Jacob?"

"I've got a man coming by tomorrow to look at the goats. I want them out of here by the end of the week even if I have to give them away."

Her mouth fell open. "You can't sell my goats."

"I surely can. They are on my property, and as the head of this family, I can get rid of them if I see fit."

"But . . . but . . ." She couldn't find the words she wanted. The goats had become like the children she hadn't been able to have. She loved their weird eyes and scratchy fur on their long, sweet faces. "That's not fair."

"What's not fair is me having to leave work to come home and chase them around in one-hundred-degree heat."

She stiffened her spine. "You are not going to sell my goats." Just saying the words went against everything she had been taught about being a good wife to her husband. The man was the head of the household. But Jacob was being completely unreasonable.

"I can, and I will." He started toward the door as if

he had said what he needed to say and wasn't hanging around to see if she had any feelings on the matter.

That was the problem. The realization came to her like the clouds opening up and the sun shining down after a long rain. He didn't care about her feelings. He didn't care about her goats. He didn't care how hard she worked. Nothing.

She stopped in her tracks as he made his way to the door. She was unable to move as he pushed out of the screen door and into the bright and happy Oklahoma sunshine.

But she wasn't happy. And she hadn't been in a long time. She was tired of Jacob coming home too exhausted to have a conversation with her but not too tired to scroll on the Internet on his company-provided smartphone. She was tired of him being surly and stomping around the house like an angry giant with a score to settle. Amish didn't settle scores; they turned to God. But Tess wasn't sure God was listening to them anymore. How had it gotten to this? How had it turned from simple inconvenience to outright arguing? And what could she do about it?

She eased down at the kitchen table as the tractor engine started outside.

Nothing. There was nothing she could do about it. Jacob Smiley was as stubborn as God made them. He had made up his mind. He was getting rid of her goats, and he hadn't given her feelings even half a thought. She might not be able to divorce him—wasn't even sure if that was even a consideration if she could—but that didn't mean she had to live under the same roof with a man who had already forgotten the vows they had exchanged.

She pushed to her feet. She was going home. Back to Clarita. Back to her family who loved her and cared for her.

And her goats? As sad as she would be to see them go,

she knew this was about more than goats. This was about two people who should have never gotten married to begin with.

Mind made up, she walked over to the cookie jar and extracted the money. With any luck she would have enough to get a driver to take her home.

Chapter Four

The tears started halfway between her house and Obie Brenneman's. They ran down her face without so much as a sob or a hiccup. Tess supposed it was because she was more mad than sad. She was hurt and felt wronged. She wiped them away with the back of her hand and kept going.

The bag she had packed was beginning to get heavy. She hadn't taken all of her things, just essentials. She could send for the rest later. She had to get away and fast, before she lost her nerve, before Jacob came home and talked her out of it.

As much as she hated it, this was the only solution she could see. He was never going to change. And she needed him to.

She was tired of looking at all of her friends and their wonderful husbands and boyfriends. Caroline Fitch, Emily Riehl, Sadie Kauffman, and Abbie King, even Lorie Kauffman. She might live with the English now, but Tess could see how much she loved her new husband and how much he cared for her. Was it too much to ask to want a little of that romantic, undying love?

She dashed back a few more tears and moved farther onto the side of the road as a car whizzed past. Jacob had been loving and kind when they were dating. Of course, things had been different then. They had all lived in Clarita and her parents were right next door. But when his parents had decided to come to Wells Landing, Jacob had wanted to remain close and chose to move as well. Tess hadn't bothered to point out to him that if they moved he might be closer to his parents, but she would be farther away from hers. She hadn't said anything because they were looking for farmland and Wells Landing seemed to have more of it available than Clarita had. At the time. Apparently they weren't the only ones looking for land, and the demand outweighed the supply. They had moved but weren't able to afford the house and land they had both dreamed of. Now they rented a house and scraped and saved every penny in order to be able to afford a house with property as soon as possible.

Now it was all for naught. She was going home tomorrow. Or as soon as she could get a driver.

A few cars passed her as she walked, but thankfully no one on a tractor. She wasn't sure how she could explain her actions to another church member. She didn't know how she was going to tell Clara Rose and Obie, but she would think of something.

Their mailbox came into view before she had the words formed in her mind, but she trudged down the lane toward her friend's house. How ironic. She had just been less than a quarter of a mile down the road for the quilting circle meeting only an hour or so before. Now she was back again, but not for the same reason.

"Tess?" Clara Rose must have seen her through the window. Her friend rushed out onto the porch, greeting her before she could make it halfway across the yard.

"I—" She had no words.

Clara Rose's eyes flicked to her suitcase, then back, snagging her gaze with soulful eyes. "I think you'd better come on in the house."

Neither one said a word as they made their way up the porch steps and inside. Once upon a time the house had belonged to all of the Brennemans, but once Clara Rose and Obie got married they took it over. They bought a double-wide and placed it behind the main house, the perfect Oklahoma *dawdi* house. Now Paul and Obie's two brothers who still lived in Oklahoma were living in their new trailer.

"Where's Obie?"

Clara Rose led her into the living room. "He's out in the barn. He has some new puppies. Just born last night."

More babies. Never mind that they were dogs. She wondered how proud and happy the mama dog was. "I'm going back home."

Clara Rose frowned. "But you just got here."

Tess shook her head. "I'm going home. Back to Clarita. Tomorrow. But I need a place to stay until then."

Clara Rose's frown deepened as she mulled over everything that Tess had just said. She took so long that Tess was afraid that she would just tell her no without hearing what she had to say.

But what did she have to say? That she didn't think her marriage would work? That she had made a mistake? That she missed her family, and if Jacob didn't appreciate her she was going back where she knew people who would?

How could Clara Rose understand any of that? She had the perfect marriage. She was having a baby. She had a wonderful house, land to farm, everything that Tess herself didn't have.

"I-I'll have to talk to Obie." Clara Rose stood and smoothed her hands down the front of her dress. She sucked in a deep breath as if she was having as much trouble as Tess in deciding what was next.

"Rosie?" Obie's voice floated to them from the back of the house.

"In here," Clara Rose called in return.

"I thought I heard someone." He smiled at Tess. "How are you?" he asked, then his eyes widened as he took in her tearstained face. At least, that was what Tess thought he was looking at.

She wiped at her cheeks, feeling new moisture. She had thought she had stopped crying. Apparently her eyes had other plans.

"Obie," Clara Rose started, "can I, uh, talk to you for a minute? Alone. In the kitchen." She all but took him by the arm and bustled him from the room.

Tess sank back into the couch cushions, the weight of the world pressing down on her. She knew that Clara Rose was talking to Obie about her wanting to stay. How could Clara Rose tell him what was going on when Tess hadn't had a chance to even tell her?

She pushed to her feet and followed the path they had taken until she was standing outside the full swinging door that led to their kitchen. One hand placed to push her way inside, Tess stopped.

"I don't know, Rosie."

"Please."

"It's a lot to ask."

"Do it for me?"

What were they talking about?

"Why do you think me talking to Jacob will help?"

Talk to Jacob? About what?

"I don't know. I think they are having problems. Why else would she come here saying she's going home?"

Obie heaved a huge sigh, one large enough to be heard through the kitchen door. "Fine. If you think it will help."

"I do." Clara Rose's voice rose on the end. Tess could almost imagine her leaning up on her tiptoes and giving her husband a quick kiss on the cheek. When was the last time she had kissed Jacob like that? For no other reason than she wanted to? It had been a long time. Perhaps even before they had moved to Wells Landing.

But another thought crashed through her head. Jacob didn't know she was gone. She hadn't left a note or anything stating her intentions. She hadn't thought about letting him know where she was going or why. He could figure that out on his own. Maybe then he would understand where she was coming from.

Or maybe not.

Suddenly remembering that she was eavesdropping, Tess hustled back to the couch and sat down just in time for Clara Rose to come through the door.

"Well, now." She came back over to where Tess sat and perched on the sofa next to her. "Would you like to talk about this?"

Obie never came through the door, and Tess supposed that there were two ways into the kitchen. A tractor started outside and she knew that was Obie heading over to her house.

"I can't do it anymore," Tess said. It was the truth, but only part of it. Tess couldn't tell her friend that she wanted what she had. What they all had. Emily, Mariana, Caroline, Sadie. They all had men who loved them. Truly loved them. "Jacob doesn't love me any longer."

Clara Rose shook her head. "He said this to you?"

"Well, no. But he doesn't have to. I can tell. Things have

gotten worse since we moved here. Every day. He gets up and goes to work. He comes home late and plays on his phone. He doesn't want to do anything with me, saying he's too tired."

"He works hard, Tess."

"Every day?" Her tears started again welling up in her eyes and spilling down her cheeks. "I know it's wrong, and I've prayed about it."

"What did God tell you to do?"

"He never answered me." Tess sniffed.

"Maybe He did."

"How?"

"By not answering."

Tess shook her head. That philosophy was more than she could comprehend right now. Not with her heart breaking.

She had left her husband. She had run on some internal unknown energy when she left and all the way here. But now that she was facing the truth of the matter, she was scared.

Her hands trembled and her insides quaked. "Clara Rose . . . what am I going to do?"

Her friend took her hand, squeezing her fingers with an understanding that only friends have. "You could go back."

Tess shook her head. Her prayer *kapp* strings tickled her neck and sent shivers down her spine. The sensation was ominous. "I can't go back."

"Just because you argued—"

"It was more than an argument. He wants to get rid of my goats and we're never going to get out of that house. We're never going to have a baby."

Clara Rose sat back a bit. "Well, that certainly can't happen if you're here and he's there."

"Will you be serious?"

"I am."

"My goats. He said that if he couldn't sell them, he was going to give them away."

"I can't say that's the nicest thing I've ever heard him say, but Jacob is a reasonable man."

"He's not," Tess protested. "Not since . . . well, not in a long time." Since they moved here. Since he took the job with the English company. Since he got the cell phone.

But the worst part of all was she looked at her friends' marriages and she wanted a piece of that for herself. She hadn't been happy in so long she had almost forgotten what it felt like. And today was the last straw. Her goats were the only thing she had left, and if he took them away . . .

"If you move, he'll for sure sell your goats."

Tess shrugged as if it were no matter. But the words made her stomach hurt. "I'll just get new ones."

Clara Rose patted her hand encouragingly. "Don't let your pride get in the way of your marriage."

Pride wasn't her sin. It was jealousy, but she couldn't tell Clara Rose that. She had prayed and prayed for relief from the feelings but they always remained, hovering just below the surface, ready to rise up and take control of her every thought and emotion. But even as much as she knew the jealousy went against everything she had been taught her entire life, it was there all the same.

She wondered what Jacob was doing. What he was going to eat for supper and if he was really going to sell her goats. She hoped not. Or maybe by leaving she would shake him up and make him see that he needed to do more for her. Quit playing Internet games and working so hard. Was it too much to ask for him to play cards with her every once in a while? Or even just sit and talk. Share his day. She didn't think so.

But she couldn't ask him to play with her now. She had made her move and there was no backing out. She had taken that first step; she wasn't going back again. Not without Jacob promising that there would be some changes. And since she was headed home tomorrow, the chances of that were slim to none.

She had to keep her focus, remember what she wanted from her life. And it surely wasn't a husband who ignored her and sold her goats. She wanted love and respect.

"So can I stay?"

Clara Rose hesitated just slightly then gave a small nod. "Obie and I talked and we think you should stay here tonight." Her words hung expectantly in the air, as if more should follow but she wasn't ready to say them yet.

"Oh, *danki*." Tess hugged her friend close, so relieved. She would have a place to stay tonight. Then tomorrow she would find someone to take her over to Clarita. She had come this far. There was no turning back now.

Obie returned an hour or so later. He came into the house only long enough to tell Clara Rose and Tess that he had returned, then he went back to the barn and his newborn puppies.

Clara Rose kept the conversation light as she and Tess worked side by side cooking supper. Tess was thankful, though she really wanted to know what Clara Rose thought about Obie's visit with Jacob.

Instead she let the conversation flow naturally from one mundane subject to the other. What the pattern might be for the next quilt the quilting circle would make to donate to the Clarita School Auction.

She would be home in time for the auction this year. She hadn't been able to attend the last two years. Jacob's schedule had been increasingly hectic this time of year and he hadn't been able to get the time off work. That only added fuel to her dissatisfaction. Why couldn't he take time off? He wasn't the only employee there. And he deserved a vacation from time to time. The only answer she had was that he hadn't really wanted to go back. He had family members still living in the area, but not immediate ones. Just a few cousins and an aunt and uncle or two. His parents had moved to Wells Landing around the same time they had. It wasn't like he had to travel miles and miles to see his *mamm* and *dat*.

The more she thought about it, the madder she got. She was practically fuming inside by the time Clara Rose turned off the burner under the potatoes.

"Can you set the table while I wait on the bread?"

Tess nodded as Obie came in through the back door. The two of them, Obie and Clara Rose, shared a look so loving that flames of jealousy seared through Tess. Obie gazed at Clara Rose as if she was the moon and the sun all rolled into one. Tess couldn't even get Jacob to take her home to see her mother and father.

She snatched up the stack of plates and stormed from the room, giving the happy couple the privacy they deserved.

The first plate hit the tabletop with a resounding thud. Tess took a deep breath. She might be upset with Jacob, but she didn't have the right to take her anger out on someone else's dinnerware. Emotions in check, she placed the plates on the mats and started for the kitchen and the silverware they would need.

"How'd it go?" Clara Rose's voice stopped Tess in her tracks. She would surely have to pray extra hard for forgiveness tonight. After all, the day wasn't over and she had already listened in on two conversations.

Then again, if the conversations were about her, why shouldn't she know what was being said?

"Fine, I guess." It sounded like Obie was eating something as he spoke, most probably a slice of the cucumber Clara Rose had just cut. She had told Tess earlier that cucumbers were Obie's favorite.

And what is Jacob's?

She pushed that thought aside as Obie continued. "I mean, he doesn't know why she left or what's wrong with her. He didn't even know that she *had* left. He went back to work and when he came home she was gone."

"He went back to work after they had argued? Jacob said he was going to sell her goats."

"*Jah*. He mentioned that to me. I got the impression that the neighbors have been complaining about the smell and the fact that they tend to get out a lot."

A fact that could be remedied if Jacob would take the time to build her a decent pen. She might not have many goats, but they deserved a good place to live. How many times had she asked him to do that for her?

Well, she hadn't exactly asked him outright. But that was because he was never at home these days.

"I'm sure it'll blow over by tomorrow," Clara Rose said.

Obie made a grunting sound that might have been in agreement or it might not have been. To Tess it wasn't a positive sound, as if Obie didn't think it was going to blow over any more than she did.

Tess took that opportunity to push her way back into the kitchen. They both started as if caught in the act of doing something they weren't supposed to be doing. If Tess hadn't already known that they were talking about her, their guilty expressions would have tipped her off right away.

"Silverware?" she asked. "Napkins?"

Clara Rose moved to grab them off the island counter-top and thrust them at Tess. "Here you go."

Feeling somewhat dismissed, Tess hustled back into the dining room and started placing one at each seat. She would try not to listen in. She shouldn't have done so already. But that damage was done. From here on out she would do her best not to eavesdrop. Even if those who were talking, were talking about her.

Chapter Five

"Did you want to lay out any clothes for tomorrow?" Clara Rose asked.

They were standing in the Brenneman spare bedroom. Already, it was starting to show signs of change. Signs that a baby was coming. Furniture had been pushed to the side, the closet had been emptied and boxes stacked on chairs. Clara Rose had told her that she was moving the baby into the sewing room downstairs, which was the room next to the master bedroom, and then this room would become the sewing room. To Tess it seemed like an awful lot of shifting, but she was certain it would all be worth it when Clara Rose held her baby in her arms.

"I guess so. I mean, I'm just going back to Clarita."

"Well, you should always look your best, *jah*?" Her voice was overbright and Tess noticed her gaze darted around the room, never settling and never meeting her eyes. It seemed as if Clara Rose was hiding something. Or perhaps something was up and she wasn't ready to tell Tess about it. Or maybe she was just uncomfortable knowing that Tess was leaving Jacob and she wasn't coming back.

Tess grabbed a dress from her bag and hung it in the near-empty closet. It looked forlorn just hanging there with nothing else around. And it was her favorite dress. A beautiful green like fresh-cut limes. Her mother said the color made her brown eyes take on a golden glow. Tess worried it just made her freckles stand out a little bit more. Still, she loved the dress, which was a little on the fancy side, as she had stitched a row of hearts around the sleeves. She had done the work by hand and had wondered at the time how Verna Yutzy made such tiny stitches when she quilted. She assumed it had a lot to do with age and practice. One day Tess hoped to make those pretty stitches like the eldest member of the quilting circle.

"What about your apron?" Clara Rose asked.

Tess gave a quick shrug. "I guess I'll just wear this one."

Clara Rose's eyes widened. "You can't wear that. It's got stuff all over it."

Tess looked down at herself. Somehow in helping Clara Rose with supper, she had managed to pick up a few extra stains. She gave a small shrug. "I'll spot-wash it tonight."

"Do you have another?"

"I'm sure it's fine."

"We should always look our best."

"I'm just going home."

"*Jah.*"

But something in her tone made Tess wonder if Clara Rose knew something she didn't.

Bright morning sun worked its way under the shades covering the windows to shine directly in Tess's eyes. Perhaps it was God's way of telling her that it was time to get out of bed. But she hadn't slept much the night before.

She'd tossed and turned to the early hours of the morning, finally drifting off to sleep just before dawn.

She should be content with her decision to go back to Clarita and her family, but all she could think about was Jacob.

They had loved each other, of that much she was certain. So what had happened?

She had done everything in her power to bring that Jacob back. She had tried to get him to go on dates like they had when they were courting. She had connected with their old youth group in Clarita and set up a reunion, but he had refused to attend. She had even asked him to go to marriage enrichment classes, but he had claimed to be too busy at work. She hadn't brought it up again.

The old Jacob was lost to her.

A light rap sounded on her door. "Tess?"

"*Jah?*" She pushed herself up in bed. There would be no more sleep for her. Not that she would have been able to stay in bed much longer. The day was wasting. She had to find a driver and get back home.

Clara Rose nudged the door open and eased inside. "Breakfast is ready."

Tess's stomach growled in response. She hadn't eaten much the night before and it was catching up with her. "*Danki.* I'll be right down."

Clara Rose hovered by the door, her expression expectant. "Do you want some help with your hair?"

Tess shook her head. "I can manage." Just as she had done for years.

"*Jah.* Okay then. See you downstairs." Then Clara Rose was gone.

Tess pushed out of bed and padded across the hall to the bathroom. Clara Rose and Obie's bedroom was downstairs, so she had no fear of running into him while she was still wearing her nightclothes.

Once she had taken care of her morning necessities, she made her way back into the spare room to get dressed.

Half an hour later she made her way into the Brennemans' kitchen.

Clara Rose seemed almost relieved to see her. "Have a seat and help yourself," she said. "Everyone else has already eaten."

"Everyone else?"

Clara Rose turned bright pink. "I mean Obie. Do you want an egg?"

Tess shook her head and slid into one of the chairs there at the kitchen table. Her appetite was suddenly gone, but she knew she should eat. She had a big day ahead of her and she didn't need a headache from lack of food.

She buttered a biscuit and added a piece of sausage to make a small breakfast sandwich. With any luck she would be able to eat it all. That would at least get her home.

"I've got coffee brewed if you want some." Clara Rose lifted the pot.

Tess shook her head. "But *danki*."

"Well, it's here if you change your mind." She set the pot back on the burner, then wiped her hand on a dish towel. "I guess I'll go hang the laundry out."

She bustled out of the room, leaving Tess to wonder what her hurry was. It was barely eight o'clock, and she had already made breakfast and run a load of clothes through the washer.

"Hello, Tess."

She whirled around in her seat. Jacob stood in the doorway.

She wasn't sure but she thought he might be more handsome today than he was yesterday. She hardened her heart against him. She couldn't let him get the better of her today. She had made up her mind. And she was sticking to her plan.

"Go home, Jacob."

"I will. Once you say you're going home with me."

She searched his tone for any signs of sincerity, but could find none. He merely wanted her to come back home. "I'm going back to Clarita," she said and turned back to face the front. She managed to take another bite of her biscuit sandwich, though it had lost all its flavor.

He nodded. "That's what Obie said. But it's time to come back home."

"No." Not until he realized that their marriage was in trouble, that they needed to work on it. That he needed to get rid of his phone and pay more attention to what really mattered.

He shifted in place, then exhaled. She could almost feel his frustration.

Well, fine. She was frustrated too.

"Tess, now is not the time to be difficult."

"Difficult? You think I'm being difficult?" How blind could one man be? "You said you were selling my goats."

"*Jah.*" He nodded as if everything was normal. "They are more trouble than they're worth."

"But they are mine."

"You don't need them."

She wanted to yell her frustration to the ceiling, but she had been raised better than that. "I use their milk for cheese and soap. For lotion and all sorts of things."

"I'm well aware of all your hobbies."

"Hobbies?" She could hardly believe her ears. Did he not know how hard she worked with the goats and making the products? And she still managed to quilt for the needy, have supper on the table each night, and her house ran like a clock. There were no hobbies to be found. "I'm saving that money to help with the house fund."

He crossed his arms. "I believe you've mentioned that before."

"I'm surprised you remember." She felt out of control, as if someone else had taken charge of her mind, thoughts, and body, leaving her a spectator to her own actions. She crossed her arms and pressed her lips together. She was angry, unhappy, unsatisfied with the way things had turned out, and she wasn't backing down. She had come this far.

"Get your things and tell Clara Rose good-bye."

"No." Her chin rose to a stubborn angle. "If you are selling my goats, I am going back to Clarita."

Something unidentifiable flashed through his eyes like the flames of an out-of-control bonfire. But as quickly as it came, it disappeared again. A muscle in his jaw twitched, but otherwise he made no other move. Then finally, finally he gave a stern nod. "If that is how it's going to be."

Somehow she managed to raise her chin another notch higher and still maintained eye contact. "It is."

"So be it."

His footsteps boomed like the reverberating sound of a gong. One, two, three, and he was gone.

Tess sank back into the chair behind her and kept her chin up and her tears at bay until she heard his tractor start. It seemed to take forever before she heard the sound. He was leaving. Her heart tripped over itself in her chest. Leaving.

She didn't care, she told herself. But she felt as if with the slightest touch she would break into a million pieces that could never be put back together again. How had it come to this? Where had the love gone? The dedication?

The promises and vows to work together through any problems that could arise?

"Tess?"

She nodded at the sound of Clara Rose's concerned voice.

"I guess that didn't go as planned."

Tess burst into tears.

What happened to the sweet, mild-mannered Amish woman he had married?

Jacob wiped the sweat from his brow and adjusted his hat a little lower on his forehead. He knew he was scowling, and there was nothing he could do about it. Seemed like he spent most of his time these days frowning about one thing or another. And the last thing he needed was Tess losing her good sense over a bunch of mangy goats.

Okay, so they weren't actually mangy, but he hated the creatures. They bleated all day long on the weekends and got out during the week, most always when she was off doing something with her friends.

At least she had the time to make friends. He had barely gotten to know anyone in the church district, having only the hour or so after church every other week to cultivate those relationships.

"Jacob?" Obie Brenneman came out of the barn, a concerned frown on his face. At least his wasn't angry.

"I'm sorry, Obie." He wished he could say more, but the words seemed blocked behind the lump in his throat.

"There's no need for you to apologize."

Jacob stopped halfway to his tractor and allowed Obie to come up next to him. "I don't know what to say. She's not coming home." He shook his head. "She says she's going back to Clarita."

Obie shook his head. "Clara Rose and I have already talked about that. We're going to do everything in our power to keep her here until whatever this is blows over."

"*Danki*." It was all Jacob could manage in response. He didn't know what bee had gotten into Tess's bonnet. Though she had been acting strange lately, not at all like herself.

He appreciated Obie's help, but how would they know if things were back to normal if they didn't know what was bothering her? He surely wasn't going to ask.

"I don't want her to be a bother to you." He and Tess had been married for going on three years, but Obie and Clara Rose had been married less than a year. And most of that had been spent getting their house ready and living with his father and brothers. He knew they needed their alone, married time and hated that something in his life was taking that away from them.

"She's no bother. In fact, I think having Tess around might be good for Clara Rose. She's used to a gaggle of females surrounding her, and she doesn't get that much here on the farm."

Jacob gazed out over the open land that constituted the Brenneman farm and had to tamp back his jealousy. One day . . . one day he would be able to quit work at the roofing company and farm for a living. He wanted to take seeds and dirt and with the good Lord's help turn it into something more—tomatoes, wheat, soybeans. A living for him and Tess. But there never seemed to be enough money, or the property wasn't available. He spent every spare moment he had scouring the county for property to farm. He wanted a goodly piece of land but was afraid that he might have to settle for something much smaller. A compromise he wasn't willing to make just yet.

"Why don't you come by for supper tonight?" Obie asked.

Jacob shook his head. "She's not really talking to me much right now." And he had no idea what to do about it. The elders would only let this go on for so long before they put a stop to it.

"She surely can't talk to you if you're not here."

"*Jah*, I guess that's true."

"I know it is."

Jacob nodded. "I will come, but only if I can bring food."

"That sounds like a fine idea." Obie smiled.

"Kauffman's fried chicken okay?"

"I do believe you just read my mind."

"Don't you think I should go out and call the driver now?" It was well past midday and Tess was beginning to think that Clara Rose didn't want her to leave.

"You can call him anytime." Clara Rose waved a dismissive hand.

"*Jah*, but I don't think anyone is going to want to drive me to Clarita and then turn around and drive back here in the dark."

"*Ach*, it doesn't get dark until way after nine. And I really need help getting these cucumbers in." She straightened and stretched her back a little. Tess was sure it was full of kinks from bending over to search the prickly plants for cucumbers.

"If you're sure."

"I'm su—would you look at this one!" Clara Rose held up the biggest cucumber Tess had ever seen. "I'd better hide this or the men will think they can use it instead of a bat in their baseball games."

Tess smiled at the exaggeration, realizing that it might actually be the first time she had smiled in days, maybe even weeks. "It's a big one all right. But it probably won't be fittin' to eat."

"I know," Clara Rose exclaimed. "Let's make pickle relish. I've got *Mammi*'s recipe. So good."

Tess eyed the cucumber. "You're going to need more than one."

"I'm sure there's another one in this mess." She motioned toward the overgrown cucumber plants.

Just then Tess found another huge cucumber. Her mother had always told her that very large cucumbers tended to be bitter and full of seeds, but they would be perfect for pickle relish, and Jacob lov—

She reined in her thoughts. Jacob had come by and they had solved not even one of their problems. She wasn't making pickle relish for him no matter how much he loved it.

"Say you'll stay tomorrow and help me make relish."

"I don't know . . ." Tess started.

"Please." Clara Rose did a little dance in place.

How could she say no? "*Jah*, okay."

"Goodie!" Clara Rose gave her a quick hug. "And you can have some to take home for you and Jacob."

She shook her head. "I don't think we have a home."

Clara Rose's demeanor immediately sobered. "Don't say that."

"It's true." She wanted to ask how much of their earlier conversation her friend had overheard, but she couldn't bring herself to rehash it all. Conversation . . . who was she trying to fool? It was an argument, plain and simple. Every time they tried to talk these days, they ended up arguing. She wasn't sure how other couples managed to keep their relations together. What had shifted between her and Jacob? Clara Rose and Obie didn't fight all the time. At least they hadn't argued even once since she had been there.

"You and Jacob will work this out." Clara Rose sounded much more confident than Tess felt. Her relationship with Jacob was like trying to hold on to a greased eel. It was slipping through her fingers no matter how hard she tried to keep ahold of it.

But what have you really tried?

She pushed the nagging thought away. She wasn't to blame if Jacob was being completely unreasonable. They had loved each other once upon a time, but she had no idea how to get it back.

"Are you sure this is going to work?" Jacob shifted as Obie adjusted his suspender straps.

"No." Obie laughed. "I barely got Clara Rose to consider me. I have no idea what I'm doing."

Neither did Jacob, but at least Obie had plans that seemed like they might help. Straight down to instructing Jacob to bring flowers as well as supper.

He did as he was told, stopping by the small florist there on Main Street before hitting Kauffman's. He had missed New Food Tuesday, the day Cora Ann Kauffman got to experiment with recipes and different foods, but that was okay. He was after fried chicken. Tess loved fried chicken. At least he thought she did. Hadn't she told him that when they were dating? He couldn't remember. Too much had happened between then and now. A lot of living went into three or so years.

Obie's puppies whined from the corner of one horse stall, but they were tiny things. They didn't even have their eyes open yet. A few of the bigger pups had been romping around in the hay when he had arrived, but they stood now, waiting for the chance to jump if he happened to drop any of the food. He had to admit the chicken smelled delicious.

"Do you think she'll like the flowers?" Jacob asked. He hated spending money on such frivolous things. He was doing his best to scrape up enough money to buy them a farm of their own. Flowers seemed like an unnecessary expense, but Obie said that was what he needed to do, so that was what he did.

"I think she'll love the flowers." He dusted imaginary specks from Jacob's shoulders. "Are you ready to go in?"

Jacob took a deep breath. Was he? "*Jah.*" He had to be if he was going to fix the problems in his marriage. How had it come to this?

"Let's go."

Together he and Obie walked toward the house, the older puppies trotting alongside. His heart pounded in his chest and his palms began to sweat. He hadn't been this nervous since he had first asked Tess if he could take her home from a singing.

Up the porch steps and into the house, his mouth was dry, his knees quaking.

"What are you doing here?"

He nearly dropped the sack containing their supper as Tess spied him from the other side of the dining room. She marched toward him, her jaw tight and shoulders stiff.

Obie nudged him in the side. "Flowers," he whispered.

"I, uh . . . I brought you flowers?" Now, why did he make it sound like a question? He took a step forward, extending the blossoms toward her. They quaked with the trembling of his hand.

She eyed them as if they were a snake about to strike.

Where was the trust? Where was the love? This was his wife, the one person in the world he thought he would be beside forever, and now he was having to court her all over again. The thought left a bad taste in his mouth.

Finally, she reached out and took them, raising them to her nose to see what scent they carried. "*Danki.*"

Did they smell good? He didn't know. He hadn't thought about that when he bought them. He hadn't thought about anything. Did she like daisies? Why didn't he know? And why hadn't he noticed they were such bright colors? Were they even real colors? Or had they been altered by a clever florist?

Obie nudged him again.

"Oh, and supper. I brought us supper."

Tess lowered the flowers and gave him one last look, then she turned back to Clara Rose. "When you said you were having a guest . . ."

Clara Rose gave a delicate shrug. "How are the two of you going to work through your problems if you're not even together?"

Tess seemed to think about it a moment. "I'm calling the driver in the morning."

So she was still planning on going back to Clarita.

"You don't have to."

Obie stood stock-still as Clara Rose bustled toward Tess.

"I could really use your help again tomorrow," Clara Rose said. "There are a few more cucumbers to pickle, and the tomatoes need to be gathered and canned before they blister out there in this heat."

Was Clara Rose dreaming up ways to keep Tess from leaving? Why hadn't he thought of any of these things? He had been too busy working. Too busy earning a living. He didn't have time to hold Tess's hand every day—

literally or figuratively. They had plans to see through. Couldn't she see that?

"I should get home," Tess protested.

She said the words and he started forward. Her home was with him. What there was of it for now. But soon . . .

Obie reached out with one hand and stopped Jacob in place. This was not turning out the way he had planned. At all.

"Let's be reasonable here. Jacob has brought us a fine meal from town and we planned to sit down and eat it together. I can't think of a valid reason why we shouldn't follow through. Am I right? Then we can let tomorrow take care of itself."

For a moment he thought Tess might protest, then she gave a stiff nod. "*Jah*, okay then." But Jacob had the feeling she would rather sit down with a table full of lions than dine with him. Why? Hadn't they eaten supper together just a few nights ago? Maybe not. How long had it been since he had eaten a meal with his wife?

In the mornings he grabbed a quick bite that he could eat on his tractor while he drove to the meeting place. Lunch was eaten at work, and at church he ate with the men. Still, there were plenty of times when he ate supper with Tess. But right now he couldn't think of one.

Clara Rose smiled encouragingly and waved him on into the room. It was then he realized that he was standing as still as the statue in front of the Wells Landing library. His legs were stiff and his knees threatened to buckle with each step he took. But somehow he managed to make it to the table and deposit the bag there.

This was worse than courting. He had messed up with Tess, and he didn't have a clue as to what he had done. Maybe her goats. But she had to see his reasoning eventually. They spent almost as much in food and lost wages as they made with her goat's milk products. It was ridiculous to have them at all. And when they were gone, that was just one less stress for her to worry over.

"Tess, you sit here." Clara Rose directed his wife to the place just opposite him. He could reach across the table and touch her hand. Why did that seem so intimate? He had sat across from her countless times. He knew it. But for some unknown reason he couldn't remember the last time. Maybe that was why it felt familiar and brand-new all at the same time.

Clara Rose started unloading the sack and organizing the containers as Obie took his seat. Jacob tried not to stare as he watched Tess snap her napkin and place it in her lap. Really, she was the prettiest thing he had ever seen, dark brown hair and big brown eyes. She had on her green dress. He couldn't say it was a favorite of his, but it made her freckles stand out all the more, and for some reason he found it utterly appealing.

"What?" She lifted her napkin and dabbed at her chin.

He had been staring. "Nothing." He ducked his head and Clara Rose took her seat.

They bowed their heads for prayer.

He should have told her that she looked pretty. That he had forgotten just how pretty she was. But the moment was gone. If he said it now, then it would just be awkward. More awkward than it already was.

They raised their heads and Obie started passing around the food. Fried chicken, mashed potatoes, gravy, and green beans with enough biscuits on the side for them each to have a couple.

"So, Jacob," Clara Rose started, "did you see Obie's new puppies in the barn?"

How could he not? "Of course." But he hadn't really been thinking about puppies. He had been trying to figure out how he was going to get through tonight and reach wherever it was that his wife had gone off to.

But now he was thinking about Obie and the opportunities he had made for himself. Raising puppies. But that wasn't all that he did. Like many other Amish men Obie had spread his talents about, creating a string of cottage industries in order to make ends meet. It was admirable, to say the least. Maybe when they got their property and he started to farm he could do something similar, maybe breed cats or something.

Or goats.

The thought came to him in a flash, but he pushed it away as soon as it arrived. Goats were not the answer.

"How are things in the roofing business?" Obie asked.

How were things? "Busy." Oklahoma had suffered a rougher than usual spring. Strong winds, tornadoes, and various hailstorms had made for a heavier workload than normal. He had barely been able to keep up. The company was more concerned with getting the job done than the actual job itself. They produced quality work, but to Jacob it always felt rushed. What he wouldn't give to be able to walk out and never look back. He didn't mind the work. It was working for someone else and on someone else's terms that didn't set well with him.

"Busy is good, *jah*?" Obie asked.

Jacob glanced up and caught Tess's gaze. She looked so sad that for a moment he wasn't sure he could answer at all. He swallowed his bite of chicken and the lump in his throat. "*Jah*."

Tess couldn't tear her gaze from Jacob's. His eyes were filled with such sadness. How had so much sorrow gotten there and what had she been doing as it happened?

Finally, Jacob looked away and Tess dropped her gaze to her plate. The look on his face was enough to make her stomach hurt. It surely wasn't the food. Kauffman's was always a fantastic meal. But tonight . . .

The conversation turned away from work and onto other topics: who they suspected was getting married in the fall, the latest baseball game after church, and what store might go in the empty space next to the post office.

They finished up supper and played a couple of hands of Uno, but Tess had trouble concentrating. All she could think about was Jacob.

"I win!" Obie threw his last card on top of the discard pile and sat back with a satisfied smile.

Jacob tossed his cards into the middle. "That's it. Time for me to go home."

"So soon?" Clara Rose asked.

It was almost nine and it was nearly dark. It would definitely be safer if he headed out now.

"Walk with me to my tractor?" Jacob stood and waited expectantly for her answer.

"*Jah.*"

Clara Rose and Obie shared a look as Tess rose from her chair. She got the feeling this was what the two of them had been waiting for all night.

Crickets chirped and night birds called as they stepped out onto the porch. The dusk held an expectant air and the wind was still, as if the world was holding its breath in anticipation.

"I had a good time tonight." Jacob loped down the steps ahead of her, then extended his arm to steady her for her descent. It was such a gallant gesture it almost brought tears to her eyes. Why hadn't she realized it before? They had lost sight of each other. Maybe it wasn't as tragic as

she had first thought. Maybe they could recover some of
what they had lost.

She still wanted—no, needed—for things to be different, but this was definitely a step in the right direction.
Tonight gave her hope.

They walked together toward his tractor and she noticed the closer they got, the slower their footsteps
became. Was he thinking the same thing she was? That
the night was special and she never wanted it to end?

But it had to end, and that frightened her for tomorrow.
What if tonight was just a unique time and tomorrow everything went back to the way it was before? What then?

"What are you thinking?"

Jacob's words startled her out of her thoughts. She
couldn't tell him what was really on her mind. "Nothing."

He nodded, but she knew he didn't believe her. At
least he didn't press. He stopped at the tractor and turned
to face her. She dropped her hand from his arm and
sucked in a breath as she waited for him to say something,
anything.

"Well, good night, then."

That was all? Maybe she was mistaken. Maybe nothing
between them had changed. Why oh why had she thought
otherwise? Because she had seen the look in his eyes. She
knew that tonight was special. But maybe it was better to
leave it alone. Especially if everything was going back
to normal tomorrow.

"Good night." She couldn't keep the dejected tone from
her words.

He stared at her and she was certain the world stopped
turning. She stared back, waiting, watching.

Jacob raised one hand to the side of her face. The
fingers were rough and familiar against her skin. He raised
the other hand and cupped her cheeks in his palms. The

night hung, suspended in that one moment. It seemed as if the entire evening had been leading up to this moment.

Tess closed her eyes, exhaled, and then his lips touched hers.

It was the sweetest kiss, like sweet strawberries in May, the touch of butterfly wings, and all good things rolled up into one.

Jacob's lips on hers brought back memory after memory. Their first kiss, their wedding day, the very moment when she knew he was the one. What happened to those feelings? What happened to them?

He lifted his head and she was certain for a moment she felt the night wrap comforting arms around her.

"You don't have to stay here tonight." Jacob's words were no more than a whisper. And she wasn't certain if he had actually said them or if it was another part of her past memories.

She opened her eyes. He watched her, his expression intense.

"What?"

"You've proven your point."

Tess shook her head. "I don't understand."

Jacob flashed her a grim smile. "Amish women are getting more and more independent. We all know that. So you've proven your point. But that doesn't mean you have to stay here. You can come back home."

She felt as if she had been doused with a bucket of ice water. The beauty of the night disappeared with his words. "What?" she asked just to be sure. She wanted to be wrong. She wanted to not have heard him correctly. But somehow she knew that she wasn't wrong.

"You've made your point. Now come home."

That was what she was afraid he had said. With a sad sigh, she took a step back. His arms dropped to his sides.

"What?" he asked.

"You just don't get it." She managed to make the words soft-spoken instead of the roar of frustration she felt bubbling inside her. Tonight had been so perfect. Well, almost. "This isn't about making a play for independence. This is about me and you and our marriage." She wanted to cry as she said the words, but she managed to keep her tears at bay. "I thought it meant more to you than this. I guess I was wrong." She turned on her heel and started back to the house.

"But—"

She faltered a bit as he said the words, but she managed to keep walking without looking back.

"Tess," he started, but she wouldn't allow herself to turn around. This was too important. Too much was at stake. If she wanted a marriage like her friends had, she had to keep to her plan.

But she was never going to have that. Not with Jacob. Not with anyone, because Amish marriage was forever.

Jacob working all the time, him selling her goats, that was all she was ever going to have in life, and it wasn't enough. No matter how much she loved him, she wanted more.

The tears started as he said her name again, but she didn't turn around as she made her way up the porch steps and into the house.

"That was some kiss."

Tess nearly jumped out of her skin as she entered the house. The living room seemed dark and quiet. Almost as dark as her thoughts, but not even close to the turmoil in her mind.

"Sorry." Clara Rose stepped from the shadows.

"It's okay." Tess wiped the tears from her cheeks as discreetly as possible, but Clara Rose was too observant not to notice.

"After a kiss like that, why are you crying?"

The dam broke, and Tess was left without words. Her tears flowed, but she couldn't tell her best friend what the problem was, not when her friend had everything that Tess herself wanted.

She sank down on the couch, savoring the warmth as Clara Rose eased down next to her and pulled her close.

Tess allowed her tears free rein, for a few minutes then caught herself. "Where's Obie?"

Clara Rose rolled her eyes affectionately. "He's in the barn with his puppies." Which meant he wouldn't come in on them. Still, Tess was tired of her shame being out there for the entire world to see.

She wiped her tears away and stood. "I'm going to bed."

Clara Rose was on her feet in an instant. "Are you sure? We can talk about this—"

Tess shook her head. "No, *danki*. Good night."

She could sense that Clara Rose wanted to protest, but her friend remained silent as Tess climbed the stairs to the bedroom where she had been sleeping. She needed to leave. Tomorrow. It was better that way.

She undressed and crawled beneath the covers, forgoing washing her face and brushing her teeth for the comfort of the bed.

Just before she had gotten married, her mother had given her all sorts of advice, but nothing came close to this. Her mother had never said this might not turn out the way she hoped, the way she planned and dreamed.

Her parents' marriage was good enough, she supposed. Her mother seemed to not want for anything. Not that

Tess had noticed anyway. At the time, everything had seemed the way it should be.

Just as it had when Tess and Jacob were courting. Everything had seemed fine, perfect even. But now . . .

When had the change come into their relationship?

Just after they were married.

And it had only increased when they moved to Wells Landing.

It was time to go home.

Chapter Six

"Tell me again what happened."

Jacob shook his head. He didn't think telling Obie again would help. He wasn't even sure why he took the time off from work to come over here and talk to the man. "I told her that I understood. That I knew Amish women were trying to gain a little more independence. That she had proved her point and it was time to come back home."

"And this was after you kissed her?"

"*Jah.*"

Obie whistled low through his teeth. "What made you think that was a good idea?"

Jacob frowned. "I thought that's what women wanted. Someone who understood. I was trying to be understanding."

Obie gave a small chuckle. "It seems to me all you did was make her madder."

He couldn't argue with that. "Where are the women now?"

"Clara Rose convinced Tess to ride into town with her and look for material for new dresses."

Jacob nodded. That was a surefire way to get women

into town. They loved looking at material. He knew Tess could stand for hours to pick out the right shade of blue. He didn't pretend to understand it, but he acknowledged it as a fact. Surely that was something in his favor.

"I guess I better get going before she sees me here."

"How are you guys going to be together if you avoid her?"

"I don't know." He didn't have the faintest idea about anything these days. One day his marriage was flourishing and growing, and the next thing he knew his wife was storming out, determined to move back to her family in Clarita. More than anything, he wanted to get her home before church on Sunday. But it was certain it had already gone through the grapevine of rumors and gossip throughout the entire settlement in Wells Landing. Everyone would know by now that Tess was staying with Clara Rose and Obie. And if everyone knew, he was certain his parents knew as well. It wouldn't be long before his *dat* came to talk to him and give him advice. He could well imagine what that would be. His father was a bit old-fashioned. He would tell Jacob to get his woman and bring her home. Even though Tess had sworn up and down that this had nothing to do with her play at independence, he knew that telling her to come back home now would only make her stay away longer.

"When did women get so complicated?" Jacob asked.

Obie clapped him on the shoulder in a gesture of sympathetic friendship. "Soon as you get married, that's when everything changes."

"All I'm saying is you shouldn't be hasty." Clara Rose cast a quick look over her right shoulder, snagging Tess's gaze. All Tess wanted to do was go home. She hated this feeling of limbo, somewhere in between being married and going home. Plus, she didn't want to put Obie and Clara Rose out any more than necessary.

"I'm not being hasty. I'm just trying to surround myself with people who support me."

"And Jacob doesn't support you?"

Her thoughts filled with Jacob's threats to sell her goats, to give them away if he had to. She thought of the cell phone and the Facebook account. "No." But as she said the word, she couldn't help but think about how hard Jacob worked. He supported her in many ways, that she couldn't deny. But it seemed as if he didn't support her in the way she needed the most. "I don't know how it got to this."

"Just because we marry forever doesn't mean we don't have problems. It's how we handle our problems that sets us apart."

Tess let those words wash over her. She couldn't say she'd handled the situation properly. The truth of the matter was she didn't know how to handle it, and she didn't feel like she could get through to Jacob these days. What happened to all those wonderful nights sitting on the porch talking, holding hands, and enjoying each other's company for the sake of the company, nothing more? Why did things have to change when people got married?

"I asked him to go to marriage enrichment classes." She hated how accusing her words sounded.

"One time?"

Clara Rose's words made Tess feel lower than a snake's belly. "I should ask him again?"

Clara Rose smiled. "If it were Obie, I would ask him and ask him until he agreed. If that's what you think would solve or help these problems between you, that's what you should do. Isn't your marriage worth that much?"

Maybe she had given up too easily. Maybe she should ask him again. Maybe this time he would even say yes.

"Just do me one favor, okay?" Clara Rose asked.

"Okay."

"Don't go home yet. Stay with us as long as you need to. If you go back to Clarita now, Jacob will have a very hard time. He won't be able to see you as often, and if you can't see each other, how are you ever going to work your problems out?"

"What if the problems can't be worked out?"

Clara Rose shot her a sympathetic smile. "If they can't be worked out, then they can't be worked out. But you have to be absolutely sure. Promise me?"

Tess swallowed hard and gave a quick nod. "Promise."

When they got back to Clara Rose and Obie's house, Tess called Bruce Brown's cousin and told him thank you, but she wouldn't be needing his services for the next day. Clara Rose might be onto something. How could she and Jacob work out their problems if they were miles and miles apart?

After a morning spent looking at fabrics and notions, Tess and Clara Rose made another batch of sweet pickle relish.

"I really should go check the blueberries," Tess mused. And her goats. She really missed her goats. If they were still there. And if they were there, who had been taking care of them? The thought sent a flash panic through her. "I need to go home."

Clara Rose's eyes lit up with promise, but Tess shook

her head. "My goats. I mean, what if he didn't sell them or give them away? Who's been feeding them and milking them?"

"You don't think Jacob would allow them to suffer just because you're not there."

Well, when she put it like that, it was hard to believe, but Tess knew how much Jacob hated the goats. She wouldn't put it past him to have given them away just so he wouldn't have to take care of them. And there was only one way to find out.

"Do we have time to go to my house before we have to get supper ready?"

"I believe so." Clara Rose wiped her hands on a dish towel. "I'll go tell Obie, okay? I'll meet you at the tractor."

The ride over to Tess's house seemed to take forever. Maybe it was because her heart was pounding in her throat. How had she forgotten her goats for days? It was unforgivable. She'd been so caught up in her own problems that she hadn't even given them a second thought. She only hoped she hadn't added fuel to Jacob's threats to sell her goats.

She breathed a sigh of relief as Clara Rose turned into their short drive. She could see sweet Millie standing on top of the small house she had constructed for them to sleep in. She had known the goats climbed up there, and with only a small leap, Millie would be out in the yard, free to roam and pester the neighbors. "So that's how she gets out," she muttered to herself.

Clara Rose chuckled. "That's some goat."

Tess smiled. "*Jah*, she is." But Tess was even more excited that the goats were still there. And Jacob was gone, no doubt on the job site, though she worried about him when he worked in the heat like this. She knew his boss provided them with plenty of water, but it was still incredibly hot and heatstroke was a constant concern.

"They don't seem to have suffered from your absence," Clara Rose noted.

And she was right. But that could only mean one thing. "Do you think Jacob milked them for me?"

"It appears so. But what has he done with the milk?"

"I usually store it in the refrigerator in the barn. Any extra I have that I won't be able to make into soap or lotion or cheese, I put in the freezer."

"So let's check the refrigerator in the barn."

Tess gave Millie one last pat on the head, then followed Clara Rose into the barn. She opened the refrigerator door to see bottles of goat's milk stored there, milk that hadn't been there when she left.

Tears filled her eyes. Jacob had done this for her. There was no way around it. He had worked and worked at his regular job and yet he had come home and milked them at least once a day, but from that amount of milk in the refrigerator she would have to say twice a day for sure.

Suddenly she felt ungrateful, mean, and spiteful. She had been lamenting the things that she wanted not realizing that she had a lot already.

"I think it's time to come home." Clara Rose smiled.

"I think you're right."

There was nothing worse than having to redo a job that had been done right the first time. But that was exactly what Jacob had spent the entire day doing. Ripping off perfectly good shingles to replace them with other, perfectly good shingles that were one shade darker gray than the ones that had been used. The worst part? No one on his team had made a mistake. It was just someone being extra picky—wanting more, being difficult, not being satisfied with what they had. Nothing irritated him more. So not only did he have to redo the work, which made him extra tired, but he was aggravated as well. He pulled his tractor to a stop next to the carriage house. He would put it up later. Right now he had too many things to do.

Tess had left, and though he had threatened to sell her goats, he hadn't found a buyer yet. Well, that wasn't exactly true. He hadn't really looked for one and he surely hadn't given them all away. So now he had to milk them.

He hopped off the tractor, grabbed his water jug, and headed for the house. Something seemed different as he made his way up the porch steps, but he couldn't put a finger on what it was. His heart gave a hard pound in his chest. There had been a few break-ins in the county, and most times the culprits were high school kids, bored and rambunctious.

He slowed his steps and cautiously opened the door. The smell of blueberry pie filling scented the air, mixed in with what could only be meat loaf. He had heard of thieves and vandals, but he'd never been told of ones who, once they broke into a house, started cooking.

Just then Tess moved into view. He resisted the urge to rub his eyes and make sure his vision was correct. "Tess?"

"Hi, Jacob."

"Hi." Not exactly the most intelligent thing he had ever uttered, but his thoughts were tumbling over themselves. Each one wanted to be spoken first. "What are you doing here?"

"I live here." She chuckled. The sound was apologetic.

"I know that, but does this mean you've come home?" After last night he wasn't sure she would ever return. He had started to make plans with Obie to come to supper tonight again, doing everything in his power to court his own wife.

"*Jah*," she said. "I've come home."

Jacob had never heard sweeter words. This was what he had prayed for, that somehow she could find peace or whatever it was she needed to bring her back home where she belonged.

He crossed the room to stand in front of her, hesitating only a moment before he pulled her into his arms. He hugged her close, cradling her to him. He didn't kiss her, just rocked her back and forth, his chin resting on the top of her head, her nose buried in the crook of his neck. Tess had come home and the world would be right again.

Tess loved the feel of Jacob's arms around her. She loved being close to him. His embrace was warm and comforting. He took a step back, plucking his shirt away from his skin. "I need to take a shower."

She smiled. "Supper will be ready in about twenty minutes."

He nodded. "Then I've got plenty of time." He seemed not to want to take his eyes from her. He backed from the room, finally turning and heading up the stairs.

Tess turned back to the stove. It felt good to be home. She had left what clothes she had at Obie and Clara Rose's. She could pick up her bag later. The most important thing was coming back home and being here when Jacob got off work. He missed her. He might not have said the words, but she could tell. Actions always spoke louder. He hadn't sold her goats, and somehow she knew everything was going to be just fine.

Jacob came back downstairs as Tess was setting the table. They sat down and prayed, tears stinging the back of her eyes with the beautiful familiarity of it all. As they ate, Jacob told her about his day at work and his frustrations with some of the customers. She listened, so grateful to be able to share his day with him once again.

They got up from the table, and Jacob headed for the living room while Tess cleaned up. Half an hour later, she joined Jacob in the living room to find him immersed in his phone.

She sat down across from him. She wasn't going to get upset. This wasn't about getting upset. She would give him a few minutes to notice her, then he would realize that he was placing the phone over their relationship and he would put it away for the night. They would play a game together and everything would be just as it should be.

But after five full minutes of staring at him, he hadn't taken his attention from the phone even once.

"Jacob." She tempered her voice so it didn't sound chastising. But she wanted his attention.

"Huh?" He didn't even bother to look up, though he smiled at something he had seen.

"Jacob," she said, louder this time.

"*Jah*?" he responded with his attention still centered on the tiny little phone.

"Jacob." Somehow she managed to keep her tone below an out-and-out yell.

Exasperated, he set his phone in his lap and met her gaze. "What is it?"

"You're doing it again."

He frowned. "Doing what again?" His gaze went straight back to the phone though he didn't lift it from his lap. It was obvious he wanted to.

"Playing on your phone all night and ignoring me."

Some strange light flashed across his face, but it was

gone so quickly she wasn't able to discern what it was. "I'm ignoring you?" She couldn't read anything into his tone, though the words were dark and heavy with warning.

"*Jah*, that is what I said. You are playing on your phone and you're ignoring me. I'm not going to have it anymore."

"You're not going to have it?" Just the fact that he repeated her own words was enough to make Tess realize he wasn't happy with her demands. But she wasn't happy with a lot of things. All the elation she had felt over the fact that he had taken care of her goats while she was at Clara Rose and Obie's vanished in an instant. In its wake it left regrets and sadness.

Tess stood. What was it Verna Yutzy was always saying? In for a penny, in for a pound. She had started this and she would see it through. She'd given in to a moment of weakness this afternoon, but it seemed as if things weren't nearly as different as she had thought.

"That's right. I won't have it."

Jacob was on his feet in a heartbeat. "You can't make demands like that. I don't make demands on you."

"Of course you do. You make demands all the time. It doesn't feel like demands to you because you're the one making them. You don't like my goats. You don't want me to go to the quilting meeting. You don't want me to do anything except go visit your parents. I've had enough of that. We're living your life, Jacob, not our life, and I don't want to do this anymore." The words fell between them like a stink bomb in a one-room schoolhouse. He stood there, stock-still, as if trying to assimilate everything she had just said.

"Fine then." His words were like cast iron, dark and heavy. "If this is the way you want it, it's the way you can have it." He exhaled through his nose like a bull snorting out a challenge. "In fact, why don't you just take your things and go back over to Clara Rose and Obie's. Isn't that what you want?"

Was that what she wanted? She didn't know. Well, that wasn't true. That was not what she wanted at all. She wanted her Jacob back. But it seemed as if she wasn't going to find him. That Jacob was gone, and instead she had the man before her. And though this man looked like her Jacob, he didn't act like him. He didn't want the same things, and he sure didn't seem to love her. Wasn't that what love was about?

Heart breaking, she stared at him for only a moment and started back for the door. She was leaving tomorrow. She would get a driver and she would go back so quick that everything else would just have to wait.

Jacob watched as if viewing two other people. He watched as Tess ran from the room. The door slammed behind her and then she was gone. Wasn't that what she wanted? Why else would she question everything he said? Everything he did? It seemed he couldn't be the man she wanted. The only thing left to do was to let her go.

It had been just a day since she had walked from her house to Clara Rose and Obie's and yet here she was again. This time she had no tears. This time she couldn't blame anyone but herself. There weren't many couples who ended up living apart even though they were married, but she knew it wasn't unheard of. She just never thought she would be one of those mentioned in the conversations of couples who didn't make it. And only after three years. She would just have to accept that this was what God had planned for her.

Eyes dry, she made her way back to the Brennemans'.

"Tess!" Clara Rose's call was one of complete surprise. "What are you doing here?"

Once again Tess was overcome with the need to tell someone, and yet the embarrassment of telling someone was almost more than she could take. Especially someone like Clara Rose, whose marriage was so utterly perfect.

"I just need to stay tonight."

Clara Rose and Obie shared a look that once again sent tentacles of jealousy reaching through Tess. It was as if the two of them shared a common language that no one else on earth knew. How badly she had wanted that with Jacob. They had had it once upon a time, and then everything had fallen apart. Well, no more.

She would be the one that everyone talked about, the crazy lady who was married but didn't live with her husband, who lived at the end of the lane. She could take in excess sewing, maybe make pickles, can blueberries for people, and a variety of other things to make ends meet. Maybe her mother and father would even let her move into the *dawdi* house. Whatever was her fate, she knew it did not lie in Wells Landing, and it was not with Jacob Smiley.

"Tess," Clara Rose started, her voice soothing in both tone and manner, "come sit down. We can talk about this."

Tess shook her head, barely registering the fact that Obie disappeared through the kitchen as she and Clara Rose talked.

"There's nothing to talk about."

"Then why do you need to stay here?"

Tess studied her friend's face. There was no malice

there, only concern. And she knew that if she gave Clara Rose a valid reason for needing to stay, then she would be welcome for sure.

"It's Jacob. I can't do this anymore. I can't stay with him. I can't live there."

Clara Rose took Tess's hand into her own and led her over to the living area. She eased Tess down into the wooden rocker that sat off to one side, then perched on the edge of the sofa nearest her. "This is going to be hard for me. But I think we need to talk about this."

Tess nodded, unsure of what Clara Rose was getting at, but willing to share what she needed to with her friend.

"I've noticed lately that you've been very unhappy, and it has me really concerned."

"*Jah*," she said. "I've not been happy, and that makes it so hard."

Clara Rose nodded reassuringly. "I know it's not enough to be worried about you and now . . ." She shook her head. "Now that he's come here twice, it makes me wonder."

Tess frowned. "Wonder about what?"

Clara Rose squeezed Tess's fingers. "This is not an easy question to ask, but did Jacob hurt you?"

Tess drew back.

Clara Rose stumbled over herself to qualify the question. "I mean, you come here twice and you seem distraught. Yet you love him and you go back. I just don't know how to help you if I don't know what the problem is."

Tess jumped to her feet and wrapped her arms around herself. "And so you would automatically assume that he would hurt me?"

"Oh dear, I'm making a mess out of this." Clara Rose shook her head. "I don't want to think that he would hurt you. I don't want to think anything like that could happen in a marriage, but I have to have some place to start to help you."

Tess nodded and bit back the bile that had risen into the back of her throat. "Jacob would never hurt me," she said. "Never."

Clara Rose nodded. "Is he drinking?"

Tess shook her head incredulously. "No. Of course not."

"Gambling?"

"No." Why was she asking all these questions?

"I'm afraid I don't understand, then," Clara Rose said. "What has he done that makes you want to leave?"

"He doesn't spend any time with me. Not like Obie does with you." Even as she said the words, they sounded petty and small. But inside her head they had seemed enormous.

Clara Rose grabbed her fingers and pulled Tess back into the rocking chair. "Maybe you'd better start at the beginning."

Tess nodded and that was what she did, outlining for Clara Rose all the times Jacob had played on his cell phone and ignored her, all the times he worked late, everything and every infraction he'd made since they moved to Wells Landing, topping it off with the fact that he didn't ever want to go see her family and yet she had to see his on a regular basis. When she was finished she felt lighter than she had in years, but still a small nagging thought dug at the corners of her mind. Was that all he had done? Were all those little things worth her marriage?

"And that's it?" Clara Rose asked.

"Isn't that enough?" Tess jumped to her feet and threw her hands in the air. Her earlier frustration rose to the surface once again. "I don't understand. I look around me and I see how happy everyone is, and I want that happiness. Then I go home to Jacob and the happiness is not there. Why is the happiness not there?"

Clara Rose stood and took her hands into her own. "Honey, you have to make your own happiness."

Tess stopped as still as the eye of the storm. Make her own happiness? Was that even possible?

"You can't compare your relationship with Jacob to other people's relationships with their husbands. It's not healthy."

Tess shook her head. "But I want that. I want what everyone else has. I want a husband who does things for me, who wants to be with me, wants to spend time with me, and doesn't spend all his time playing on Facebook. Is that too much to ask?"

"No. Of course not."

"See? Even you admit it. Obie doesn't spend all his time on his cell phone."

He picked that moment to walk back in through the kitchen door. He had a cell phone pressed to his ear. He walked with it as if he'd been born to talk on that phone. Tess somehow managed to keep her jaw from hitting the floor.

"But he has—"

"A cell phone," Clara Rose said. "Yes, and a Facebook page. Three, actually. One personal page and then one for his business with his puppies and one that he shares with Gabe Allen Lambert."

Tess frowned. "Titus's brother?"

"*Jah*."

"But—but . . ." Tess faltered. It wasn't just about owning a cell phone. It was about more than that. It was about completely ignoring her. It was about the relationships that other people had. She wanted that happiness. Why couldn't she have that happiness?

* * *

She would have to pack if she was leaving. But there was a part of her that hoped maybe some of what Clara Rose said was true. Could she make her own happiness? Were her comparisons unhealthy for her relationship with her husband, or were those the thoughts of a person who had no idea? She just didn't know.

Her heart gave a quick thump as her house came into view. Not her house, but Jacob's.

He came out onto the porch the minute he saw her walking up the drive. "Tess? What are you doing here?"

"I came to get a few things. I think I'm going back to Clarita."

"You think?" Jacob asked.

"Well, I don't know for sure." Why couldn't she come up with a coherent response?

"Why don't you know for sure?"

Tess shook her head. "I am. I am going back." But her heart clenched in her chest as she said the words. She didn't want to go back. *Jah*, she wished she lived closer to her family, closer to her *mamm* and *dat*, but she really wanted to spend her time with Jacob. Just not the way they had been spending time together lately.

Tell him, the voice inside her said. They couldn't work anything out if she didn't tell him.

"I'm not happy, Jacob."

She watched his Adam's apple bob as he swallowed hard. "Okay. Why aren't you happy?"

Tess outlined all the reasons why, beginning with the fact that he never seemed to be available to her anymore and ending with his Facebook page. But even as she said the words they sounded petty. No matter how many times she said them, it seemed as if she was a small child stomping her foot in order to get what she wanted. And all she wanted was a good marriage. That child in her rose up again. Why couldn't she have that? "I look around me," she continued. "Everyone around us has things. They have fancy tractors, big houses, faster horses. They have everything. And the people who maybe don't have everything financially"—she shook her head—"they have each other, and that's a lot, as it's more than we have."

Jacob frowned. "How can you say that?"

"I say it because I don't have my face glued to a cell phone every waking moment I have off."

"Now we're getting somewhere."

"What's that supposed to mean?"

"You've not liked my phone since the first day that I got it."

"Why should I like it? It does nothing but bring me pain. Once you get on there you don't want to do anything else."

"Once you stick your head in a seed catalog I never see you again," he countered.

"The seed catalog is a far cry from the cell phone."

Jacob gave a quick nod. "That very well may be, but the end result is the same. You sit in your chair and ignore me and so I get out my phone for my own entertainment."

She shook her head. "No, you get on the phone first. Then I get out the seed catalog." Or the goat books or even a romantic library book. Suddenly it became a little clearer to her. Could she have been ignoring her husband as much as she was accusing him of ignoring her? The thought was unsettling.

"Everyone's happy. I want that happiness," she said, once again feeling like a small child stomping her foot in order to get her way.

Jacob took a step toward her. "Are you saying you're unhappy?"

"Yes, I am. I mean, sometimes."

"What are you unhappy with?" Jacob asked.

She was unhappy with a lot of things. "Like how you come in and tell me you're going to sell my goats." There. She'd said it.

"They're so much work for you. Why should you do that much extra work?"

"Because I want to. Because I enjoy them. Because I want to contribute to our house."

"But I've told you time and time again that it's not necessary."

"Just like you tell me time and time again that we can move, but only if we have enough money."

"It's more than that. We have to have property to buy as well. And until something becomes available, we have to stay right where we are."

"I think I should leave now." It was the only way she could imagine stopping this argument. They were going around in circles with no end in sight.

Jacob opened his mouth as if to protest, then shut it again. "Fine," He turned on his heel and stormed back into the house.

One day passed and then another. Sunday came and it was time for church. Tess could feel the pitying gazes as she walked through the throng of people, but she kept her chin high. Not even once did Jacob try to talk to her. That was when she knew it was well and truly over.

Clara Rose had talked Tess into staying through to the

next quilting meeting. She even promised to pay the driver herself if only Tess would stay.

So Tess stayed. It wasn't about the money. She wanted to stay, see her friends one more time before she left.

She felt like a shell of herself going through the motions. She had nothing to offer. She did what she had to do. But at least she would be home for her sister's wedding. The thought should have been a happy one, but it wasn't.

"I tell you, this is the hottest summer I ever remember." Verna Yutzy shook her head, then turned her attention back to her plate of treats. They had quilted for a while, then switched their attention to food since this was a sort of going-away party for Tess. She only wished that Mariana could have been there too.

"The heat makes people do all sorts of crazy things," Clara Rose added.

"We need some rain," Eileen said.

They did, but rain would mean Jacob would have to take a day off from work. Not that it mattered to her any longer. She had a driver all lined up. This afternoon she was heading back to Clarita. Back to her family.

Jacob hadn't reached out to her even once since that day on their front porch. Correction, *his* front porch. It wasn't hers any longer. And neither was he.

"I'll tell you," Verna started. "The heat used to make Abraham do all sorts of weird things."

Clara Rose shook her head. "Please don't tell us. He was my *dawdi*, after all."

Everyone laughed. Everyone but Tess. She couldn't get a handle on the fact that she was leaving. She should be happy that she was going. She was getting her second chance. Well, as much as she could and still be married. And that was what she wanted. Wasn't it?

She just didn't know.

Everyone talked and laughed around her, telling jokes and trying to lighten the mood, but all Tess could think about was how unhappy she was. This move was supposed to make her happy. She wanted the perfect life of the people around her, and by leaving . . . she still wouldn't have it. And the worst part? She wouldn't have Jacob at all.

Her heart did a dive in her chest. She was leaving. Leaving! And it was changing nothing. She would be without Jacob, and that was something she didn't think she could bear. It was hard enough to love him and feel that she had lost him to the phone and Facebook, but it was another matter altogether for her not to have him at all.

Her shortsightedness hit her like a ton of bricks. Her breath caught in her throat, and suddenly everything that Clara Rose had been telling her became real.

She couldn't compare her marriage to those of the people around her. Obie had a cell phone. She should ask and ask Jacob to attend marriage enrichment classes until he finally said yes.

Her marriage was worth more effort than she was giving it, than she *had* given it. She should be ashamed of herself, and she was. Jacob worked hard. He wasn't perfect, but he deserved better than a wife who pledged her all but didn't deliver.

She looked from Clara Rose to Eileen and threw her half-eaten goodies into the trash. She had been taught her entire life to take only what she could eat and eat everything she took, but this was another matter altogether. "I have to go."

"Go where?" Eileen asked, casting a quick glance into the trash.

"Home." Her lips stretched into a wide smile.

"Is Bruce here already?" Clara Rose asked.

Tess shook her head. "No. I'm going home to Jacob."

There was no sense in prolonging the inevitable. Tess wasn't coming home, and it surely wasn't a home without her.

Jacob looked into the long faces of her precious goats. He didn't want to sell the beasts. Not now, anyway. He had heard rumors that Tess had already gone back to Clarita, but he had also heard that she was scheduled to leave today. The date might still be in question, but the intent to leave was clear. And just when he'd found the perfect property.

It was in their budget, the exact size they needed, and there was plenty of room for her goats. The man who was selling the land actually had a few more goats to add to her herd, but now that wouldn't be the case at all.

In fact, he was letting the house go completely and moving in with his parents. It seemed like such an act of failure. But he hated his roofing job and he wanted to work the land. He could help his father much more and be happier than scrimping and scraping, trying to get a farm that no one would live on.

His cell phone buzzed in his pocket. He pulled it out and checked the screen. It was the number for the Realtor. She would want to know his decision on the property.

He hadn't been able to tell them outright that his wife had gone. And some little part of him hoped that she would return. He wrestled with the idea of finding her and telling her about the land and about all their dreams that were about to come true, but he didn't want her that way. He wanted her to come because she wanted to come. Not because of what he could give her, but because of him.

He shook his head at himself. He'd been hanging out with the English too long. *Jah*, that was for sure.

He thumbed the screen to answer the call. "Hello?"

"Jacob? It's Margie Anderson. Have you thought any more about the property? My seller's getting a little antsy. He thought you really wanted it."

He had really wanted it. He had wanted it for himself. He had wanted it for Tess. And he wanted it for the family that he thought they would have, but somehow everything had gone awry. "I just wanted to think about it a little more." He wanted that property so badly that he couldn't bring himself to tell her that it would never be his. And that made him a big, fat chicken.

"Jacob!"

He turned at the sound of that voice to see Tess running down the driveway. The wind caught the tail of her apron and sent it flapping behind her. The strings of her prayer *kapp* floated behind as well. From here her expression looked happy enough, but she ran with such speed that he knew something had to be wrong. Terribly, terribly wrong. As he watched her, he started to tell the Realtor that he needed to go, but the words wouldn't come.

"Are you there, Jacob?" Margie again.

"I may have to call you back, Margie."

Tess continued to approach. The closer she got, the more he could see, and the more he could see, the more she looked . . . happy.

"Don't hang up, Jacob. This is important. I have another buyer that's interested in the land."

"Oh, Jacob." Now that she was within ten feet of him, her steps slowed. But he saw a sparkle in her eyes that he hadn't seen in a long time. He hadn't seen it since he moved her from her home.

Suddenly all the problems, all her issues, all the unhappiness that they had suffered slammed into him. He should've never moved her from Clarita. He should've never moved her from her home. But he had been selfish, wanting to stay near his family, and he hadn't given a thought to hers. Maybe it was time to move back.

"Give me just a minute," Jacob said into the receiver.

"Jacob, are you—"

"I'll call you right back," he said, his gaze locked with Tess's. "Give me fifteen minutes. Just fifteen minutes."

"Okay," the Realtor said. Then Jacob hung up. He slipped the phone back into his pocket.

"Hi," he said. Not exactly the most intelligent thing he had ever uttered to Tess, but it was all he could muster. She was supposed to be gone and yet there she stood. He didn't want to blow it.

"Hi."

They stood for a moment just looking at each other, then they both started to speak at the same time.

"I've got a confession—"

"What are you doing here—"

Tess shook her head. "You first."

"What are you doing here?" Then he realized how his words sounded. "I mean, I'm glad you're here. More than happy that you're here."

Tess sucked in a deep breath. "It seems I've made a mistake. A big mistake."

"What kind of mistake is that?"

"Well, it seems as if I may have given up on my marriage before I even gave it a chance."

His heart skipped a beat. "*Jah?*"

Tess nodded. "And even worse, I started comparing it to other people's marriages."

"And then what happened?" He swallowed hard. This conversation wasn't going exactly the way he thought it would. But she was still smiling; she was still there; she was still his Tess.

"I thought it was lacking."

It was official. His heart was broken in two. The words cleaved it in half. "You don't think our marriage is good?" His words were barely a whisper.

Tears rose in Tess's beautiful brown eyes. "For a while there I didn't. But today I realized something very important. I realized that I can't compare our life to someone else's. I can't wish for what someone else has." She wiped her tears away with the back of one hand. "It took me days to realize it, weeks even. But I was so mad about your phone and your job. Then I looked at Clara Rose and Obie and all the other girls I know and saw all the wonderful things that they had. I just wanted something as wonderful."

"And you still feel that way?"

"I already have wonderful. You have provided for me, loved me, given me a beautiful house."

He shook his head. "I've let the house go."

Her eyes widened. "Why?"

"It's too big for just me."

The crestfallen look on her face was enough to make his heart lift. "Where are we going to live?"

"I thought you were going back to Clarita." He had to hear her say it.

She shook her head. "No, I don't want to move back to Clarita. I belong right here, in Wells Landing. With you."

He looked from the house to the goats to his wife. "I'm

supposed to move in with my parents next week. I thought you were gone."

Tess shook her head. "I'm staying, and I don't care where we live, as long as we're together."

"You really mean that?"

Tess nodded. "I was a fool. There's no other way to say it. I was childish and immature, and I don't know . . . I guess I'll just blame it on the heat. It makes people do all sorts of crazy things, you know."

"I know." He took a step toward her and it was all she needed. She closed the distance between them and flung her arms around his neck. "I mean it, Jacob," she said as she held him close.

He snaked his arms around her waist and pulled her nearer still.

"I don't care where we live, I just want to be with you, but you have to promise me one thing."

"What's that?"

"Promise me that you'll go with me to marriage enrichment counseling. If not for you, then for me."

Jacob pulled away to look into her eyes. "Anything for you."

He lowered his head and placed a small kiss on her waiting lips. Then he drew back. "There is one thing." He released her long enough to fish his cell phone from his pocket.

A cloud crossed her face. He knew she hated the phone. But this time she might make an exception.

He hit redial and put the phone on speaker. It rang three times before it was picked up.

"Margie here."

"Margie? It's Jacob Smiley. About that land . . ."

"Yes?"

"I'll take it."

"Wonderful," she said. She started chattering away about papers and inspections, but Jacob only had room in his heart and thoughts for the woman in front of him.

"Land?" Tess asked. Her voice was soft and tentative, as though if she said the word too loud, it might not come true after all.

Jacob nodded. "I've already given my notice at the roofing company. I was going to farm with *Dat*, but now I'll farm on my own. With you."

"Oh, Jacob. Really?"

"*Jah*." He smiled. "For you and me and a few kids and as many goats as you want."

Tears spilled over and ran down her cheeks.

"Jacob, are you there?" Margie again.

"So you forgive me?" Tess asked.

"As long as you forgive me too."

Tess threw her arms around Jacob once again. He returned her embrace, dropping the cell phone into the grass.

Margie continued to talk about whatever Margie needed, but Jacob only had time for Tess, and that was just the way he wanted it to be.

Content to be unmarried and plain-spoken,
Kathryn "Kappy" King is an odd-woman-out
in the Amish community of Blue Sky, Pennsylvania.
But she's skilled at making the special *kapps*
local women need to cover their hair.
And she might be the only one who can unearth
the danger hiding in this peaceful valley . . .

When Kappy's neighbor, Ruth Peachey, turns up dead
in her yard, everyone in Blue Sky believes it's a tragic
accident. Until the *Englisch* police find the gentle dog
breeder was deliberately struck down—and arrest her
mentally challenged son, Jimmy, for the crime . . .

Jimmy's sister, Edie, returns to Blue Sky to clear his
name, yet no one will speak to a shunned former
Amish woman, much less give her information.
Determined to help, Kappy starts digging for
the truth among her seemingly innocent neighbors.
But suddenly a series of suspicious "accidents"
threatens Edie and the Peachey farm—property Edie
is determined to protect for her brother's future.

Now, as danger looms large in the small community,
Kappy must bait a trap for a killer snapping hard at her
heels. And Edie must decide whether to make a home
once more in the town she thought she'd left behind . . .

**Please turn the page for an exciting sneak peek of
Amy Lillard's first Amish mystery,**

KAPPY KING AND THE PUPPY KAPER,

coming soon wherever print and eBooks are sold!

Kappy King took one look at her front door and promptly marched back down the porch steps to her buggy. She didn't even bother to take the new bolt of sheer, white organdy into the house. She tossed it onto the seat next to her and climbed in. Thankfully she hadn't unhooked the mare when she arrived back at the house. Heaven only knew why. Maybe the good Lord was directing her footsteps and He knew she would be needing it sooner than she thought.

Sooner, indeed. This needed to be taken care of and fast. There was only one person she knew in the valley who would have the audacity to paint her front door blue without permission and that person was her across-the-road neighbor, Jimmy Peachey.

She clicked the horse into motion and took a deep breath to calm her raging emotions.

Audacity wasn't the right word. *Clueless innocence, misguided helpfulness, unwanted good intentions.* All these described Jimmy and more.

He was as sweet as pie, stubborn as a mule, and cute as a button on a shirt. He was wily in his own way, despite the fact he had Down's syndrome. Kappy didn't know much about the ailment, only that it made Jimmy look a little different than other folks and act a little slower as well. But that didn't mean he wasn't smart. He was too smart by far, but in ways different than everyone around him.

And it had started off to be such a nice day too.

The Peacheys weren't her closest neighbors, but they only lived less than a quarter of a mile from Kappy. Normally she would have marched over there on foot, but since she had just returned from the bulk goods store and her horse was still hitched to her buggy, this way was much faster.

The tall stalks of corn rustled as she drove across the main road to the driveway on the other side. Mountains framed both edges of the valley as the clouds created shadows across the green. Blue Sky was one of five boroughs nestled between Stone Mountain and Jacks Mountain. The entire area was around thirty miles long, but only four miles wide. And most all of that was farmland: wheat, corn, and more. She supposed if she had walked it wouldn't have taken anytime at all to get to Jimmy and Ruth's but this way was much more acceptable. Even if she was coming to find out exactly why Jimmy had felt the need to add color to her door.

She shook her head. She knew why he had done it. She just didn't know *why* he had done it.

It was a common misconception that a blue painted door in the valley meant a girl of marriage age and availability lived there. She supposed since she and Hiram Lapp had called off the wedding she was technically available, but she had already settled herself to being an old maid. Everyone in the valley thought she was odd anyway. Why not add old maid to the list?

The Peachey house seemed strangely quiet as she pulled up the drive. Corn stalks surrounded them on each side, land that belonged to Ruth and had been leased since the year Amos Peachey had passed. Ruth was nothing if not a shrewd businesswoman. But necessity had made her that way.

How long had it been now since Amos had died? Twenty years? Kappy couldn't remember. A long time ago at any rate. Her family had been alive then and Ruth's daughter Edith had still been in the valley. Maybe fifteen. *Jah*, closer to fifteen since Jimmy hadn't yet started to school.

Kappy pulled her horse to a stop and set the brake on the buggy. From the barn she could hear the dogs barking as if on the hunt for something sinister. She shook her head at herself and got out of the buggy. She really needed to quit reading those detective novels. But they were just so interesting. She had never been any place but Kishacoquillas Valley, Pennsylvania. And she would probably never go anyplace else. But she could live a little through books. As long as the bishop never found out. She was certain Samuel Miller would not approve of a pipe smoking Englishman who solved mysteries with the help of his good friend, Watson.

Once again, Kappy was overcome with the sense of quietness. No, that wasn't right. It was more of a stillness, an expectancy, as if the farm was holding its breath waiting for something else to happen.

She shook the thought away. That was ridiculous. Something else couldn't happen because the first something hadn't even happened yet. But as soon as she found Jimmy it would. And once she left he would know with great certainty that she did not need nor did she want her door painted blue.

"Silly tradition," she muttered as she stalked up the

porch steps. Whoever came up with such a custom should be hauled before the church. Maybe even hauled into jail. It was just plain silly. Yet now that her door had been painted, she could only hope that not many people saw it or she would be the laughingstock of the community before church on Sunday.

Not that it would be the first time.

She ignored the quiet that didn't really exist, and the noise of thirty or so barking dogs and knocked on the front door. She shifted from foot to foot waiting on someone, most likely Ruth to come to the door.

She knocked again, uncomfortable just walking in as most of her neighbors were prone to do. No one walked into her house uninvited and she couldn't see doing the same. If that made her an odd duck, then so be it.

No answer. Surely someone knew she was there. How could they not with the dogs barking like crazy? Unless no one was home.

Kappy took a step back and eyed the door thoughtfully, as if the little bit of distance would provide some answers.

The paint on her door had still been tacky to the touch when she had pulled up to her house which meant it hadn't been long since Jimmy left. But how long? And had Ruth allowed him to cross the street by himself? She didn't think so.

The noise of the dogs grew louder as if they'd found another reason to bark. What was going on over there? She had been over to the Peacheys' plenty of times, and never had she heard the dogs acting like this. With one last look at the door—the nice, plain, *white* door—she skipped down the porch steps and around to the back of the house.

Like her house, the Peachey place was a two-story white structure with a large barn off to one side. An open hay barn sat a little farther back, but now it held the yellow-topped buggy that belonged to Ruth Peachey. But that would mean . . .

Ruth was somewhere in the house or the barn. And since there was no answer at the house . . .

Kappy started across the side yard to the barn which sat in the green grass, a red jewel shining in the sun.

She stopped for a moment, thinking she'd heard something, then she shrugged it off and continued across the yard.

The barks grew louder with each step she took and for a moment Kappy wondered if Ruth had gotten some new stock, dogs that weren't familiar with the noises of the valley.

It wasn't like they were friends or anything, her and Ruth. Just friendly enough neighbors. Truth was, Kappy wasn't friends with many people in Blue Sky, but was that any fault of hers? Not in the least. She couldn't help what people thought of her. She couldn't control it if someone believed she was a bit on the odd side. The good Lord knew what was in her heart and that was all that mattered. Wasn't it?

Kappy resisted the urge to cover her ears as she stepped into the barn. The barks were almost deafening. Yet amid the woofs and howls, she thought she heard another noise, this one distinctively human. "Ruth?" she called.

Not a reserved person, she surprised herself by easing cautiously forward. "Ruth?"

Still no answer.

Light filtered through from the other side of the barn. The door was open, but Ruth's horse was nowhere to be seen, most likely put out to pasture for the afternoon.

"Hush!" she hollered toward the large pen containing Ruth Peachey's prized beagle pups. They were so loud she could barely hear herself think! The dogs quieted for a moment, then started back up again.

Kappy shook her head, then rounded the corner that led to the pasture. She stopped short.

Jimmy Peachey stood there, his feet nearly buried in the hay. Tears ran down his reddened cheeks. He twisted his hands in his straw hat, crushing it as he sobbed.

"I'm sorry. I'm sorry. I'm sorry," he chanted as he rocked back and forth.

His mother lay prone at his feet.

Kappy rushed forward. Jimmy didn't move, didn't stop chanting as she knelt beside the woman. Ruth's storm-gray eyes stared unblinkingly at the rafters overhead.

The dogs continued to bark, blocking out all thoughts. Kappy moved by instinct, holding a hand under Ruth's nose to see if she was still breathing. No warm breath brushed her fingertips, no rise and fall of Ruth's chest. No movement of any kind.

Just the dogs barking and Jimmy chanting and rocking back and forth. Back and forth.

Kappy checked her breathing once more unwilling to accept her first answer. But there was no breath. And that could only mean one thing.

Ruth Peachey was dead.

Connect with Us

Visit us online at
KensingtonBooks.com
to read more from your favorite authors, see books
by series, view reading group guides, and more.

Join us on social media

for sneak peeks, chances to win books and prize packs,
and to share your thoughts with other readers.

facebook.com/kensingtonpublishing
twitter.com/kensingtonbooks

Tell us what you think!

To share your thoughts, submit a review,
or sign up for our eNewsletters, please visit:
KensingtonBooks.com/TellUs.

Books by Bestselling Author
Fern Michaels

Available Wherever Books Are Sold!

Check out our website at **www.kensingtonbooks.com**